I0699704

★

MOTHERLAND

MOTHERLAND

NICOLE
BRELAND
AANDAHL

MOTHERLAND.
Copyright © 2024 by Nicole Breland Aandahl.
All rights reserved.
Published and printed in the United States of America.

The Library of Congress has catalogued the hardcover edition as follows: LCCN 2024920965

Names: Aandahl, Nicole Breland, author.
Title: Motherland/Nicole Breland Aandahl
Description: First Edition | 2024.

Hardcover ISBN: 9798218510923
Ebook ISBN: 9798218510930

Author photo by the Jaxon Photo Group, @jaxonphotogroup
Cover and book design by Jonathan Sainsbury // 6x9design

Copies of this book may be purchased at:
https://motherland-book.com
and local bookstores upon request.

Who knows what women can be when they are finally free to become themselves?

—Betty Frieden

Chapter 1

MARYANNE

February 2, 1968
NASA Headquarters, Washington, D.C.

Maryanne zipped through NASA's main entrance, flashed her badge to the leering security, and checked her watch. *Thirteen minutes to spare*, she thought, willing her pulse to slow down. *You'll get to your desk before he does.*

It was annoying, the almost daily protests downtown that snarled traffic and slowed down her bus to work. Every day marked a new battle in the war against injustice, historic resentment was front page news, and everyone had chosen a side. But Maryanne had no time for rebellion other than her personal mission to prove she deserved her job. At just 22-years-old and the only Black and female analyst in the Office of Tracking and Data Acquisition, there was no room for error, much less tardiness.

Maryanne stopped in front of shiny display case to check her hair, which had been styled into a perfect flip save for an errant stray hair. Carefully, she smoothed the rebellious stray and wrinkled her nose at the sepia reflection shimmering in the glass like a warm wraith. Inside the case were photos of steel-jawed, serious men, doing serious things. No one that looked like her in this or any other display case in the building. She'd checked.

"Hey you, uh, girl!" said a voice that sounded like it'd been run through a cement mixer.

The hair on her neck stood up and she turned to see Pearce, a fellow analyst with whom she'd worked for at least six months. He was probably the same age but bore the smirk of an impish schoolboy. He, like most of her colleagues, never seemed to remember her name. Plus, he was always acting like he was her boss, pawning off grunt work and trying to order her around. She mostly ignored him, though fear he'd pull the emasculated whiteboy card and get her fired always poked her in the gut. He shoved a stack of paper toward her, but she firmly planted her hands on her hips.

"What's that?" she said, knowing what was next.

"Take these to the copy room and make a dozen copies, will ya?"

"I can't," she said, almost too sweetly. She imagined kicking him in the groin and smiled harder. "I've got to get to my desk. Bye!" Brushing past him, she gripped her father's leather valise to her chest like armor, toward the office, her insides burning. *The nerve!* she thought at first, then anxiety started to prick at her ears. What if he told her boss, Director Atkins, about the snub? *No time to worry about that now*, she thought, looking at her watch again. She had to be at her desk in three minutes.

If lucky, she could sneak past the conference room before Atkins threw more work at her. She just had to get to her desk before he did. She already had three intense projects going simultaneously — two from Atkins and one from a freckled senior astrophysicist whose hair stood up like he'd stuck his finger in a socket.

One minute. Her desk was just a few steps away and she started to exhale. Then, to her dismay, the conference door flew open.

"Oh! Maryanne . . . MARYANNE!" came Atkins' familiar and perturbing command, stopping her dead in her tracks. At least he knew her name.

The room from which the perpetually agitated astrophysicist emerged pulsed with caffeinated energy, generated by equally agitated men huddled around a large table and abused chalkboard. She quietly sighed to herself and turned to face him, her cheeks aching from smiling.

"Yes, Dr. Atkins?"

He peered at her over his black-framed glasses around which oily perspiration pooled, gripping his chest like he was having a heart attack.

"I've put a new set of documents on your desk. Need you to look — now. Get back to me by 3:30."

"Yes, sir. I'll get to it right . . ." but before she could finish her sentence, he shut the door in her face, causing her to lose balance and land hard on the floor. Anonymous hands helped her to her feet, asking if she was ok, but humiliation seized her tongue. It was one thing to suffer indignity in private, but another in public. Her hand flew to her hairdo, and she managed to squeak out a single "thank you" before limping to her desk, tears catching in her throat.

8:30am and she was already exhausted.

She would have given anything to be a fly on the wall in those closed-door meetings. NASA Headquarters was a constant hive of activity, with every worker bee focused on the mission of catching up to — and beating — the Soviets in space. Sure, she was lucky to have the job, but better to be in a graduate program on her way to a doctorate. On the flip side it was great NASA didn't send her to Hampton Roads, Virginia, into Jim Crow's armpit, even though that was where a lot of the research action happened. She just didn't care about beating the Soviets to the moon. She wanted to listen to deep space, beyond the confines of Earth's orbit.

Instead, her job was cranking out calculations for a program *only* focused on Earth. Boring. At least she got her foot in the door. She sat down at her desk and dove into analysis, carefully but quickly scrolling her eyes across the numbers and figures on the page. Her pencil flew across the paper, calculations dancing around frenetically in her head until finding synchronicity. It was consuming work, like deep sea diving, for once she dove in, she needn't come up for air. She'd had the office lights shut out on her at least twice.

Atkins reappeared at 3:15pm. Fifteen minutes early.

"Have my analysis?" he said.

Her stomach turned, perturbed that she hadn't gotten to him first. Every time that happened, she feared he'd think she was slacking. She handed him the work with two shaking hands, like it was a tray of full champagne flutes.

"It's right here, Sir!" she said, her cheeks burning with embarrassment over her eagerness.

He half-smirked and peered over his glasses at her work.

"Exceptional, as usual," he said.

"Thank you?" she said, her eyebrows raised. He never gave positive feedback. Or negative feedback. In fact, he'd never given her any feedback at all. Plus, she hadn't shaken off her fear that the engineer from earlier went up the chain of command to complain about her insubordination. But now she was being praised? She looked at Atkins like he was the snake in the Garden of Eden.

"You've been a real asset on this team," he continued. "A true asset." He pursed his lips into a tight smile. "But it's time for you to move on."

She knew it! Her neck suddenly felt like it was being burned by a hair dryer. She could hear herself say,

"No — no, Sir! I love my job. I love working here. I don't want to. . ."

"Calm down. I'm not firing you."

"Oh — oh, ok?" She swallowed hard, hunger and confusion threatening to dissolve her into a teary mess.

"Listen," he said in a low voice. "I'm putting together a new team. A team of men — I mean, people — I trust. I want you on that team. It's a top-secret program and your skills are needed. Your love of radioastronomy will be a real asset."

She felt her heart lift as if buoyed by hummingbirds. Radio-astronomy! He'd never shown any indication that he knew her passion. And the best labs, well, they were far from the madness that was D.C. *Has my hard work paid off?* she thought, her pulse quickening.

"Are we going to Goddard? Or California?" she said, almost out of breath.

"No," said Atkins. "We're staying in the area. But trust me, you'll be blown away by the work being done close to home. That's all I can say now. Just be here at 7:30am tomorrow and I'll take you to your new workstation."

Maryanne paused. Well, maybe not exactly what she wanted, but still, he mentioned radioastronomy. And he selected *her.* Not Pearce, or the other condescending, self-important analysts. *Her.* She impulsively reached out to grab Atkins' hand and shook it vigorously.

"Oh, thank you, thank you!" she said. "This is a great honor. I won't let you down."

His smile evaporated and he quickly pulled his hand away, wiping it on his pants. "Yes, yes," he said. "Don't thank me yet. It'll be grueling work, but you'll be at the forefront of national security."

❋ ❋ ❋

Maryanne burst from the building and skipped to the bus stop, her heart somewhere on Venus. All of her work finally noticed! She couldn't wait to find out what the actual job was. Plus, Atkins had let her go home early, so she'd surprise her mother with the news. She'd tell her father too, though lately he was so entrenched in woe and self-pity the news would probably go over like a lead balloon.

Floating down the street she almost ran over Walter Hobbs, a senior scientist that worked directly for NASA Administrator Webb. She'd met him when the interns had a meet-and-greet with Webb. Unlike the other stiffs in the building, he'd been kind to her. Shivering, he was wearing just a sweater vest and jacket.

"Oh, sorry, Dr. Hobbs." she said cheerfully. "Are you ok?"

He looked stunned, like she'd slapped him in the face. He was holding something in his right hand, but she couldn't tell what it was.

"Oh, hi, um — Margorie?" He didn't extend his hand.

"Maryanne." She took a step back, suddenly mindful that she was standing a bit close. Gladys always said she acted familiar with folks too soon. Too personal. No filter.

"Oh right, Maryanne." His eyes darted around like he was expecting someone. "Is this your bus stop?"

"Yes. But I've never seen you here. Do you live in Northwest?"

"Uh, no." he said, shifting from foot to foot. "In Maryland, but my car is broken down. I was just waiting for a friend to give me a ride but they're late and it's cold and I . . "

His eyes, which had never stopped dancing, suddenly peered at something behind her. She turned her head to look. Seeing nothing, she swiveled back to Dr. Hobbs. Was that panic on his face?

Everything ok? She wanted to ask, but for some reason held her tongue.

"I forgot something in my office," he said. "I'll call my wife. Have a great night!"

He turned abruptly and jogged back toward the building, looking once more over his shoulder.

"What in the world?" she said under her breath. Looking around, she saw nothing but a couple of parked cars on the other side of the wide boulevard. Then the bus rumbled up, blocking her view. She shrugged and climbed aboard, suddenly feeling unsettled, as if she were being watched.

Chapter 2

MARYANNE

February 2, 1968, evening
Northwest Washington, D.C.

As the massive chrome bus lumbered up Georgia Avenue, Maryanne peered out of her window at Howard University's distinguished iron gate. Campus appeared quiet despite the events of the past year. D.C. was saturated with racial tension, reflecting a nation being forced to confront its sins by people who'd had enough. When she was a student at Howard, the culture changed so dramatically Maryanne wondered if she graduated from the same school in which she enrolled. Once reserved and compliant students now openly challenged the administration and seemed to protest everything. Racial injustice. The Vietnam War. The curriculum. School policies. School policies on protesting. Campus nearly exploded when four students were disciplined for burning an effigy of the Dean during an anti-draft demonstration. Her father, also an alum, opined to everyone and no one, that every protest tarnished the school's image. He reserved a special venom for afros, picks, head wraps, and Dashikis, which seemed to be everywhere.

Maryanne felt a longing to participate — to stop straightening her hair, to add her voice to the symphony of voices declaring "Black is Beautiful." But what would that do to her career? She avoided the turmoil, keeping her head down and record clean. The federal government was pretty much the only place Black degree-holders could get a decent job and she knew it.

She arrived home right before sunset, the liveliest time of the day on Oglethorpe Street, a hamlet of Black, educated D.C. The smell of stewing greens and fried fish filled the air as children darted back and forth across the street without care. The men, just home from breadwinning, sat smoking on every porch, having been greeted at the door by their perfectly powdered and coiffed wives with a kiss on the cheek and whisky on the rocks. Few mothers worked outside of the home in this neighborhood, much less 22-year-old girls, so she was used to being stared at in judgement as she walked down the street carrying her masculine valise.

Her father was holding court in the living room with Mr. Reeves, an economist who worked in a 'good-for-a-Negro' position at the Department of the Treasury. They, like everyone on the bus, were talking about the front page of the Washington Post showing a poor man being shot in the head in Vietnam.

"Hi Sweetheart," said her father demonstratively. "Didn't see you there. How was work today?"

His cheeks were already ruddy with intoxication, and he made one of those *huh-huhs* which meant he wasn't taking her seriously but trying to hide it. She bristled at his tone and reconsidered announcing her promotion, deciding to tell her mother first.

"It was fine. Thank you." She respectfully paused, but leaned forward on her front toes to make a break for the kitchen as soon as she could.

He peered at her through a cloud of smoke.

"So, I hear you are going out tonight on another date with the Walker boy?"

Mr. Reeves raised his eyebrows.

Oh shoot! she thought. She'd forgotten. Truth was, she wasn't quite sure what to do about THE Martin Walker. Not yet.

———

"Yes. But with Gladys and Eric. It's a double date." She started lightly bouncing on her front foot like a sprinter at the starting line.

"Remember he's a good one," her father snorted. "A real good one. You're lucky. Be on your best behavior."

She knew what that meant. Whenever she chewed Martin's ear too much about her love of space and career ambition, he'd tune her out, even start flirting with someone else. But he kept asking her out, and she kept saying yes. They'd kissed, but hadn't necked, not really, and she could tell he was getting angsty. More than once, she'd had to remove his hand from her thigh. But she just wasn't ready to go further. If she wasn't careful, he'd give up. She'd return home dejected, and it would be all her fault. *Spinster.*

Her mother was in the kitchen, looking tidy in a wool shift dress with a bric-a-brac apron around her waist. She was staring at the dishes in the sink, unmoving, like a statue.

"Mommy?" said Maryanne, cautiously. Lately her mother seemed more melancholy than usual.

Her mother blinked and gently smiled. In Maryanne's middle class, educated, Black community it was common for women to call their mother's "mommy" well into adulthood. "Mom" would be too disrespectful, and "mother" lacked affection. Her mother's skin was creamy caramel, topped with doe eyes, impossible lashes, and a scatter of freckles across her nose. Maryanne was petite and slender like her mother, though with a more athletic build after years of playing field hockey.

"Hello, Sweetie," her mother cooed. "Are you all set for tonight?"

Maryanne could detect a bit of resignation in her mother's voice. She never pressured her to find a man, instead, her mother was her biggest advocate and frequently defended her against Father's criticisms.

"Well, yes, I'm just running a bit late. But I have something to tell you."

"Yes?"

"I got a promotion! I mean, I was selected for a special job."

Maryanne's eyes twinkled, like she was sharing a delicious secret.

Her mother grabbed a towel to dry her hands and flew over. She wrapped Maryanne in a soothing, musky rose embrace.

"I am so proud of you!"

Maryanne didn't want to pull away, but if she didn't get upstairs soon Gladys would have a conniption. Gladys never seemed to trust Maryanne to dress for dates on her own and would come over to make sure her look was on point. Conveniently, Gladys lived with her perfect husband Eric just a few blocks away. The model couple, beautiful, successful, and loving. Maryanne thought about her date, and her smile wilted as if she had an upset stomach. Why, again, did she keep saying yes to Martin when she felt no spark? Oh, that's right, because Martin Walker was the Mount Everest of catches.

"I have to get ready," she said as cheerfully as possible, giving her mother a peck on the cheek and bouncing off. Once clear of her mother's view, malaise seeped back into her soul and she mounted the stairs as if they led to the stockade. *But maybe this night will be different*, she said to herself. Maybe Martin kept asking her out because he was starting to love her for who she was, like Eric loved Gladys. A man for her like that had to be out there somewhere. Maybe it really was Martin and she just needed to open her eyes.

Gladys stood at the top of the stairs, hands on her hips and foot tapping impatiently.

"So glad you finally decided to — and — oh! Look at your hair and your clothes! Tragic!" Gladys snapped her fingers. "Let's get to work."

"Just get this over with," quipped Maryanne, giggling. What would she do without her big sister?

❊ ❊ ❊

Most-eligible-bachelor Martin was the only son of Dr. Henry Walker, who was a Cardiologist at Howard University Hospital. They lived in one of the few large, detached homes in their neighborhood. Mother also worked at the hospital, but as a proper married woman never accepted Dr. Walker's invitations for a ride or drink after work. Martin was known to have a refined and gentle nature, though he also had the reputation for being a bit of a cad. Maryanne raised this concern with Gladys who quipped, "All men can be tamed by the right woman."

Maryanne felt a surprising jolt of excitement when she saw Martin behind the wheel of a brand-new Mercury Cougar, which he parked in front of her house. He got out, impeccably groomed, and opened the passenger side door as the parents looked on, her father with a smug grin and her mother smiling cautiously. Maryanne ignored the stares and whispers that seemed to swirl in the air as she slipped into the car, her lips in a tight but pleasant smile. There was a reason women swooned over Martin. Smooth talker, smooth face, smooth movements. The leather seats were slick, so she kept her legs tightly closed and hands in her lap, shoulder pressed against the door. She looked over at Gladys and Eric in their Chevy and wished they'd all gone in the same car.

"Why're you sitting so far away?" he said. "I won't bite."

"Oh, I didn't realize . . ." She shifted her hips over an inch and tried to look relaxed. *What's wrong with me?* she thought, her stomach twisting.

They went to Billy Simpson's Supper Club, an exclusive spot for the Black elite, and she tried to ignore a feeling of unease. As usual, Martin was charming and attentive, never taking his eyes off her, save for an occasional glace at some bright young thing that crossed his path. The couples wined, dined, and danced until near closing. Eventually she found herself swooning a little, laughing too enthusiastically at his jokes and flipping her hair. Gladys took notice and squired her off to the Ladies' Room for a status check.

"Look Maryanne, he really likes you!" said Gladys, furiously powdering her nose. "I mean, really, REALLY likes you. It's been what — a month? What's your deal?"

"I guess so?" Maryanne stared at her reflection, and noticed she was a bit flushed across the bridge of her nose. "I mean, I told him about my new job, and he didn't ask me anything about it. Didn't even congratulate me. He only likes to talk about himself, his father, or Muhammed Ali, who may as well be his father. He never wants to hear about my interests or, you know, my aspirations."

"Aspirations?" Gladys shook her head. "You know you can't expect any man to want his woman to have aspiration other than looking pretty and popping out babies. And for a boy like Martin, that means gracing the pages of *Jet* magazine as his devoted wife."

"Well, why I can't I look pretty and pop out babies and have a career too?"

Gladys looked at her sister up and down.

"Have you lost your mind? I know your head is in the stars but keep your feet on the ground. Just keep acting cute and maybe he'll start talking about the future."

How much of myself would I have to abandon to be Martin's girl? she thought, the queasiness returning. Suddenly, it hit her. She *was* putting on an act. And she wasn't attracted to Martin, not really. Because despite his effusive affability, or his astonishing good looks, he had zero interest in who she really was. She spent every moment with him in a state of self-censorship, careful not to be too this and too that, to do nothing but bask in his saccharine glow. It was exhausting and boring at the same time.

She had to break it off, no matter how disappointed her father and Gladys would be.

The two couples parted ways after dinner, and Martin promised to deliver Maryanne home safely. How many cocktails had it been? Not more than three, but strong enough to send her swaying into his eager arms.

"Steady girl," he teased as he helped her into the car.

"I'm fine, just tired," she said, feeling ridiculous. She'd wait until he dropped her at home and break up with him then. She just hoped he didn't want to go necking. "I really need to go right home."

Fighting to keep her head up and eyes open, she leaned against the window to regain composure. He peeled out and shot toward Georgia Avenue, and it felt like she was on the deck of a ship. A cold shock on her thigh and she was suddenly awake, watching Martin's class ring creep under her skirt.

"What are you doing?" she snapped, recoiling. "Not today, please."

He scowled and stared straight ahead. Something about his stony silence filled her with dread. She sat up straighter and pulled her skirt back down.

"I need to go home now. I'm tired," she said sweetly, though something was just — wrong.

He yanked the wheel and they turned into the wooded darkness of Rock Creek Park. The opposite direction of her house.

"Where are we going?" she said, fighting to keep her voice steady. "You turned the wrong way." She felt every nerve in her body, and her fingers twitched. She told him no. What was he doing? The walls of the car cabin felt like they were closing in and she looked at him with pleading eyes.

He just sneered and slowed down.

Maybe I got through to him? she thought, feeling her shoulders drop. For a moment she thought he might make a U-turn, but instead he pulled into a narrow break in the trees and parked, cutting the lights. She stiffened and her heart throbbed in her ears.

"Martin," she croaked, "I need to go straight home. Gladys will be waiting and so will my mother ...."

"Girl," he snickered, "you know Gladys and Eric went home and your dad is passed out in front of the television." A menacing smile crept across his smooth face. "And your mother? Your mother ain't home. She's working tonight. At the hospital. With my *father.*"

His salacious suggestion was enraging, and it caught her off guard. *How dare he say such things about my mother,* she thought. She sat up even taller in her seat and craned her neck to make eye contact, her tongue suddenly spiked with venom.

"Martin," she spat. "Take me home. Right now." She was in control, but her rage was building, cheeks hot. *Need to get help,* she thought, her heart seized with panicked anger, and reached across him for the horn. But he grabbed her wrist and squeezed so tightly her fingers grew numb.

"Ow!" she cried, eyes wide in disbelief. She yanked hard, her skin burning in his grip. "Let go!"

"Either you finally give me what I want," he hissed as he tugged harder, "or I'll break your wrist."

Maryanne felt every bit of good girl escape her body. She wanted to haul off and punch him in the face, if she could. A slap wouldn't be enough. Her fear was eclipsed by sheer, unbridled anger. She wiggled to free her other arm, which was stuck between them.

"Go ahead," she said. Her eyes shimmered, but without threat of tears. "Go ahead and try. I can't even feel it. If you break my wrist, I'll tell everyone what you did. Everyone. I'm not afraid of you." Her mouth was hot, as if filled with fire. She looked him dead in the eye, pulling so hard she braced to hear her wrist snap. But she didn't care. She would get away.

His smile dissolved into disbelief, and he let go. Her freed arm flew across her body and smacked hard against the door handle, but she felt nothing. Her heart racing like cornered prey, she yanked the door open and leapt out, never taking her eyes off him. Martin fired up the car and backed out, leaves and dirt swirling as he tore off into the park like he was being chased, the passenger door still open. Maryanne stood frozen, hands balled into a fist, her chest heaving, ready to fight if he changed his mind.

"We're over!" she screamed after him. It felt like she was on fire. Looking down, she saw her throbbing hand and wrist were turning from red to purple. *Just bruises*, she thought defiantly. *They'll heal.* Letting angry tears flow, she was grateful that she'd escaped, the alternative outcome too horrific. When his car lights were no longer visible, she turned toward the glow of streetlights up the hill in front of her and willed her feet to start marching.

Father was snoring in his lounge chair when she finally arrived home, her legs jelly, wrist throbbing, and spirit depleted. Her rage was somewhere back on Missouri Avenue. Exhausted, she was grateful her mother and Gladys were not there — how would she explain the bruises, running mascara, and dirty dress? It had been a near perfect day, and yet again, a man ruined it.

Maryanne was done with men. Nothing but work now. Nothing but her dream.

She quietly crept up the wooden stairs, cleaned herself up, and sunk into a sleep, momentarily awoken by the roar of an engine coming to life outside her window.

Chapter 3

MIKHAIL/MICHAEL

Mikhail waited, parked between streetlights across the street from the Black girl's house. He'd followed her bus home, then again after she got into that shiny car with the equally shiny young man. But he couldn't follow them into the park without being seen, so he drove back to her street and cut the engine. Surveillance on residential streets was risky, especially in neighborhoods where everyone seemed to know everyone else, but after dark it was more manageable. He'd donned one of his favorite disguises, a short, Chestnut brown curly wig with whisps of gray, brush-on tan, very uncomfortable brown eye lens, penciled in a few crow's feet, and used the extra car he kept at the warehouse. He looked like a racially ambiguous 40-year old instead of a foppish blond haired, blue eyed 27-year-old. A much better fit for this 100% Black community.

Such comfortable lives, he thought to himself as he scanned the row of connected homes, each with a porch and small yard. No one in Moscow had homes. Only cold, concrete high-rise apartments clustered around barren courtyards. It had been marginally more comfortable in the barracks during KGB training, but that seemed eons ago. By comparison, his apartments in D.C. were downright luxurious. And heated.

He shivered, pulled his coat tightly around his neck and sunk down further in his seat. Where was the girl? He looked at his watch — it had been almost an hour since she descended into the darkness of Rock Creek Park. Something was not right. She was drunkenly hanging on that man's arm, and he practically tossed her into the car, his lips curled like a Cheshire Cat. Mikhail briefly entertained the idea of going to look for her, but decided it was better to stay put. If she didn't show up, just abandon the operation and find another target.

Then, he saw his girl at the end of the street. He whipped out his small, but powerful binoculars, and focused. As she drew closer, he could see the outline of errant hairs sticking from her earlier perfect style, clothing sullied and molested. Tears streaked her ruddy cheeks and her face was twisted into a furious storm. She didn't look a girl who'd had a good time. He was unexpectedly ambushed by the urgency to burst from his darkened car and rush to her side, ask if she was ok, but instead steeled his jaw, pulled out his camera, and snapped a several pictures. What was it about her that stirred up such a reaction? Chivalry was not an instinct he was born with, unless it was his mother, or a means to an end. Besides, maybe he could use the photos against her later. He waited until she closed the front door behind her and drove off, chuckling silently. Until that day she'd just been eye candy, an enjoyable distraction from his gallery of disaffected male targets who he'd observed fighting with their wives, drunkenly gambling, and picking their noses. Now he knew she was a bit more.

Seeing her talking to Walter Hobbs — code name "Orion"- she might also have access to the Administrator's office. Orion clearly knew her. What information would she have access to? Maybe she'd do what Orion wouldn't, like plant listening devices. Maybe, she was a secretary in need of money or easy to blackmail, who could slip in and out of Administrator Webb's office.

He'd make his case to secure Center approval to pursue her.

It would be a welcome change. He was growing a bit tired of his current cadre of turncoats — disgruntled, entitled men. There was Roger, a chain-smoking, philandering middle-aged CIA officer on loan to NASA, code name "Marlboro." And Orion, who was as jittery as a squirrel in the middle of traffic. Sure, they were the prime targets, eager to provide more and more information (for money, of course.) And they had *access*. Access and hubris. But this girl, with her confident, easy familiarity with someone as highly positioned as Orion, meant she was worth watching. And she looked unlike any other woman he would check out. Twice.

The next morning, he told Roman, his Station Chief, what he'd learned.

"I saw her with Orion, you know, my asset," he told Roman, his Station Chief. "She must have access to information about a variety of areas of concern — the space program, maybe satellite surveillance. Plus," he said flatly, "she looks young and vulnerable."

Roman sniffed.

"Fine. See what you can find out about her and if there is anything we can exploit. She might be a good target for strong incentive. But," he said with a smirk, "no honey. That won't work on Negroes — they're too suspicious of Whites. Plus, they're all criminals in the eyes of their own government, so be extra careful."

"Got it," said Mikhail, hiding his excitement at the plan forming in his head. He couldn't wait to get started.

Chapter 4

MARYANNE

February 8, 1968, morning
NASA Headquarters, Washington, D.C.

t seemed the lights at NASA never went off. The building always pulsed with the frenetic energy of engineers and mathematicians, as well as elephantine computers, churning data from the collection of space craft deployed to put a U.S. man on the moon and explore the cosmos. Conference doors slammed open and shut, expelling wafts of burnt coffee and cigarette smoke. Everyone was so focused on work she wondered if they were aware the country was in a state of utter turmoil. Every night there was coverage of another protest, the war in Vietnam was worsening, and despite desegregation and voting rights, Jim Crow still hadn't been evicted from the South. No one at NASA seemed to notice or care.

Maryanne trudged to her desk at 7:15 am, slapping her cheeks to wake up. She'd risen in the early morning darkness, still seething with anger, but also filled with excitement about the new job. She sat down for a few minutes, but her legs wouldn't stop bouncing, so she stood up and paced. Not knowing what the job was — well — that was killing her. That, and not being able to tell her sister what happened yet. At least she had time. Gladys would probably ask about Martin later, and she'd tell her everything. Just talking to Gladys always made her feel better.

She stopped and shook her head to clear the racing thoughts. Sitting down, she rubbed her blistered fee, still swollen from last night's uphill hike. But she'd gotten away. *I'm not going to let what happened defeat me,* she thought to herself. It could have been much worse. Today was too important.

Atkins materialized out of nowhere. As usual, he had no time for pleasantries, but he seemed — cheerful?

"Come with me," he said.

He marched down the hallway at a fast clip, lifting his heels, as if leading a band. Maryanne eagerly kept pace, trying not to slip on the freshly mopped floor. After an excursion around several corners, down a set of stairs, and around another corner, they arrived at a steel door with a combination pad. She winced in pain, her feet throbbing. Luckily, Atkins was focused on unlocking the door. Once inside, she saw a large room filled with cubicles, offices and conference rooms lining the perimeter. There was no sign of a window, natural light, or anything other than aggressive electric lighting. It was the kind of room where everyone focused on work because there was nothing else interesting to look at. Atkins flipped a switch which activated a rotating red light. Whatever conversation inside that had been ongoing instantly ceased and she felt the burn of anonymous eyes trained in her direction.

"What's the light for?" Maryanne asked, clutching her valise tightly to her chest. She could not shake the feeling she was in some sort of trouble.

"It's just to indicate that someone without the proper clearance is in the area. We're working on yours now."

Atkins knocked on a couple of open doors as they passed, and they were soon joined by two more men, one who looked like a younger version of Spencer Tracy, and the other who had a grey pallor, smelled strongly of tobacco and a had grease stain on his shirt. He had two badges clipped to his jacket - one for NASA and the other one had a crest she recognized but could not place.

"Daily lunch run to the Waterfront, eh Roger?" Atkins teasingly pointed at the evidence on the man's sullied shirt.

Roger shrugged. "Were you there?"

"No, just we all know how often you sneak off for something fried." Atkins smirked. Roger formed his mouth into a little 'o', but as he was about to say something Atkins slapped him on the back.

"I'm just giving you a hard time. Relax."

Maryanne was dumbfounded. She had never seen Atkins in a state other than anxious, annoyed, and impatient. Now he was jovial, light, and damn-near jolly.

He waved at her to come nearer. "This is Maryanne. She's a junior physicist on my team and is about to graduate, from, where again?"

"Actually, I already graduated," she said, her tone raising slightly. "Almost two years ago." How many times would she have to tell him?

Roger looked at her and grunted.

"She's been helping with the Geo data and doing a great job," said Atkins. "She's faster than anyone here at analyzing data and explaining her findings in plain English. She'll be able to interpret the technical briefings and data and put together our briefing materials for the higher ups."

"I will?" she blurted. It was the first time Atkins had articulated what her job would be.

Roger looked at her and smirked. "Are you sure you understand this stuff, girl?"

Her cheeks burned with the familiar sting of a man trying to put her in her place. She peered at him, suddenly recognizing the crest on his badge. It was the Central Intelligence Agency. She narrowed her eyes and looked him up and down. This guy - he looked nothing like the cool, dapper spies on T.V. Too oily, too frumpy. She could feel the corners of her mouth twisting into a smirk. "Mary, you always wear your heart on your sleeve," she could hear Gladys chastising in her head. Gratefully Atkins whipped out a stack of reports — reports she'd written and stuck them under Roger's nose.

"She has the expertise and smarts we've been looking for.

In fact, she found something that has eluded us for months." Atkins declared.

Maryanne's face brightened. "What did I find?" she asked, then felt silly for not knowing.

"Well, I guess I can tell you a bit before, you know, your security credentials come through. You found one of what we suspect is a Soviet signal, probably comms between satellites or back to their ground locations. That means you recognize patterns and data faster than I've seen — we usually have to send info off to one of the labs for clarification, which means we lose days before we can brief the higher ups. We need that information to brief them so they can decide what action to take. Having you here has saved us days of waiting."

Maryanne had no time to process Atkins' accolades because Roger suddenly leaned forward in his seat to grab her memos.

"Let me have a look," he said as if no one would challenge him.

Atkins snatched them back. "Now Roger, let's keep this in *our* family for now, ok? Don't want you stealing her off to Langley. She's on my team."

They suddenly seemed to remember Maryanne was there, her mouth still open, processing the discussion. Young Spencer Tracy quizzically looked at her.

"You ok?" he asked.

"Yes, fine," she managed to say.

But she wasn't. She was in a windowless room with a couple of men haggling over her as if she were their property. They were taking her talent and locking it away for their exclusive use. Hopelessness piqued her heart. What would it take for her to prove she was good enough to do real research? She wanted to be under the stars — not stuffed in some underground bunker.

"Alright boys," said Atkins. "We've got some work to do." He gently took Maryanne by the elbow and led her to the door, oblivious to her disappointment.

"Why don't you go home now but come back on Monday to clean up your old desk area and get your paperwork done. Report to me first thing Tuesday morning. Make sure to come directly to my office." She looked at her reports, which he had tucked under his arm. "Don't worry, I'll lock these in my office," he said. "We'll get you badged and you'll work down here from now on."

She nodded, but her head felt like stone.

"You have a bright future with this agency." He extended his hand.

Maryanne took it and they shook.

"Thank you, Dr. Atkins. I won't let you down." She walked away with a Barbie smile across her face, willing her legs to walk forward instead of collapsing to the ground in tears. Why was she being so unrealistic? Of course, they'd never give her the opportunities she craved. It's not as if she hadn't made it clear every time she had the chance to chew Atkins' ear. The analyst job was just her entré into NASA. Sure, she was grateful, but she had zero interest in humans, be they Soviet or otherwise. But listening to space itself, the planets and energetic bodies, and forms of light and movement yet to be discovered — that was the future of radioastronomy. She wanted to analyze data gathered from the giant antennae in the desert, and to sit under them while gazing at the stars. There were so few people doing the work, they had to be open to welcoming more into their ranks no matter if they were man, woman, Black, White, or polka-dot. She just needed a chance to prove herself in a PhD program first.

Maryanne stopped in her tracks and ran toward a quiet corner, letting bitter tears stain her powdered cheeks. Annoyed men swerved around her, off to important work. *I won't give up,* she thought, dabbing her tears with a sweater sleeve. Then she marched back out into the hallway, fighting to keep her chin up with dignity.

Chapter 5

MIKHAIL/MICHAEL

February 9, 1968
Southwest Waterfront, Washington, D.C.

Mikhail spoke into the phone receiver with the clipped, direct confidence of the American Man, which he had practiced incessantly to replace his native tone of Soviet condemnation. "Right-O Mr. Sullivan, my guys will be there at 6am sharp."

He had long abandoned 'yessiree' because it sounded childish and had not yet tried out "right on" because he had only heard the Black men saying it. "Right-O" seemed to be widely accepted, though somewhat overused, so he was careful to only use it once or twice a week. Roman said it would take a full year before he was completely comfortable with D.C. slang, so his cover as a Long Island, New York boy who was new to the Nation's Capital would suit him well. It had taken him over a year to eliminate his Moscow accent, and now he was so comfortable with English, as well as French, Czech, Spanish, and German, that he only slipped into Slavic parlance when actually speaking Russian.

Although *Stevenson Builders LLC*, his construction and development company was a front, it was necessary to build a solid customer base and in stay high demand. Anything else would have drawn suspicion. He looked through the coffee-stained window between his back office and his team, all hunched over phones, pencils moving furiously. They worked from morning to night, fielding orders and work requests for the Southwest revitalization project, which had kept his small construction firm comfortably legitimate. Geoffrey, his *not his real name* business partner, had not yet arrived to take over for the afternoon. Mikhail impatiently tapped his foot against the edge of his desk. He was scheduled to meet up with Marlboro, aka "Roger", at the Waterfront. If he got back home in enough time, he could also look for an opening to engage that curious girl.

At this point he didn't need to conduct any more surveillance. He knew how to assess a target quickly, gathering enough information to make initial contact meaningful and lay the foundation for rapport.

> Data: Target at NASA every day of the work week. Arrives at 08:00 via bus and typically leaves at 16:45. Always carries a valise. Sometimes works late. Lives with two older persons — likely mother and father. Another young woman (verified: sister) visits often. Sister married. Target often stays overnight at sister's apartment 0.5 miles away. No apparent close friends or romantic relationship.

Mikhail was going over his first contact plan when Geoffrey finally showed up. He threw his coat over an empty chair with an exasperated grunt and shut the door.

"Hey, man. How's it going?" said Mikhail, his spine stiffening in anticipation of one of Geoffrey's angsty soliloquies.

"It's been quite a day," said Geoffrey, in his adopted flat Midwestern accent. "But nothing of concern to you." He turned on a large, noisy fan and placed it behind the phone and radio, then moved his chair closer. Even though they only spoke English, anything they said could be overheard and considered suspicious. And Washington, D.C. was crawling with not only the FBI and CIA, but intelligence outfits from all over the world.

"We have information that the Americans have obtained imagery over Kazakhstan," said Geoffrey. "We need your man to find out what they have."

Mikhail's shoulders relaxed and he nodded. NASA satellites were up in space looking for Soviet missile and bomber sites, but they'd had yet to intercept the images.

"I'm going to meet my tobacco-steeped friend for a late lunch, so I'll ask him," said Mikhail, wincing at the thought of having to watch Marlboro eat. Always with his mouth open, sandwich in one hand and cigarette in the other. Better to clear his mind and shift back to his new target plan.

He turned away from Geoffrey and put a finger on his temple, closing his eyes. The girl wasn't anything like other Blacks he'd tried to engage, albeit with little success. Even the card-carrying Communists looked at him with skepticism. The Center said that Black revolutionaries, hungry for money, would willingly and eagerly offer to serve as bag men or drivers. But that hadn't been his experience. The select times he'd made overtures they treated him with as much disdain as an American White man. As for Maryanne — well, it seemed she was a good girl with bad tasted in men, a favorite target of spies worldwide. It was worth a shot.

When Mikhail worked his way into being selected for KGB training it was mostly to make his mother proud, and to defend the Motherland. But it was also because he'd been a consumer of bootleg American cinema since childhood and dreamed of operating in the U.S. Steve McQueen was his idol, and he studied his speech, demeanor, mannerisms, and swagger so convincingly that "McQueen" became his nickname at the Institute. His electric blue eyes didn't hurt. But not once did he ever consider pursuing a Black female target, nor did he expect to find any target intriguing. He'd have to tread carefully.

* * *

Mikhail held his collar tightly around his neck with his left hand and shoved his right hand in his pocket. It was a cold day — not Moscow cold — but still a wet, cloying chilliness that one could never shake. By comparison, Moscow winters froze you to your core, thickening the blood. If you stood still long enough, death by freezing was inevitable. In Russia it wasn't unusual to discover a human popsicle who'd gotten drunk the night before and passed out against the side of an apartment building in the early mornings.

He kept his chin down, like he was gazing at the ground, but his peripheral vision was in full effect. Park to the right where the girl liked to have lunch was empty as usual. To the left, an elementary school, quiet despite hours earlier being filled with mostly Black schoolchildren. At night, it was not unusual to be eyeballed by the several illicit street corner entrepreneurs, and he had even been approached and threatened by desperate addicts after dark. But it was late afternoon - a different scene. From sunup to sundown, everyone from federal employees to construction workers made the short trek to the river for the fresh fried seafood and steamed crabs stands. As much as he missed his homeland and its hearty stews, he had become comfortably addicted to the Chesapeake Bay's bounty, and he swore Americans had stolen their idea for coleslaw from the Ukrainians. Despite the frigid temperature, when he got to the river all counters were already packed with hungry men of all stripes who'd just got off work.

His asset Marlboro stood facing the counter at one of the barges, hunched over a plate of fried fish and sliced white bread. A cigarette burned in an ashtray to his right, the smoke drifting directly into the eyes of the fry cook, who winced with annoyance but dare not challenge a White man in public. The cook saw Mikhail and knew exactly what to prepare.

Mikhail slid into the spot next to his asset and looked straight ahead. "Do you have an extra square?"

Marlboro reached into his pocket and pulled out a near-empty pack and placed it on the counter in front of him. "There's only a couple left, but you can have'em." Mikhail put the pack, which had film rolled into cigarette shape, in his pants pocket.

Marlboro continued to pick at his plate as Mikhail's usual order of shrimp steamed with Old Bay and fried clam strips was placed in front of him. After tucking his napkin under his chin Mikhail said, "We need you to find something new," and shoved a peeled shrimp in his mouth. Marlboro leaned in a little too closely and Mikhail pulled back slightly. "We need to find out what images have been captured by your satellites over our territory."

"Our satellites take lots of images," Marlboro said. He could be annoyingly standoffish for a man being crushed by debt. "It takes a while for the reports to reach my desk and I can't possibly get everything."

"We don't need everything. Just get whatever was taken in the past two weeks."

Marlboro let out a long sigh, like a like a kid who'd just been told to clean his room. "Fine. But this will be risky. I want double the usual payment."

Mikhail raised his eyebrows. *Is he serious?* he thought. Marlboro had been useful and kept him up to speed on the program's progress, even cueing him in on how the film was retrieved. Lately he hadn't shared anything of high value, getting lazy maybe. But Mikhail knew once an asset is acquired it was nearly impossible to cut them loose, because like a jilted lover, they wanted revenge, which often meant telling all to U.S. authorities. He'd already been dispatched to cull a loose-lipped asset of another agent.

"I'll see what I can do," said Mikhail. As they ate silently, he mused over his handling of this vexing, but important asset. Marlboro was not timid like the others. He seemed to be drawn to danger and pushing boundaries. In fact, he'd marched right up to the Soviet Embassy and demanded to talk to "whoever might be interested in information." Mikhail trailed and investigated him for two weeks to make sure he was legit and not part of a sting operation. He had to stroke his ego but also occasionally put him in his place, which Marlboro seemed to respect. Most of the time.

Mikhail gathered his trash and started to walk away. He had to restrain himself from retaliation when Marlboro grabbed his elbow, mouth open to say something else.

"Be careful," Mikhail warned in a low voice. "You never know who is watching." He looked at the fry cook, who he suspected might be on someone's payroll. "Or listening."

"I need double. Or I won't help you," said Marlboro.

"Just get what we want. I'll make sure you're taken care of."

Mikhail thrust a toothpick in his mouth and turned on his heel, cursing in his own head. *Who does he think he is?* Then he looked at his wristwatch and realized it was too late to execute his plan to initiate contact with the Black girl. He dragged his feet in the light snow that was accumulating on the sidewalk, taking his time to walk a circuitous route toward his apartment so he'd pass her bus stop. But when he turned the corner, his heart skipped at the sight of her walking in his direction. He made a snap decision, realizing providence was suddenly on his side.

Chapter 6

MARYANNE

Maryanne was so busy working she'd completely lost track of time. Again. There were a few loose ends to tie off and work to leave for her successor, whoever that might be. The new job was starting the next day, and it was all she could think about. Heck, she'd probably be up all night with excitement.

Might need to sneak a nip of Daddy's scotch to get sleep tonight, she thought to herself.

The sun was setting when she stepped outside, and the street was eerily quiet. She hoped she hadn't missed the last bus — if so, she'd have to walk all the way to The Mall for a pay phone to call Gladys to come get her. She looked nervously down the street, then closed her eyes and prayed.

When she opened them, a tall, solid figure with square shoulders was confidently striding up the icy hill in her direction. He was looking out into the distance it seemed, not turning left or right. There was no way he saw her sitting there. Or did he? She'd never liked being alone in the dark unless it was under a sky full of stars. Definitely not at a lonely bus stop at night. She looked at him out of the corner of her eye, because ladies did not stare, especially at strange men. She clutched the valise close to her chest and held up her chin, masking the fear curdling inside.

She was therefore unaware of how close he'd gotten until she decided to briefly turn her head under the guise of looking for the bus. He was almost an arm's length away, looking down at his watch. She quickly tried step out of his way, but it was too late — he slipped and fell directly toward her. In his flailing grabbed the valise, leaving her standing in the "hands up!" position and him flat on his face.

"Are you ok?" she said, cautiously crouching down. He rolled over and she wrinkled her nose at the sight - he had not one scratch, and his blue eyes seemed almost unnatural. He sniffed and scrambled to his feet - he was taller than she'd realized. She immediately felt tiny.

"I'm fine, just my pride is hurt, I guess," he said, smiling warmly.

She caught his gaze for a mere second and felt as if she were standing under a spotlight in her underwear.

He blinked and looked away quickly.

"Oh no, I'm so sorry," he said. He picked up her valise and brushed it off. "I broke your bag. Wait — I didn't even ask, are you alright?"

"I'm fine. You're the one that fell - flat on your face." He was movie star handsome — especially his jaw, which was impossibly chiseled, and deep-set blue eyes. The ground felt like sand under her feet, and she willed them to steady. "The devil is a lie," Pastor would say every Sunday.

"I sure did. I'm such a klutz." He looked at her bag again, squinting.

"It's ok," she said, but noticed the corner of a document was poking out. She was taking work home — a big no-no — but promised Atkins she'd finish her summary of several reports by Monday. She quickly tucked it back in.

"Can I try to fix that?" he asked, pointing to the broken

handle.

"Oh no, it's fine, really, it's just an old bag." She held it tightly. *He's handsome, but you don't know him, be careful,* she thought.

"Well at least let me compensate you." He reached into his coat pocket and pulled out a wallet. "How much is it worth?"

"Oh, please, don't, it's not worth anything." Her eyes darted around, looking for harsh, judgmental glares and invisible condemnation. Even though they were the only ones at the stop, how would it look if someone saw a man handing her money at a bus stop at dusk? That was the paranoia attendant with being Black — the constant fear that you'd get into trouble, even if you were doing nothing wrong.

"I won't take your money. But thank you." She gathered the coat tightly around her waist and looked straight ahead. *He'll get tired of this — of me — and go away soon,* she prayed. Never in life had she felt so idiotic.

"I'm sorry, I didn't mean to offend you." His eyes softened and the corner of his mouth sloped downward, as if he were deeply apologetic. She unconsciously wiggled her nose and held her breath. If the bus didn't come soon, she'd burst.

Gratefully, the glow of bus lights crested the hill and Maryanne felt an uneasy relief. His eyes grew large, and he quickly extended his hand.

"My name is Michael. What's yours?"

"Maryanne," she replied and offered her fingertips, a ladylike gesture which she hated but seemed safest. *He's just a man,* she thought to herself, looking down to avoid eye contact.

"Nice to meet you, Maryanne." The bus pulled up and the doors opened.

"Likewise." She slowly mounted the steps, wanting to break into a full sprint.

"Hey," he said. "I work around here - maybe we'll run into each other again?"

He's flirting, she thought. *Oh my goodness, he's flirting.*

"You gonna get on or what?" The bus driver's sharp command vaporized her brief reverie.

"I hope so," she shouted back at Michael before thinking,

and quickly found a seat. The doors closed.

She looked out the window and saw him standing there, looking in her direction. She giggled into the collar of her coat, and it felt like a fever was setting in.

It was fully dark by the time Maryanne arrived at her stop on Georgia Avenue. She disembarked quickly, keeping her eyes straight ahead to ignore the human vultures who hovered in front of the liquor store on the corner. Her neighborhood seemed a world away from the hustle on the avenue and after today, she was eager for the quiet of her room, where she could process what had happened. But as she rounded the corner onto her street, she saw a buzz of activity. Then it was as if she was watching a movie scene, and it was right in front of her house.

Maryanne broke into a full run. Familiar faces milled about, going up and down the front stairs, gathered in small huddles on the sidewalk. She wriggled through them, though without a care about niceties. Whispers propelled her forward and her eyes landed on Eric and Gladys' new Pontiac at the curb, its side mirror broken and what looked like blood on the door.

Pulse throbbing in her ears, she pushed through a sea of people to get inside. When she made it to the living room, she saw the horror and froze. Eric was laying on the couch, holding a bloodied towel to his head, with Gladys at his side, gripping his free hand. Her father was pacing the floor, his lips moist with whisky. A few younger men, including Martin, stood with arms crossed, their brows set and nostrils flaring. The entire neighborhood seemed to be in their living room. Her mother breathlessly emerged from the kitchen, flour dusted cheeks stained with tears. She handed Eric a towel filled with ice, and when he swapped it with the old one Maryanne saw the gaping wound across his brow.

"What happened?" she managed to croak, her knees turning to jelly.

"Eric's job sent him across the river to Virginia for the day," said Martin. Maryanne wasn't sure if her nausea was because of him or because of what happened to Eric. "And when he was coming back some state troopers though it would be fun to stop him on the 14th Street bridge and play 'beat up the Black man', right before crossing into D.C."

Another neighbor cleared his throat, the manly way of holding back tears. "The crazy part is they beat him *after* he showed proof of ownership. Those pigs were just mad that a Black man would own a nice car."

Maryanne balled her hands into fists, outrage coursing through her veins. It was a feeling with which she was intimately familiar, one that would cause her heart to twist in pain at the endless stories of daily injustice. And now, Eric.

"I hope I don't lose my job," Eric muttered, which would seem a ridiculous thing to worry about except that for a Black person being a victim equaled guilt. There was no point reporting a crime because the police would treat the victim like the criminal, or, even worse, shake them down. Maryanne's gaze shifted from Eric to her sister, who was shaking but her eyes were on fire, one hand on her husband and the other balled into a fist. Maryanne knew better than to engage her at this moment. The helplessness she must feel, the helplessness Maryanne felt, the inescapability of the injustice of simply being Black.

Mrs. Cooper, the neighborhood nurse, masterfully stitched his wound shut. "A total of six stitches," she announced with authority, "but no bone fragments", which led to a crescendo of sighs and sobs from the neighbors that now filled every inch of the first floor, including the front porch. Dr. Walker, who had been an importantly useless observer, pat Mrs. Cooper on her backside and she 'accidentally' elbowed him in the groin.

The energy in the house was suffocating. Several of Eric and Gladys' friends were there, including Gary, a former editor of The Hilltop, who aspired for big time journalism but wasn't even offered grunt work at the Washington Post. Undeterred he continued to pitch stories, especially about rampant police brutality, but they were only interested in cases where it resulted in a race riot. Just an ordinary, law-abiding Negro minding his business? No story. Nevertheless, the Quixotic journalist blinded an already traumatized Eric with his flash camera and rushed home to write the story that would *this time* be picked up by the Post. In the kitchen a few young men planned to march in protest, but then remembered they had jobs and livelihoods and did not want to put an even larger target on their backs. They raised their fists in solidarity with Eric then paid respect to Gladys, looking over their shoulders as they went home, wondering if they would be next.

After the house exhaled the last guest, and Gladys took Eric home, Maryanne sunk into the couch, across from her father. She looked at him with pleading eyes, wanting to say something, but what? *Daddy, I understand your anger and pain? Daddy, we need to bond together? Daddy, I still love you?* He looked at her with the sorrow of a condemned man, and without a word got up and trudged upstairs. No matter how many times he mocked or shunned her, it stung.

Maryanne let the hot tears flow, her soul begging her run into the street and scream out into the heavens. But the sight of her beautiful broken mother, hunched over a broom, trying to sweep away any memory of what had happened, woke her from the enraged stupor. She ran to the kitchen to get the trash bin. Empty bottles and filled ashtrays seemed to cover every surface. Bloody rags had already halfway filled up the bin and Marianne wanted to scream again.

"What they did to him.," her mother was saying, shaking her head. "I'm so glad he will be alright. And poor Gladys - she was a wreck!"

No, he will NOT be alright! And neither will Gladys, Maryanne thought. But her mother needed peace, so she bit the inside of her cheek and took a deep breath, tucking her anger down where her rage was stored. She had a surplus, that was for sure, and it never seemed the right time to unburden her psyche.

"Gladys is a good wife," said Maryanne, changing the subject. "She takes really good care of Eric."

"Yes, she does. Those two, whew!" Her mother's tone lifted, and her eyes lit up. "You can see it when they look at each other. They're so deeply in love."

"She's lucky." Maryanne felt her lip start to tremble.

"Oh, sweetie, you may not have found your Prince Charming, but look at you! Top of your class and a career girl. You don't need a man right now."

"But what if I want one?"

Maryanne almost choked the words back down her throat. Just a week ago she wanted nothing to do with men. Gladys was so lucky — no — divinely blessed — to have found Eric. He listened to her dreams, her hopes. Supported her career. Never tried to change her to be more like a "good" wife. Stayed with her during their fertility problems. Even after all of the disappointment, and the violence that was Martin, was there someone out there like that for Maryanne? The only love that was true — the only love she felt could rely on — was her love of space. But her encounter with Michael — well, there was a spark. It made her uncomfortable, but excited. And if she felt that with him, there had to be someone Black that would inspire the same reaction.

"You'll find him when the time is right," said her mother.

"But what if I never find anyone? Would you be disappointed if I - if I never got married?"

Her mother took a step back and looked her straight in the eye.

"What kind of talk is that? Why are you afraid you'll never get married?"

"Well, I'm afraid I'll never find a man that I *want* to marry. I mean, how did you know you wanted to marry Daddy?"

"What makes you think I wanted to marry Daddy?"

Maryanne shook her head as if there was water rushing between her ears.

"What do you mean?"

Her mother reached above the cabinet and retrieved a pack of cigarettes, a habit in which she had never indulged in front of her children. She opened the window over the sink and lit the cigarette on the stove. Maryanne stood with her mouth agape.

"Let me tell you something," said her mother, blowing a stream of smoke toward the window. "I never wanted to get married - especially not to your father."

Maryanne swooned and it suddenly felt like the ground was soft. She grabbed a chair and sat down. "Then, why?"

"Because back then we didn't have a choice. Black girls didn't have careers or aspirations. Well, we might have, but where would we work? Live? Plus, if you were a Black girl, the only jobs were washer woman, nanny, or typist, if you were lucky. Not enough to live on."

"But you had a career - you were a librarian."

"Not a real one, no, mostly clerical and hardly enough to get by. Then I got pregnant with Gladys."

Maryanne had never done the math, but her mother did look a bit plump in the wedding photos. She looked at her mother as if she were an actress on screen.

"Your father was - how do I say this - a rolling stone - a real *Tom Jones*. I wasn't his only girlfriend. He even tried to deny the baby was his." She blew another cloud of smoke. "My friend told me about this doctor who could take care of it - you know - the pregnancy if I got to him early enough. So, I set up the appointment. But the night before I was scheduled I found out three women had died in his basement clinic, and I changed my mind. I marched right into your father's office and threatened him with castration if he ignored his responsibilities."

Maryanne's jaw felt like it was in her lap. Her mother, the pillar of modesty, the model wife and mother, was now pouring a glass of whiskey, admitting she had sex before she was married, even undoing her chignon to literally let her hair down. Suddenly the cold linoleum looked inviting.

"So, you only married Daddy because you were pregnant?" said Maryanne.

"That's right," said her mother.

"And you never would have chosen him otherwise?"

"Wasn't even in love."

"So, all of this - this is just a lie?"

"Oh no, sweetie, not at all. God has a plan for us all. And you - and your sister - well, the two of you were written in the stars. I never imagined feeling the kind of love I feel for you and Gladys. It's more than I would ever have for your father - or any man. That being said," she stubbed out her cigarette. "I will not be disappointed if you never get married. Because if you do, I want it to be for true love. The kind of love you can't live without. Head over heels love. But that kind of love, well, is one in a million. So never forget you have what I didn't."

"What's that?"

"A choice."

Chapter 7

MARYANNE

Maryanne had not slept well, anxiety scratching all night like wool pajamas. The conversation with Mother on Friday left her reeling, but strangely hopeful. Maybe it didn't matter that Martin, or any other of her dismal dates hadn't worked out. It wasn't her fault she never fell in love. She just hadn't found the right man. Of course it wasn't that, ugh, *White* man at the bus stop. Clearly, he wasn't *truly* interested, just getting some kicks toying with a Black girl. That's how men generally treated her — she was ignored, patronized, teased, put down, or demeaned. But the flirting was fun. Exciting.

Her thoughts swirling, she gave up sleeping, slipped out of bed and turned on her desk lamp. A draft report for Atkins was still sitting on the blotter, so she got to work.

Too easy, she thought to herself, just 45 minutes later. Looking up from her desk, she caught her reflection in the vanity mirror. Dark circles swam under her tired eyes and all her curlers had fallen out overnight, so her hair was bouffant on one side and flat on the other. "Silly girl", she muttered, and stuck out her tongue. Nothing attractive here. No, she was wrong, that mystery White man wasn't *really* flirting. He was just playing with her. But the job — the job was real. She flopped back on her bed and dozed off for a few hours, pulled herself together at dawn, and set out into the chilly morning to catch the early bus.

She was going to take control of her fate — yes, she would — because now she was on an important project, and she was trusted with a clearance, and her hard work and intellect would be recognized and rewarded, not feared, maligned, or ignored. It wasn't the job she wanted, but it was a step up. As she walked into NASA and settled in with the wave of scientists, policy wonks, military officers, and secretaries, she felt almost like she belonged. A surge of pride filled her chest as she strode past her old desk and the bloated conference room, toward the elevator.

Maryanne navigated to the locked door, rang the bell, and looked over her shoulder. After last week's events she kept waiting for someone to pop out and declare "gotcha!" putting her back in her place. Instead, the door clicked and swung open. A skinny 20-something with acne squinted his eyes at her, as if having to open the door ruined his life. "Follow me," he grunted, handing her an envelope marked "TOP SECRET," then slinked away without looking in her direction.

No red light today. She was legitimate.

The secure area conference room was indistinguishable from the one by her old desk, except there was a much smaller group present. Atkins was sitting at the table talking with Roger who was wearing an Air Force uniform, and a brill-creamed everyman with thick black glasses. Three other men huddled at the far end of the table. Maryanne stood in the door, unsure where to go when Atkins slammed his notebook down and said in a voice too loud for the small room,

"This is Maryanne. You make sure she has access to any information she needs to do her job. Come see me if you have any questions." The men shifted in their seats as if trying to hold back flatulence, wincing in agreement. Atkins looked at her. "Go ahead, take any seat, and read the memo in the envelope you got — sign it then return to me. Then we can talk."

The men got back to whatever they were doing, completely

ignoring her again, which was a relief. There was nothing she hated more than being stared at or put in the spotlight. And now she felt as alien as a Martian, in a lab of smart men. It was only a matter of time before they began to resent her intellect as well as her race and gender. Well, she didn't care. She wasn't there because she was a shrinking violet. She wasn't there to be the help. She was there because she deserved to be. She gave one hard look around the table and signed the memo promising not to disclose information to any unauthorized person under pain of the law with a flourish. Atkins looked at her with mild amusement, then began.

"We have known for several years now the Soviets have deployed spacecraft into outer space to orbit and relay back information on Venus and Mars. We've been at it too, you know."

"What kind of information?" asked Maryanne, leaning forward in anticipation.

"Mostly Geo-type data. Pictures. Scientific and intellectual study. But then we started thinking — what else might they be doing? Because you know, when the Russians say they are doing one thing, they are really doing something else. And their number one objective is beating us — on Earth and in Outer Space."

"But we're winning right?" said Maryanne. "Doesn't the next Apollo launch again soon?" She sat up straighter. "We'll make it to the moon before them, and no one is close to sending men into outer space." She felt eyes on her again, but less harsh, more curious. She sat up straighter.

"It's not just manned missions we're worried about. There are other ways of extending U.S. power into space. You understand, right? This is why your interest in radioastronomy is useful here."

Maryanne nodded her head. She still could not believe he had any idea what her research interests were since he had never asked her directly. This was their first real conversation in her entire six months with NASA.

"Yes, uh, I specifically want to listen to and study the electromagnetic waves emitted by celestial bodies . . .there is so much to learn about our Solar System and outer space . . . " She paused. Everyone in the room was again intently listening to her.

Atkins half-smiled. "We think the Soviets might be trying to use their deep space links to create a seamless communication stream between their spacecraft and military ground stations, able to serve as a way to cut short the distance information would have to travel to Earth." He pushed his glasses back into position. "You, my dear, with your keen eye for obscure patterns, seem to be really good at identifying their signals, albeit in an unconventional way."

She twisted and turned her findings around in her mind, inducing a minor headache. Sitting down, she placed her hands on the table, fingers tracing invisible numbers. All that data, the waves and lines — they told a story, just like the math games she used to play with her father. All she had to do was thread them together. Roger slid a legal pad and pencil in front of her.

Show them what you can do, she thought.

"But the satellites just take images — I know we have antennas on the ground, but we need to get close enough to hear," she said, looking up, catching sight of Atkins's mild aggravation. "Oh, I think I understand. You're trying to get close enough to their signal to *hear* what is being communicated."

"Bingo." Atkins leaned in so closely she almost recoiled, but instead she squeezed her thighs together and drew her lips inward. He lowered his voice "Now, what I am about to tell you is very sensitive. You can't even tell anyone else at NASA, got it?"

Maryanne nodded, suppressing a triumphant smile.

"Ok," he said. "So, you need to know that NASA does not spy. Nope." He shook his head. "But we do work with our military and intelligence community. And there is a new game in town, called the National Reconnaissance Office."

She blinked. "What's that? I've never heard of them."

"They're a special intelligence function that does nothing but satellite work, getting information from space-deployed satellites focused on finding out what our enemies are doing on the ground, so we can defend ourselves. The Air Force used to do this," he snorted. "But they could never get their act together."

Roger twisted his mouth like he had just swallowed vinegar. "Calm down, Roger," Atkins continued, "the higher ups — they had enough — so NRO was founded."

"We've observed the Soviet's ground stations with satellites, which are like the ones you are familiar with, but are more sensitive and better positioned." Atkins leaned back in his chair and looked up at the ceiling, then swooped forward and slammed both hands on the table. "There's information coming from all over the place, which makes it hard to pull together succinct reports and briefing papers for the higher ups." He swept his arms over the piles of paper on his desk. "You're speedy at pulling together and understanding every piece of information put in front of you, and your calculations are spot on. Maryanne, you're going to help make sure we continue to get support for our work. And that NASA," he looked in the direction of Roger, "stays in the lead."

Maryanne rubbed her temples, careful not to disrupt the edges of her hairstyle. Helping the government spy on the Soviet Union? That had absolutely nothing to do with her interest in outer space. It wasn't that she didn't care about the Russians, but daily injustices, violence, and threats to her and her community were more pressing. It was as if Atkins hadn't heard a word she said.

"Sir," she said. "After, or maybe while I do this work, can you help me find placement at one of the labs, or in a graduate program, or . . ."

"Hold your horses, kiddo," he said, looking slightly annoyed. "We have crucial work to do here." He started to walk away, but suddenly stopped and turned to face her. "Look, if you do well here, if you do the work I know you are capable of doing, you'll continue to have a future at NASA."

Her heart was sinking, but she wrestled her thoughts back to the positive. It wasn't exactly the job she wanted, but it was still important, and he trusted her. If she kept her head down and helped Atkins achieve his goals, she might be — no — she *would* be rewarded. She had to believe that. She closed her eyes and visualized her picture behind the glass of a display case on

NASA's main hallway, in front of a team of the men who'd once ignored her. She was another steppingstone closer to the promised land. She would not fail.

Maryanne looked at the wall clock and blinked hard. Was it really 5 o'clock? She looked around the office, rubbing her right hand which was cramping from non-stop writing. Half the staff had left, and she hadn't even noticed. She'd whizzed through her work with precision and confidence, double-checking to ensure perfection. No more meaningless calculations that went into a black hole. She now had full access and was part of a team. She locked up her work and bid goodbye to Atkins, who kept his head down and merely raised a hand in reply.

She got to the bus stop early and took a seat on the bench. It was warm enough for her to pull out *Murder on the Orient Express* and rejoin Hercule Poirot in his interrogation of Princess Dragomiroff. She looked up to ponder a clue and instead saw — was it — Michael? Her stomach fluttered. He walked with the same cocky stride as the day before, but fortunately the ice had melted. He was waiving at her and smiling, as if they were old friends. She felt as if she were glued to the bench.

"Hello, Maryanne!" he said heartily.

She saw the taut lines of his square jaw, accentuating sharp cheekbones. She smiled back and felt her face flush with warmth, but kept her lips tightly closed, which always made her otherwise clandestine dimples pop.

"How're you today?" he said, standing right next to her. He looked taller than she remembered, but then again, she was sitting down.

"I'm well. How are you?" she said, closing her book.

"Oh, just groovy. Good day — busy. Hey!" He pointed at the valise in her lap. The thread around where the handle used to be attached was fraying. "You haven't fixed your bag."

"It's fine. I'll get a new one soon." She shifted in her seat, unable to get comfortable. Why was he talking to her again? Like *that*. He seemed harmless, if not a bit chatty. Friendly, but with a little extra. "That thang," Gladys would call it. She could feel herself starting to blush and wished she could just bury her head in her coat.

"You work around here?" he asked.

Maryanne caught herself. *I don't know this man,* she thought. *And now he' asking me where I work? No, wait, he's seen her twice at this bus stop. Just a normal question. Small talk.*

"I work here," she said. "At NASA."

"Wow. That's groovy. What do you do? Are you a — secretary?"

She felt her face change temperature. "No. I'm a scientist. An astronomer." She turned and faced forward.

"I'm sorry that was so — stupid of me. I promise, I am NOT a chauvinist pig."

She continued to avoid looking at him, fighting the broad smile forming in her chest. Had he read Betty Friedan? Gladys had once tried to shove *Advice to a Young Wife from an Old Mistress* under her nose, but she'd picked up *The Feminine Mystique* instead. She couldn't wait to tell Gladys it had paid off.

"True," she said emboldened. "You are no pig." She stunned herself with the harshness of her words. "Oh, I'm sorry. I didn't mean to . . ."

"No, I'm sorry. I should have known better than to assume that you were not — important."

"Do you mean to say that secretaries aren't important?"

"No — no — not at all, what I meant to say was that you look smart . . ."

He looked at his feet like a kid who'd just trampled a flower bed.

What are you doing? she scolded herself.

Maryanne packed up her book and stood, nose in the air, but unsteady on her feet. She looked at him with cautious amusement, watching him trying to recover from tripping over his tongue. The bus was on its way toward her stop, and she secretly hoped it would break down.

"Um, Michael?" she said. "The bus. It's almost here."

He gave her a look that she recognized — yes — it was one

of those James Dean, Steve McQueen smoldering looks, and she suddenly understood why their female co-stars turned into starry-eyed martyrs.

"I'll see you again?" he said as the bus doors opened.

All she could manage was a smile over her shoulder as she mounted the stairs. She slid into an open seat and wrapped her arms around herself, wishing she could sink all the way down, or just lay down and die. Once again, she'd gotten caught up the energy of a situation, like drinking too much good wine, then feeling hungover. Peaking over the edge of the window, Michael was still standing there, looking in her direction, a delicious smile on his face. She pinched herself.

Chapter 8

MIKHAIL/MICHAEL

izdets! Mikhail said to himself as he slipped into his car for the drive across town to his second apartment. Maryanne fearlessly worked to put him in his place. He'd never seen a woman shift so quickly to seductive aggression. At least, not a Western one. It was enjoyable. Well, perhaps a bit more than just enjoyable.

He let it happen, of course. She was quite clever, but he knew exactly what she was up to. He'd never let anymore, much less a woman, knock him off his game. He'd left beautiful, seductive women of all ages in pathetic tears on two continents, getting only as much as he needed from them to complete his missions. He almost had to kill one who got too close and wouldn't take no for an answer, but fortunately she killed herself and spared him from doing his most hated task. Mikhail was only 27, but knew he was a skilled lover, with an iron wall around his heart. Love was transactional, never real. A means to an end. He'd never really fall in love. The only woman deserving of his heart was his mother. And the Motherland had his undying devotion.

He started walking home. As far as he knew, he had the night off. It would give him time to recalibrate his strategy. He knew it could take some time to get Maryanne to warm up, because in his over-eagerness, he almost lost her. Good thing he'd baited her to reveal a little bit more about herself, her personality. He'd never presumed a girl like her would be a feminist, but you never could tell these days. Also, her comeback was totally unexpected. It was cagey, smart, and unafraid. There was no question — she'd been the most interesting experience he'd had since arriving in the U.S. His training had not prepared him for an intelligent, Black, female, and outspoken mark. And her beauty, it was stunning. He would not have to fake attraction.

An exceptional target.

Mikhail parked in the alley driveway behind his rowhouse near U street, across from Meridian Hill Park. It was a marginally integrated slice of neighborhood directly on the invisible line between Black and White D.C., populated with academics, artists, and well-off bohemians. Ironically, the park had been built on top of an established Black neighborhood and all of the residents were displaced decades before. Mikhail's apartment was on the second floor, giving him a decent view of the park where he had several drop spots.

"What's happening, man?" he heard over his shoulder once he entered the tiny vestibule. Mikhail braced for a fight even though he knew who was speaking.

"Hey, Leroy," said Mikhail, turning to face his first-floor neighbor, holding out his hand for a quick palm slap and slide, a gesture he'd come to respect. "It's good to see you back on your feet, man."

Leroy was a fellow bachelor who seemed to favor wearing red, black, and green. It didn't take long for Mikhail to identify him as an activist, given his penchant for Patchouli, black berets, and the Che Guevara poster that hung over a threadbare gold velvet sofa. He was about the same height as Mikhail, but leaner, with deep copper skin, and an incredibly dense afro.

Leroy pointed to the sling that cradled his left arm. "I can stop wearing this piece of useless fabric tomorrow," he said.

"Shoulder's still a bit stiff but almost 100%."

"Fucking pigs," said Mikhail, his lips curling in disgust.

"They couldn't take me down," said Leroy, jerking his chin up, then looking at Mikhail. "I never thanked you."

"Didn't help much," said Mikhail. "You still got shot."

When they first met, Leroy was unsurprisingly cold and dismissive. Mikhail tried to ingratiate himself by spouting radical rhetoric, but his neighbor's response was lukewarm, at best. But then one night Mikhail was walking to the apartment and saw Leroy and his crew of fellow revolutionaries being stalked by a shiny-faced police officer with bugged out eyes. Seizing on the opportunity to 'prove' himself, Mikhail walked casually past the cop and as he passed Leroy he whispered, "Pig on your ass, directly behind me." Within seconds the men took off running in different directions. The cop yelled for backup and bolted after Leroy.

Seconds later Mikhail heard shots and his heart sunk — not because he cared about Leroy's wellbeing — but because he didn't want to have to start all over with a new Black radical. It was a lot of work for little benefit. The KGB had long targeted Black activists, easily exploiting endemic racism, violence, and economic inequities to foment utopian idealism about communism. But successful engagement was rare, as civil rights activists tended to be democracy zealots, and radicals trusted no White people, no matter from whence they came or what pipe dreams they sold. If tipping Leroy off to the police gave Mikhail an in, and if Leroy turned out to be worthy of his trust, the Center would be pleased. If dead, well, no way to know if the tactic worked.

But then Leroy was back, out of the blue, saying he was in a "light coma" for several days. Mikhail didn't think it necessary to verify. Those people were getting shot or beaten by the police almost every day it seemed.

"Up for a beer?" said Leroy. "I've got ice cold Schlitz in the fridge."

"Sounds great," said Mikhail, mentally patting himself on the back. Leroy was now loose and friendly, and this was the first time he'd invited Mikhail into his home.

"Come on in, brother," said Leroy.

Yes, Mikhail said to himself. *He called me brother, this is good, this is good.* He looked around the living room. "Nice place," he said. Same basic layout as his place upstairs, but a world apart. Leroy's apartment was a love letter to Africa, complete with masks, rattan furniture, and large leafy plants. Books from writers such as Ralph Ellison and Amiri Baraka sat in neat stacks around the room, and a flier for the American Communist Party peeked out from under the coffee table. Sunlight streamed through bamboo blinds and heady incense hung in the air.

Leroy emerged from the kitchen with two cold beers in his free hand. "Have a seat," he said, handing Mikhail a bottle. Mikhail sat on the worn but comfortable couch. Leroy sat across from him in an ostentatious peacock chair.

"You look like a king," Mikhail said, half-jokingly. *I hope he doesn't think I'm mocking him*, he thought immediately.

"That's the whole point," replied Leroy with a broad smile.

Mikhail sighed with relief on the inside. "Did you hear what's going down in Memphis?"

Mikhail almost couldn't believe yet another U.S. city was blowing up over racial injustice. He'd arrived in the U.S. right after the hot, violent summer of 1967, brimming with righteousness over American hypocrisy, eager to capitalize on chaos. But in his short time in the U.S., the struggle for equality materialized in the form of real people he knew, like Maryanne and Leroy. It's not like he cared about them personally, no, but it wasn't right how something as stupid as skin color shaped their ability to just live.

"Of course, man," said Leroy. "Don't live under a rock, especially when it comes to my people. 'Bout time those sanitation workers went on strike."

"Yeah, those stuffed pigs in Memphis make money on the broken backs of hard-working men. Making money hand over foot. And yet those men get crushed by bad equipment, work ten hours a day, and only paid kiddie allowance money."

"Just another day in America," Leroy snorted. He took a

large swing of beer and continued. "Democracy is a lie and capitalism is the devil." He looked straight at Mikhail, eyes cold as stone.

"True that," said Mikhail, shaking his head to break the stare.

Leroy's eyes narrowed. "So, what's a nice, shiny White boy doing hangin' with an angry Black man like me?"

"Because we are both fighting oppression, and racism, and a government set up just to keep people like me in power while everyone else suffers. Because it ain't right, and because I am exactly the kind of person you want as an ally."

"Why is that?" Leroy, leaned in. "What makes you so special?" Leroy reached up, grabbed his pick, and combed out his afro a bit. Mikhail had seen other afroed men do the same. These cats were more obsessed with their hair than Miss America.

"Let's just say I want to help." Mikhail swallowed a large gulp of beer. "And I have — assets."

"Alright man, alright," said Leroy. "I don't know exactly what that means, but we can talk." He shifted in the chair and suddenly winced.

"You alright?" said Mikhail.

"Just my shoulder, you know. It aches."

Mikhail looked at his host, whose jaw stiffened like a man trying not to cry out in pain. *You got through*, he thought to himself. *Take your leave and re-engage later.*

"Well, I'll leave you be so you can rest.," said Mikhail. "We'll talk later."

"Thanks man. Yeah, later."

Surging with confidence, Mikhail bid his potential asset good night. *The door is open*, he thought. *I just walked right in.* He climbed the stairs to his apartment smiling, knowing how jealous Geoffrey would be that he'd bagged a Black asset, a communist, at that. Maryanne was next. He lay down to sleep, belly full of beer and heart full of pride.

He'd been in the U.S. for only six months, but all was finally coming together.

Chapter 9

LEROY/SPECIAL AGENT DONOVAN

February 12, 1968
FBI Headquarters
Washington, D.C.

"Leroy", aka Special Agent Gordon Donovan, sat in his windowless office mindlessly rubbing a talisman, his father's 92nd Infantry patch. It had survived two wars but was on the verge of destruction due to Donovan's nervous habit.

He hated having to lay low, but word on the street was he might be dead, so it was best to keep his "fellow revolutionaries" thinking that, at least for a while. He'd gotten in deep with a few organizations, including the Panthers, gained trust, and kept a close eye. His absence would be noticed, and the fact that he'd actually been shot by the police was painfully lucky. There were at least two other cats still on the inside, but they never interacted, or even shared information, which was unlike any other program in the Bureau.

He didn't join the Bureau to spy on other Black people. He wanted to root out communists and other enemies to America. Real enemies. Spending his school years hiding under a desk to practice being nuked by the Soviets made an impression. Couldn't do much about racism in the U.S., but annihilation wasn't the answer either. At the FBI Academy he spent the little free time he was given researching Soviet activities in the U.S., but was instead assigned to the COINTELPRO program, along with the other two Black agents in his class.

Donovan grew out his afro, rented an apartment near the action on U Street close to Howard's campus, and created a new identity around that of an activist who'd grown weary of King's turn-the-other cheek tactics. Communism curious, but not committed. It didn't take long for him to work his way into the movement, and even less time to determine he was unlikely to find any Black-Soviet connection. But when Michael, or whatever his real name was, moved into the building, he could sense something was different about him. It was the way he carried himself, looking straight ahead while his ears twitched, an easy gait that seemed practiced. Mannerisms undetectable to the average human but nakedly visible to a fellow covert operative. The FBI and CIA had so many undercover and subversive activities in D.C. it was impossible to know if this dude was a fellow Fed or foreign agent.

Then Michael tipped him off about that cop— very professionally. No Fed would have broken cover to do that. They would have just stood by, then swooped in after all the action settled down. No — Michael — or whatever his name was — went out of his way to show he was down for the cause. Donavan decided to get closer, wiggle his way in, and figure out who the hell the guy really was.

Then he got shot.

Donovan reached up to touch his injury, not wincing in pain, but at the memory of who'd shot him. At least they thought he was just a regular Black man, easy target, presumed guilty. They'd have shot twice if they knew he was FBI. No love lost between the Metropolitan Police Department and the Feds. Suddenly, there was a knock on the door, but before he could answer, his boss, Special Agent in Charge Gerry O'Connell walked in.

"How's the shoulder?" said O'Connell.

"Aches a bit but getting better every day." Donovan adjusted his sling, which made his scar itch.

"I still can't believe they shot you," said O'Connell, shaking his head. "I mean, you identified yourself, right?"

"Not until I was at the hospital. Remember, I never break cover."

"Yeah, I know, but they shot you with your hands up and in the back. You were standing against a wall! I mean, that's just crazy."

Donovan wanted to laugh and say, *oh, now you understand, jackass.* "Well, it wouldn't be the first time the police did something that wasn't quite by the book," he said instead.

"Right." O'Connell furrowed his eyebrows and turned to leave. "Oh," he said turning back. "I almost forgot why I came down. You mentioned that you may have ID'd a foreign agent?"

"Yeah, cat named Michael. Well, that's what he goes by. I've seen him around, trying to chat up some of the activists around U street."

Donovan drew in his breath to slow down. He had to be careful. Not too much detail. Especially now that it seemed Michael was prepared to offer his 'assets' to help 'the cause'. Nothing like word of shadow funding to get Hoover's juices flowing. O'Connell was decent, but even he'd blindly accepted Hoover's obsession with pursuing civil rights activists rather than actual enemies of America. Anyone challenging or criticizing racism in America was considered a radical, and anyone radical was considered to be communist and labeled 'red.'

"And has he roped in any radicals?" said O'Connell, on beat. "Anyone we should take a look at?"

Donovan's neck burned with frustration. "No. Nothing like that. But this Michael guy — something just ain't right."

O'Connell looked at him with curiosity. "Got it. Well, you just keep an eye on him and let me know if you find anything." He walked up to Donovan and leaned in so close that he could smell O'Connell's Aqua Velva. "And let's keep this between us for now, ok? Don't want the stiffs upstairs to take over yet — especially if your theory about this guy turns out to be true."

Donovan nodded. Of course, he'd keep it close hold. He was supposed to turn over all information about foreign agents to the Counterintelligence agents — COINTELPRO was strictly limited to disruption and discrediting of domestic organizations — but this could be his chance to prove that he deserved to be amongst the elite.

Michael is mine, he thought, every nerve in his body tingling with excitement.

Chapter 10

MARYANNE

February 12, 1968
Maryanne's House, Northwest Washington, D.C.

Gladys and Eric were at the house when Maryanne got home, which was a blessing, because she had not been able to organize her thoughts since leaving that sorry man standing on the sidewalk. She kicked herself the entire ride home. She could have gotten in real trouble, talking back to a White man — or any man — like that. But he played along, even struggled to recover, to say the right thing, letting her drive the conversation. She felt like a kid on her first bike ride with the training wheels off.

Maryanne tried squeezing her eyes open and shut to erase his magnetic smile from her memory, so much so the woman next to her on the bus cautiously moved to the next seat. Her cheeks flushed with embarrassment, and a giggle caught in her throat. Yes, she hoped — really hoped — to run into him again. It was crazy, for sure, but irresistible. She must have looked ill, because when she got home Gladys gave her a funny look.

"You got a fever?" said Gladys, pressing the back of her hand against Maryanne's forehead. "Woo, you're a bit warm!"

"What — no — I'm fine," said Maryanne, gently pushing her sister's hand away. "It's just — I got a promotion!"

Maryanne relaxed once it was clear her diversion worked, and basked in the effusive praise, even from her father.

But her thoughts started wandering again at dinner. What did he smell like? Were his hands rough or soft? She quickly looked around to prevent thinking about *other* things. Eric seemed like he was back to himself, though the heavy stitches across his brow made him look a bit like Herman Munster. Gladys was chatty and cheerful but kept eyeing her younger sister with curiosity. Even when they were little, Gladys seemed to be able to read her mind, but she never ratted her out. There was always a little tax to pay though, like half her allowance or standing lookout as she necked with some boy.

After dinner, Gladys pulled Maryanne into the hallway.

"What's going on with you?" she asked. "Your head in the clouds? It looks like you're having impure thoughts!"

"Don't let Daddy hear you say that," said Maryanne, trying to change the subject. "He'll know Mommy was actually taking us to confession all those years." She suddenly felt the urge to burst out laughing at the irony of her mother being Catholic.

"C'mon Mary." Gladys pinched her sister's waist. "You better talk."

"I have no idea what you're talking about." Maryanne folded her arms and jut out one hip, trying to look non-plussed. But she knew her sister wouldn't give up. She always read her like a book.

"You're lying — I can tell!"

"It's nothing, really. I just, you know, met an interesting guy."

Gladys' eyes got big. "What? Met someone? Who? What do you mean by interesting? You'd better tell me or I'll . . .."

"Girls be quiet!" their father yelled. He didn't like being disturbed during his post-dinner snooze in front of the television.

"We're not girls, we're women!" Gladys shouted in his direction. She turned back to face Maryanne. "So?"

"There's not much to say. I've only talked to him a couple of times."

"Has he asked you out?"

"No."

"But you like him." Gladys looked at her through narrow eyes. Maryanne felt like a balloon that was slowly deflating. "I've never seen you — well — infatuated." She pointed a polished finger. "You're infatuated!"

"It's just a little crush. I'll probably never see him again."

"Maryanne, if it is meant to be, it is meant to be. You're smiling too hard for it not to mean something. You'll see him again."

Gladys, as always, was a spring of eternal optimism for her sister's chances at love. The last time Maryanne felt anything close to like this was with her very first crush, in ninth grade, but the boy broke her heart by acting like he was all hers while secretly pursuing her best friend. Gladys, ever Maryanne's protector, said something to him that blanched him two shades lighter, and he avoided her for the next year. When Maryanne finally told Gladys the truth about Martin, she had to prevent her from confronting him. And what if Gladys learned she was crushing on a White man?

No, of course she couldn't go steady with a White man. That only happened with celebrities in Hollywood, and everyday Black folk would grunt in disapproval. Gladys, of course, would assume Michael was Black, which was best since she had had an almost violent allergic reaction to the movie *Guess Who's Coming to Dinner?*

"Well," said Gladys. "What does he look like?"

Maryanne swallowed hard. "Um, normal. You know, he's handsome. Tall." Maryanne's tongue caught on her teeth as she spoke, the salty blood burning her throat. She obviously couldn't say more than that.

"Well," Gladys pinched at Maryanne's waist, "before you start going steady, I want to meet him."

Maryanne laughed and nodded, torn between wanting to see Michael again and wishing he would drop off the face of the Earth.

Chapter 11

MIKHAIL/MICHAEL

February 13, 1968
Mikhail's Apartment, Southwest
Washington, D.C.

Mikhail chuckled at the news and turned off the TV. It was pure folly, the Americans' aggression in Vietnam. The Vietnamese, who had long suffered under the colonial yoke of Western imperial capitalism, had seen the light, like the Chinese had a more than a decade prior. The Americans looked like inept bullies abroad and couldn't even keep their own people in line at home. The world order was shifting, America was crumbling, and he had a front row seat.

He slipped his feet into slippers and shuffled into the bathroom to prepare for bed, running his hands over his new cotton pajamas. The fabric was downy and soft, as were his slippers and robe. He made a mental note to buy several of these sets to take home. Also, some toothbrushes, a hairbrush, and many bars of soap. The *Ivory* kind. And the green dish soap that smelled like a meadow and didn't dry out his hands. He felt a little pang of guilt, this obsession with capitalist trappings, but the Politburo bosses certainly enjoyed the spoils of their status. So why shouldn't he? Even the toilet paper was gentler in the U.S.

Home. The Motherland. He closed his eyes to conjure up

warm memories — but it was never of the place. Instead, his mind drifted always to images of his mother — toiling away over a pot of thin soup or scrubbing socks in the bathtub, kissing his dirty face after scrapping with his brothers in the square, letting him clean his father's war medals, which she kept hidden. He loved his homeland, yes, but he loved his mother more.

Even loved her when she told him she was the one to turn in his father, for being a traitor. "If I had not notified the NKVD of what he was saying about Comrade Stalin, then someone else would have, and we would all be sent to Gulag," she told him tearfully the night before he left for training. "You were just a baby, your future ahead. So, your father went quietly. He *was* a hero." At first confused, and later, bitter, Mikhail came to understand and fully respect her actions. They were driven by pure love, though imperfect, because she did it for the love of her children and not Mother Russia.

His mind drifted to his Maryanne strategy, and he felt his pulse quicken. When he thought she was a secretary, he probably would have just tried to sleep with her once and plant a bug or two, or maybe just drug her and get her to talk. But a scientist? She could prove to be more valuable than he originally thought. He'd have to genuinely get to know her, earn her trust, get her to open up. Develop a relationship.

He lay down in bed and stared at the ceiling.

It would be more complicated than if she were a White woman. Much more complicated. The Center had trained him to be charming, rugged, stoic, playful. But only with White women. They gave passing reference to "the Negroes", only that they were hyper-sexual, made good couriers and chauffeurs, and that the more they converted to communism it would be a slap in the face of Uncle Sam.

He needed to get Roman's approval to take it to the next level.

He turned off the lights and closed his eyes. Within moments he started drifting, flirting with sleep, but his swirling thoughts traced her eyes, her lips, her neck and bust, her waist. He had to get up and splash cold water on his face to settle down.

He wasn't going to be able to meet Roman for a couple of days. He'd have to keep cool until then.

Chapter 12

MIKHAIL/MICHAEL

February 16, 1968
Cleveland Park, Northwest
Washington, D.C.

Mikhail met Roman at his garden apartment, an art deco building in a pleasant neighborhood near the zoo. This was on the West side of Rock Creek Park, an area unapologetically red-lined despite the lack of any "Whites Only" signs. His handler bore the air of a distinguished older gentleman, perhaps a former diplomat, with a full head of white hair, taut jaw, and aquiline nose. Roman was affable and well-liked by his neighbors, especially the recently discarded middle-aged wife of a State Department official. He even baked for her. He kept a small kitchen garden and often helped the landscapers tend the building's lush rose bushes. Though his full-time job was managing his agents, he'd sometimes use the prime location for a little recon. He had a counterpart — a woman — who lived somewhere near the Capitol, but Mikhail wasn't quite sure where. All he knew was that she worked as a housekeeper for someone on the Hill.

Mikhail would visit at lunchtime, when most of the residents were out and the cleaning staff was on was on break. If ever confronted, he'd say he was Roman's nephew. Mikhail liked visiting because Roman was an excellent cook with cosmopolitan taste. His apartment was decorated in contemporary nostalgia, with no photographs but many American relics from the past decade, including a wiggling hula doll and his beloved jewel-colored aluminum tumblers. He had a warm, paternal demeanor, which Mikhail knew meant was to appear trustworthy and gentle.

"Here are your onions," said Mikhail, handing Roman a brown paper bag. "I even found some sour cream."

"Brilliant!" said Roman in his rich baritone, to which he'd added a note of highborn Ivy League flair. "I knew you would come through." He took the groceries to the kitchen and returned with a platter of hot tea, jam, and cookies. Mikhail sat down, poured himself a cup and swirled in a heavy dollop of strawberry preserves.

"I have an interesting development," said Mikhail. "You know that girl — the Black girl? Well, turns out she may have more value than I first thought."

Roman sat down. "Go on."

"Well, first it was her dress and the fact that she was comfortable with Orion, I thought, maybe she's a secretary? Wouldn't hurt to have another asset in the Administrator's office. Could use her to plant a bug or two in the office."

"We've done that before," said Roman, stroking his chin. "Big operation, though."

"Yes, but then, when I first engaged her, I saw that she had a classified document, perhaps irresponsibly, in her possession, in her bag, which she quickly concealed. I monitored her and she didn't appear to hand it over to anyone."

"Interesting. So, she's something more like a technical worker? Who brings her work home. You know, at home it is not so unusual for a woman to be technical, but it's uncommon here."

"She's more than technical — she's a scientist."

Roman leaned forward. "Really?"

"An astronomer."

"And you figured that out?"

"She told me." Mikhail decided the details about how he got that information was not important.

"I see." Roman looked at his watch. "Let's take a walk," he abruptly declared. He grabbed a newspaper from his counter and a heavy pen from the kitchen drawer. Mikhail had a similar pen with a camera on the end. You could take decent pictures if you got close enough to your subject. He followed Roman, mildly curious to see who they would surveille.

It was crisp and bright outside. Roman had the paper folded under his arm and held the pen in its folds. They walked south, toward the bridge to the Adams Morgan neighborhood.

"I share your concerns about how to do this," said Roman casually, waving to someone on the other side of the street.

"I've done a little research," said Mikhail, knowing better than to look toward where Roman had waved. "And what I found is that Blacks and Whites in D.C. work together, but social interaction is limited — there are bookshops and jazz clubs, and even a few restaurants where they interact — friendly and romantic. I'll keep my eyes open."

"Ok," said Roman in a tone that gave Mikhail pause. "If it becomes too much, if you feel yourself being watched or it becomes dangerous, cut her loose and walk away."

Mikhail knew what that meant. Run over by a unanimous car, carbon monoxide poisoning in the home, a staged drug overdose. An image of Maryanne's body, gray and disheveled in an alley, a needle in her arm, crept into his mind. He blinked hard to erase it.

"I'll be careful," said Mikhail. "But I won't drop her until I get as much info as I can. Something tells me she might be just what we need to jump start our mission."

As they approached the corner, a few men in dark suits with dark glasses and earpieces spilled out of a small French restaurant. The men lined the short walkway from the restaurant to cars with diplomatic license plates, each looking in a different direction. Roman slowed down and Mikhail fell into step. Then a trio of sternly smiling men emerged, chattering in French and British English. They were trailed by a splinter of a young woman with a low, blonde ponytail juggling three briefcases.

"Stéphanie, dépêche-toi!" shouted the man in front.

"Qui, j'arrive!" she responded like an angsty teenager.

The men shook hands, grabbed their briefcases, got in their cars, and took off.

No wonder this is where Roman spends his afternoons, thought Mikhail. "The French Ambassador to the U.S?" he asked Roman, lips unmoving.

Roman blinked in agreement. Then he slightly tilted his head toward the woman who was left standing there, flustered and forgotten.

Just like that, another mission, Mikhail thought, as he sauntered over to save poor Stéphanie. He was a bit surprised that Roman would put him on an assignment that had nothing to do with NASA, but he'd been told back in Moscow that in the field agents were used as needed. Roman didn't need to give specific instructions — he knew that the French had been playing both the U.S. and the U.S.S.R. on Vietnam and the crisis in Czechoslovakia and learning what they were saying to the Americans was an objective. It wouldn't be a heavy lift. But it would be enough of a break to make sure his head stayed in the game. He was at risk of losing focus if he thought about Maryanne too much.

The higher the stakes, the most focused he was. He felt a cool rush of relief as he let the pretty Black girl drift to the back of his mind.

Chapter 13

MIKHAIL/MICHAEL

February 17, 1968
Northwest, Washington, D.C.

The next morning, Mikhail blinked his eyes open and did a quick check-in to remember where and who he was. The astringent taste of the previous night's wine sat heavy on his tongue, but he had eaten plenty of *foie gras* with each glass to coat his stomach, so he wasn't too hungover. Sitting up, he looked over at the sleeping girl, Stéphanie, an *actual* secretary, from the French Embassy.

For the first time in his career, he felt the tug of something — a feeling as if he wished he were somewhere else. A day off, or even a vacation. Pure folly, of course. His kind didn't take vacation. He sat frozen, afraid to wake the snoring beauty. If he did, he'd have to instantly put on his mask again and play a role. And man, had he rendered a performance last night.

She was truly beautiful, with pouty lips, long eyelashes, and honey blond hair that cascaded down her sanguine back. But she was boring. Conventional. The kind of pliant, obedient woman that most men crave. But not him.

The day before, when Mikhail walked up and asked her if she was alright, his eyes filled with false sympathy, she immediately melted. After some cooing and light flirting, he asked her if she had a chance to eat. "No", she pouted, adding she had been mistreated one too many times by her boss, the Ambassador. Seeing an opening, he dropped a blitzkrieg of love bombs, and she eagerly joined him for dinner.

After only two more glasses of wine, she revealed that *Moscow had allies in Paris, oooh at the highest levels, and isn't that just terrible and scandalous and what about freedom and love and democracy and have you seen what the Russians are doing in Berlin?* She did not care he was only in town for the night, and her apartment was close by. After an additional post-coital avalanche of somewhat useful information, he decided to tell her he did return to DC, from time-to-time, and got her phone number. She'd be a good asset to cultivate. But almost painfully dull.

As he dressed, he let his mind drift back to Maryanne. It was Saturday, which meant she might be at church volunteering with her mother or running errands alone. She seemed to like to be alone. She would take her father's car, sometimes venturing all the way to the Union Terminal Market in Northeast, where she would grab groceries and flowers. He got up and dressed, planted a gentle kiss on Stéphanie's forehead to make sure she was still asleep, and slipped out.

Washington was quiet on Saturday mornings compared to New York where he had recently spent an entire sleepless weekend, overwhelmed by aggressively looming skyscrapers, despair, and apathy. DC, with its linear lifestyles and educated population, was much more his speed. He zipped through town and went home for a shower, shave, and change of clothes, then headed toward Maryanne's street where he could wait and tail her around town.

Smoke piped from several chimneys and a few fashionably bundled up people navigated frosty sidewalks. He zeroed in on one couple and sat captivated. Equally old and frail, they held onto each other for dear life as they walked to a well-kept Packard, the gentleman dutifully opening the passenger door for his wife. She looked up at him with such adoration, such gratitude, and he saw the man beaming back at her. Mikhail felt a warm longing seep from his heart, and he had to force his brain to take over.

Maryanne stepped onto her front porch and trot down the steps to the family car. He'd seen every member of the family drive it, including the father who last parked it halfway on the tree lawn. She suddenly turned in his direction and waved. Mortified he slumped down into his seat and prepared to take off, but when another young woman walked past his car waving, he let out a big enough exhale to power a hot air balloon. What was wrong with him? Why did he suddenly feel like he was doing every wrong, getting sloppy? He shook his head and turned over the car engine.

He followed her across town to the market, which was a bustling, comfortably integrated food hall in a part of D.C. wedged between warehouses and a middle-class neighborhood. He parked his car and followed her inside, staying close enough to observe but out of her field of vision. She was a careful and picky shopper, often walking to one vendor to review the offerings, then giving an elegant "I'll be back" hand gesture only to visit two or three more vendors before buying anything. His heart racing, he decided to make his move. He bought two Cokes, took a deep breath, and walked up to her as she was haggling over ham hocks.

"Maryanne is that you?" he said with a broad smile.

She spun around with the annoyed look of a young woman who was accustomed to being hit on, but her eyes lit up when she saw him.

"Michael? Hi! What are you doing here?"

"I was told this was the place to shop for the best food in town," he said, putting on his signature swagger. "So, I decided to come check it out."

"Oh really? Who told you that?"

"Who told me what?" he said innocently.

"Who told you that this was the place to shop for the best food in town?"

He was momentarily stunned, like he'd been slapped. What was she doing? Her guard went up so quickly, yet it was playful, biting. The way she knocked him off his game was intriguing. *Fine, I'll play your game,* he thought.

"Oh, my partner. I co-own a construction business near the Waterfront. He's from Washington, well, I mean, he's been here for a long time."

"This isn't the only market in town."

The delicate palate at her throat rippled, as if she were suppressing a giggle. He imagined nestling his lips there, and he bit his lower lip to regain composure.

"I know," he replied.

"Not even the best."

"Oh."

"So, why this one?"

Ah, she thinks she's being coy, he thought. Trying to deflect. Don't let her.

"Why not? Coke?" He held it out, making sure his hand was visibly shaking.

She looked at him with apparent pity and gently took the drink, steading his hand. He felt his cheeks flush at her touch, which would only help in this situation. There was something behind her eyes, dark pools of intensity that beckoned. He'd felt like that before, standing on a bridge, peering over the edge, and imagining flight if he just jumped. Not to kill himself, but just to experience the sensation of launching into nothingness. He mindlessly stepped toward her and right into a divot in the concrete, almost falling directly into the display of raw pork.

"That's the second time you made me trip on my own feet!" he said.

They both exploded in laughter, breaking the bubble that had surrounded them. The old butcher looked at them and rolled his eyes.

✳ ✳ ✳

Mikhail helped Maryanne shop for everything her mother needed for dinner, even buying a bouquet of flowers for the table, then helped her carry the bags to her car. They walked through the market talking about everything and nothing, casual conversation as if they had known each other for years, no longer speaking to make an impression. She appeared to be relaxed, even flipping her hair, and smiling with full teeth. Once all the groceries were loaded into her car, they stood looking at each other.

"Do you have to go home right now?" said Mikhail, breaking the silence.

"The meat might spoil."

"It's cold enough out here that nothing is going to go bad. How about we drive to the Lincoln Memorial? It's not too far and I've never seen it up close."

"Ok, but just for a little bit." Her tone was light, but he could hear a tinge of caution, like she didn't want to seem too eager. Maybe even worried about personal safety. He recommended they drive separately, and she seemed to relax. He'd used Roman's car today — not the one he usually used to surveille Maryanne and NASA — so she wouldn't potentially recognize it.

The National Mall and Ellipse were quiet, but for a few families who braved the cold to take pictures in their Sunday best. The memorial was bathed with golden sunshine, like a celestial temple. Mikhail mounted the first step and offered his hand, escorting Maryanne up the 87 steps to the top. He'd seen grand statues in Moscow to honor Mother Russia and Soviet pride. *Worker and Kolkhoz Woman* was his favorite — he always felt his head lift higher before the mighty tribute to his people. But as he stood before the formidable image of the American President and gazed at its murals and Lincoln's speeches, he was overwhelmed with admiration. They stood silently for a moment, then sat on the top steps and looked out over the Reflecting Pool toward the Washington Monument.

"We're sitting where Dr. King gave his speech, aren't we?" said Mikhail.

"Yes, we are," said Maryanne, her voice tinged with sorrow.

"Seems so long ago. I would have given anything to be here," he said.

"Me too."

"Wait — you weren't at the march? I thought most — you know — people like you were there."

"No. Not most. Many, but not most. I was still in high school. My parents didn't go either."

"Why?"

"Because they were afraid that something bad would happen, like in Selma. Like so many places. But Gladys — my sister — she snuck out. She was old enough to get away with it." She looked at her feet and twisted her lips.

Was she jealous? he thought. *Maybe she has rebellious streak. That would be gold.*

Then, suddenly, a shout behind them, along with the sound of a bottle being kicked. They both jumped and swiveled toward the commotion. It was a trio of hippies, two women and a man, stumbling around Lincoln's statue and making their way toward the stairs. The women had long hair and were clad in a mishmash of colors, textures, and tones, bundled in infinite scarves and suede. The man wore a shearling jacket and tight bell bottom jeans but was bare-chested, with long, wavy honey-blond hair. They looked as if they had fallen off the back of a gypsy caravan, then rolled around on the ground for extra effect. The young man saw Mikhail and Maryanne and stumbled toward them, a "No War" banner stuck to his left foot.

"Beautiful, just beautiful," said the bedraggled young man, pointing at the stunned couple. "Look at these two! *'C'mon people now smile on your brother . .*" he sang

"Cory, we have to go — midterms tomorrow!" said one of the women, clearly more lucid than her companions.

"Everybody get together gotta love one another right now . . "

"Coooorrryyyyyy!!!! Let's goooooo!!!"

"G'bye beautiful rainbow people," said glass-eyed Cory with a bow.

As the trio left, Mikhail started laughing.

"I still can't believe they think anyone will take them seriously," he said.

Maryanne was not smiling.

"What is it?" he asked.

"I'm just mad, I guess."

"Mad at who? Those hippies?"

"Not just those hippies. All of them. All those kids out there protesting, marching, acting a fool."

"I don't understand. Aren't they trying to change the world? Make it better, you know, against the war?"

"Who really cares about Vietnam?"

"Wait I thought that you — I mean — I've seen a lot of activists protesting against the war, even King, so I thought — "

"Yes, but not for the same reasons as Dick and Jane and Jane over there."

"Ok. I'm all ears." This was valuable information.

"For us, injustice — it's just an extension of the bigger problem of inequality. Because our young men are being conscripted and sent thousands of miles away, against their will, to fight for a country that sees them as second-class citizens. Some of the boys — they come from places where it is still dangerous for Black people to just vote."

"But these hippies, if they get the war ended, and their ideas of openness and equality catch on, well, isn't that good for all of us?"

"Not for all of us."

"Why not?"

"Because those kids have options. They have a choice. They roll out of their privileged lives into activism and try and prove they're serious by wearing dirty jeans and growing their hair. They were for civil rights for a minute, but then the war happened, and they found something new and shiny to care about, something which had nothing to do with their role in this oppressive society."

He could tell she was struggling to keep her voice down, but her frustration was bubbling. He had to be careful. Did she hate White people? No, she was spending time with him. Her anger, it was more specific. He needed to get to the heart of it, to understand. He thought about reaching for her hands, but it might upset her, blow the operation. That's right, the operation. She was only a job.

"Tell me more," he said gently.

She looked at him and he could see a shift, like a softening.

"There is nothing — nothing at stake for them," she said. "They will care only as long as it suits them. When they get bored, or the war ends, and need a place to live and food to eat, when they get a little too uncomfortable, all they have to do is take a bath and cut their hair. Dad will find them a job, or they'll marry some Tom, Dick, or Harry. And everything will be fine — for them. Black people, no matter how much we do to look respectable, act respectable, when all we do is ask for equal rights, and we do it without being strung out or urinating in public, we are still treated like trash." She sounded like she was on the edge of crying.

Mikhail had no idea what to say, or if he should say anything at all. She was opening up to him, more transparently than could be expected this early. For a moment he wondered if she might be playing him. But maybe this was what she needed, a sympathetic ear. Compassion. He decided to take the chance and took her hands in his.

"I'm sorry," he said.

Maryanne searched his eyes and he felt like he'd been struck by lightning. He wasn't ready for this.

"I'm tired," she said. "And my feet are cold."

They walked silently back to their cars. Mikhail wanted to kiss her right there, to swoop his arm around her lower back and pull her toward him. But it wasn't the right time.

"I want to see you again," he said.

Maryanne said yes, and they agreed to meet on the following Friday. She said he could pick her up by the small park down from NASA, just past the underpass, across from the townhomes, where she liked to read, right after work. He remembered to ask for details, because if he had just said 'ok' then she might figure out he'd been watching her.

Mikhail watched her drive away and then got into his car. Suddenly he felt overwhelmed with a sensation that felt like the same high he'd experienced when he learned he was accepted into the Program, an elation that also left him scared as hell. He gripped the steering wheel to catch his breath, which had quickened, leaving him feeling light-headed. Focusing on his heart, he willed it to slow down, lengthening his breaths, regaining control. This was not supposed to happen. If too emotionally compromised, he would have to abandon the mission. But he'd made it in, she was starting to trust. No, he couldn't give up now — developing assets took too much time. He'd need to get over whatever emotional effect she was having on him and focus on the mission — getting her to share information from the inside, willingly or coerced, if necessary — but with her rant it was clear her trust in him was growing. *She might be ready soon,* he thought, *to snuggle into the palm of my hand.*

Chapter 14

MARYANNE

February 17, 1968
The National Mall, Washington, D.C.

Maryanne only made it about one block before she had to pull over. She felt the urge to jump out of her car and dance in the street. *Pull yourself together,* she thought. The feeling of lightness almost overwhelmed her, as if filled with so much helium she'd float into the heavens. Michael had listened so intently, curiously, and she felt *safe*. Seen and accepted. He was curious, not judgmental. She'd never shared her feelings with anyone other than Gladys in such an open, unfiltered way — never said what was really on her mind. The stakes were too high. Black people had to be excessively careful about really speaking their minds, especially to White folks. Say the wrong thing and you'd be out of a job, accused of being 'red', thrown in jail, or worse. But Michael hung onto her every word, asked thoughtful questions, and she kept talking and talking. Nothing she said seemed to scare him and his curiosity was intoxicating. He was unlike any man she had ever met before. Was it real? It was almost too perfect. She didn't like how free she'd felt, saying anything. No man — White, Black, or purple — deserved that much trust. She could get hurt again, make a fool of herself. Or worse. But when he was sitting so close to her, and drinking in her eyes, she wanted to fold herself into him, and relinquish the control she'd fought so hard to maintain.

But Michael *was* a problem. What would her neighbors think if she went out with him? Her mother? Gladys? She risked being shunned and bringing shame upon her family. The unofficial neighborhood judgment committee already looked at her as if she were an outsider — pretty but unmarried career girl, not wife material. Martin Walker had told anyone who would listen that she was a cold fish who had no interest in men before Gladys chewed him out. She hadn't cared about that so much, but if it got out that she was dating a White man, it would come down on her family. A cold fish who'd only give it up for The Man.

But I'm not a cold fish, she thought to herself. Just didn't have time for self-centered, chauvinistic men. Michael seemed different. And he was damn fine.

She drove through the city, toward home, her thoughts swirling. *I'll turn on the radio*, she thought. *Some music will keep my mind busy.*

"This is the Sunny J. Kelsey show!" declared a melodic voice made for radio. "Cloudy with a chance of flurries today." But instead of upbeat music, more morose horns. "Still reeling from the events in Orangeburg, South Carolina, last Thursday."

Maryanne felt a tug at her heart, one that threatened to drag her downward into an angry vortex. She'd already heard about the unarmed Black teenagers and college students who were shot up by the police because of their protest against a segregated bowling alley. Shot in the back while running away, or in the soles of their feet as they lay down to avoid gunfire. Yet another glaring example of the fact that Jim Crow still rued the south, no matter what Kennedy, Johnson, or the Supreme Court did. No matter what Dr. King shouted. No matter the number of children and adults who unjustly lived in a state of fear and disenfranchisement. And the media? Well, according to them, the kids got what they had coming.

"There are now, sadly, three confirmed dead out of the 31 shot."

Maryanne turned off the radio and sat in enraged silence. *All this danger*, she thought. *All this, and I'm falling for a White man.* A horn blared behind her, and she jumped, realizing that she'd been frozen, her hands gripping the steering wheel as if for dear life. She offered an apologetic wave, put the car in drive, and continued her drive up Georgia Avenue.

But Michael seems different, she said to herself again. *He isn't racist. Can't be.*

Or maybe was that just what she needed to tell herself. Otherwise, she'd be an idiot. And she was no idiot.

"You have a choice," her mother said that day in the kitchen. The day she ignored her inner voice, her instinct about Martin. Now everything in her body and soul was drawing her toward Michael. She drew in a deep breath and exhaled from every cell in her body. *I'll go for it*, she thought. *Just keep your eyes open.*

Chapter 15

DONOVAN/LEROY

February 17, 1968
Takoma Park, Washington, D.C.

Donovan walked through the front door of his family's bungalow and the aroma of his wife's church-famous jambalaya soothed his soul. The house pulsed with comforting, domestic vibrations. He inhaled deeply and exhaled, letting his armor start to shed, the muscles around his neck and jaw softening. Home was solace, his refuge from the hell that was his life outside — as a Black man, as a Black man in the FBI, and as a Black man in the FBI trying to protect his people from the FBI. Only problem was that he couldn't be completely honest with his wife about work, so every day he shed one set of armor for another.

"Daddy!!!" His buoyant daughters, Nancy and Freda, aged 6 and 9, tackled him with hugs. He looked at their bright faces and fuzzy pigtails, catching the threat of tears in his throat. Why was he about to cry again? Lately, when he saw or even merely thought of his daughters he started to dissolve into a puddle. It was embarrassing.

"We missed you!" declared Freda.

"Bring us anything good?" pleaded Nancy.

"Of course!" he replied, dabbing his eyes and pulling two

Empire State Building snow globes from his bag.

"Ooooh, thank you!" they sang as they ran off, comparing their gifts to make sure they were exactly the same size.

"How was New York?" said to his wife as she emerged from the kitchen. Their eyes met in silent understanding, a shared secret. Shirley knew he was in the FBI and couldn't talk about his job. She never pressed him, but there was a growing fissure between them, mostly because, he suspected, she thought he was cheating. Her father had been a philanderer, which destroyed her mother and left Shirley with deep scars. What bothered — no — frustrated him, was how proud she had been once he'd graduated from the academy. He'd certainly prepared her for the life, explaining that he'd be doing work that he couldn't share with her. And what really frustrated him is that she knew his job was dangerous, but never expressed concern about his safety. All she cared about was if he was running around, which he most certainly was not. Even if he had wanted to, there was no time for anything but the job.

"C'mon over here," said Donovan, gently drawing her to him. "I missed you." But she turned her head and his kiss landed on her cheek instead of her lips. The momentary spark of affection he felt fizzled out.

"I'll be in my office," he said to the back of her head as she walked away.

He closed the door of his office and sat down at the grand walnut desk, which took up almost half of the room. It was the only piece of furniture his great uncle, a former sharecropper who'd graduated from Tuskegee with a degree in Agriculture, brought back with him from the U.S.S.R. after a five-year stint teaching Soviet farmers how to grow cotton. But his uncle was no Commie — just a smart man who was offered a lot of money and promised a land free of racism to take his talents abroad. His uncle's story of being lured by smooth-talking, American sounding Soviets capitalizing on Black anguish and ambition made a lasting impression on Donovan.

"They's always so eager," his uncle would say. "Always so keen to be your friend, know your business. Help you out. Then next thing you know you under they thumb and you bein' called 'nigger' in a different language."

Donovan opened the secret compartment on the desk's underside — the desk probably came from one of the Tsar's ransacked palaces — and pulled out a small tape recorder. It wasn't for his official notes that went into reports back to O'Connell. This was his private audio journal, where he could unload and memorialize the truth about what he really saw. Even better, he could drop the mask (code switching was exhausting) and just talk. He cleared his throat and began:

"Damn. What a day, what a damn day. I'd just got in my car after stuffing my face with a couple'a half smokes from Ben's when I see that joker Michael — or whatever his damn name is — chillin' behind the wheel of a black '67 Mustang with a dent in its bumper. Now, it just ain't right to leave a dent on such a fine car. Anyway, I ain't never see this cat during the day and last time I saw him he was in a different car, so my Spidey sense is on fire. I'm creeping behind him down U, then to Florida Ave, and all the way to Northeast to that food market Shirley likes to go to. And I'm thinking, he could either A — be food shopping or B- making a drop. I'm opting for B, because I never smell any cooking comin' from upstairs.

So, now I'm on foot, following close enough behind him to see where he's headed. I duck behind a fruit stand when he stops and turns around. He's looking for somebody, I can tell. And his head stops swiveling and locks on this fine little brown thing over by the meat counter. And I mean, she is real fine. I'd stop in my tracks too. She's foxy enough to distract him, and he makes a bee line in her direction. So now I'm thinking I'm about to get a laugh because I know that no fine black woman is gonna give some pasty white man — and he is very very white — the time of day.

I almost lost my half smokes when she smiled at him and started talking. Smilin' and talkin'. And he was smilin' and talkin'. She knew him. He bought her a drink and she took it — I eyeballed the vendor to see if he might be a front, but they emptied those bottles and dropped them off for deposit. And then — the memorial. The Goddam Lincoln memorial. So now I'm sure — he's working her. Buttering her up. She drove off with the biggest smile on her face, like she'd just won a pony. I wanted to beat the shit out of him. It's one thing to go after our country. It's another to go after our women."

"Daaaaddddyyyy! Dinner!" sang his girls through the locked door.

"Coming sweeties!" he replied after stopping the recorder.

His chest burned with outrage. That girl had no idea who her knight in white armor really was.

"Daddy, now!"

His little girls. Little Black girls who the world would try to silence, manipulate, shame, and keep down. If one of them was being used by a liar or even a foreign agent, he'd hope someone like him would protect them.

He had to pull the thread, find out who Michael really was. Sure, he was super friendly, but why really? He wasn't just another White cat getting back at dad by joining the counterculture. Donovan rubbed his chin. *Not American, already deduced that*, he thought. Plus, the FBI and Metropolitan Police only used Black folk for infiltrating Black groups. But who was most interested in getting Black folks on their side? Or, at least, causing more disruption in the community to stick a thumb in the eye of Uncle Sam? Russians and Cubans, and Michael surely wasn't the latter. *Pull the thread*, Donovan thought. *Be patient.* Once he found out what was on the other end, he'd make his move.

Then he realized he didn't even know the girl's name.

Chapter 16

MIKHAIL/MICHAEL

February 22, 1968
Southwest, Washington, DC

Mikhail was dreaming about Maryanne again. He'd be drifting off to sleep, emptying his mind, when thoughts of her would sneak in and his heart rate would take flight. At first, he tried fending her off, conscious enough to be cruel and dismissive, but so persistent the thoughts he eventually relented to the warmth that flooded him and hastily sought release. He needed to get the first date over with and hopefully move past this inconvenient infatuation. She'd do something to annoy him, and he'd be so focused on extracting information there would be no chance of him succumbing to puppy love. Mikhail could afford to be tethered only to Mother Russia, who was a jealous mistress. So long as he was in the field, unless someone was assigned to him, being alone was essential to his mission.

But he knew he needed to make an impression on Maryanne if he were to get any farther. Where should he take her? He knew more than enough about race politics to know he couldn't just take her anywhere. Fortunately, his colleague Geoffrey was half-Armenian and half-Tatar with dark hair and a sallow complexion, who seamlessly blended almost any group. But he seemed to spend most of his time with Black people, listening in on their conversations at the bookstores and coffee shops, even finessing his way into basement parties and cookouts, lifting talking points from Dick Gregory and Angela Davis. He might have some ideas, though he was visibly non-plussed about Mikhail's recent successes.

Geoffrey was chatting in a low voice on the phone when Mikhail got to the office, which was mostly empty due to the hour. Construction was an early morning job, most workers clocking off around four, and the guys were likely two miles away, on site. He hung his coat on the back of the door, sat in his desk chair and waited.

"I have a question for you," he asked as soon as Geoffrey turned to face him. "I need to find a place to take the Black girl for a nice night out."

"You mean, a date?"

"Um, yes — A — date."

"Well, how about just take her to one of those hotels, you know? Maybe something nicer than she would expect. Give her expensive wine. That should butter her up."

Mikhail bit the inside of his cheek. *What a dolt,* he thought. Spending all that time with Black people and still wed to stereotypes.

"She's not that easy," said Mikhail. "Listen — she could be an important asset, but I need to keep building her trust — make her feel like I am serious about her." He stood up straighter. "She is not like those shallow, materialistic girls I usually have to deal with."

"But she's colored. I mean, come on man, she can't be that valuable. Plus, everyone will notice the two of you together. You'll be made so fast . . ."

"That's why I need your help. You know where Blacks and Whites hang out together, right? But not those hippie places. Somewhere decent. Somewhere where we can go without being bothered."

He was doing his best to hide his frustration. Plus using the word "black" still sounded distasteful to him — in Russian it was better to call someone "Negro" because "black" meant "bad", but he was told that "colored" was even worse, and he wasn't sure how to use "Afro-American," because an afro was a hairstyle and not all of them had one. He had never seen so much angst and discussion over what to call a person.

"Got it." Geoffrey whistled and snapped his fingers, not quite in rhythm. "There's a jazz spot in Georgetown —off the beaten path and far away from her neighborhood. The crowd is mixed, and it has a real laid-back vibe. Dinner is good too and they have decent wine. Plenty of liquor." Geoffrey scribbled on a scrap of newspaper — it was less conspicuous than plain paper — and handed it to Mikhail.

"Good. I'll take her here." Mikhail rose to leave, trying to shake off his annoyance and switch to gratitude. "I'm headed over to Roman's. Need me to take anything?"

Geoffrey shook his head. It was polite to ask, though they had yet to reach a level of comradery to sherpa each other's acquisitions. Even though they were of the same cloth, you never knew if your comrade was reporting on you, or if they were, themselves, a traitor. They had been trained to trust no one, not even their fellow agents, not even themselves.

As he walked out of the office, he glanced over his shoulder back toward his desk. Through the window he saw Geoffrey on the phone, looking straight at him. *What's he up to?* he thought. Geoffrey had a different handler, and who knew what he was saying. Would he try and knock Mikhail off his pedestal? No, that would be counter to their mission. But what if they thought Mikhail was being sloppy, what if they could detect his constant thinking about Maryanne? "Never show a single emotion you do not intend to share," said one of his instructors. "Emotions are only good for one thing — manipulation."

Give them nothing they can use against you, he thought. He waved to Geoffrey, who quickly looked down. *Nothing. There's too much at stake.* He imagined ice flowing through his veins, numbing him from the inside out.

Chapter 17

MARYANNE

Maryanne frowned at the three dresses that lay across her bed. *I don't even know where he's taking me,* she thought. Suddenly Gladys burst in and flopped down on the opposite twin bed, her chin in her hands. She was beaming.

"Soooooo?"

"So, what?" said Maryanne, turning to her closet and throwing another dress on the bed. "I have nothing to wear," she said with an exasperated sigh. She'd never been so tied up in knots about choosing an outfit.

"Look at you. You're just a mess, all stressed out and nervous about a date. I've never seen you *this* worked up. Now, you have to tell me what's so special about this guy."

Maryanne caught her breath. Why did Gladys have to start interrogating her now? It was hard enough trying to concentrate on her wardrobe, and when it came to questioning, her sister was like a rabid dog on a bone.

"Uh, yes, he's kind of, you know, goofy. Well, more funny than goofy, I guess. I mean, he makes me laugh, takes my jabs . ."

"Go on."

"Let's see. What else." She picked up a camel mini dress with a red turtleneck. "He's just a bit older, not too much, but mature, not too silly."

"You said he was goofy," said Gladys, leaning in like Joe Friday.

"I said funny."

"Uh huh, so, what does he do?"

"He's in construction. Not a construction worker, but a manager of some sort."

"That's all you know?"

"What else do I need to know? said Maryanne, suddenly aware that she didn't even know the name of his company. "Look, he's not rich but seems to make good money. Nice car. Sharp dresser."

Truth was, Michael didn't talk about himself much. But he sure did ask questions, though it always felt conversational and not like an interrogation. Not like right now, with Gladys.

"He's a good listener," said Maryanne as she pulled a turtleneck over her head, muffling the tingle of concern in her voice.

"Well, you should ask him where he works."

"What about this?" asked Maryanne, holding up an outfit and hoping Gladys would move on.

"So, how brown is he?"

Oh no, not that question.

"Um, not very, kinda high. Higher than Marcus." Marcus was the kid the next street over who only needed a hot comb to lay out his afro to pass for White.

"He must be damn near White then, 'cause nobody's lighter than Marcus!" Gladys laughed, then got up and walked over to her sister. "I'm sorry for all the questions. It's just — I mean — you look so happy."

Maryanne blushed. "Hold up," she said. "It's too soon to know anything, I mean, this is our first real date."

"Ok, so you need to make a spectacular impression. Where are you going?"

"I have no idea."

"Right." Gladys looked at her sister and the three outfits on the bed. "None of these will work. Don't worry sis, I've got you."

Gladys picked out a wool sky-blue mini dress with a matching fur-collared coat. Maryanne felt a little silly and overdressed at work, but the men in her office didn't seem to notice because they rarely looked up from their desks, and almost never at her. Only Roger looked her up and down, his gray lips curled into a sneer that sent a shudder down her spine. She looked at the clock more than her work and had to rush at the end of the day to finish, which left her unsettled. She hoped Atkins wouldn't notice.

Michael's eyes sparkled at the sight of her as she approached him, leaning against his car, and letting out a low whistle. It felt as if she were filled with Champagne bubbles, tickling and popping and giggle-inducing. She looked him up and down — he was wearing a tight turtleneck, trim grey slacks, and a smart overcoat. He wasn't so much slim as he was solid, his muscles casting shadows thought his clothes. So handsome but ill-suited to her life. The opposite of what good should be. She should turn around. Walk away. But why was she still moving toward him, like a meteor propelled by gravity? As he opened the door, she looked around, nervously. She must look so silly, her cheeks on fire, tumbling eagerly toward a White man.

"You look beautiful," he said.

"Thank you," she said, falling to pieces inside as if a bomb had exploded in her chest. "Where are we going?"

"I'm taking you to a real hip jazz club I know you'll love," he said proudly.

Maryanne shook her head and felt herself regaining consciousness. Did he really just assume that she liked something? Sure, she liked jazz, but it was in the category of 'things Black people like', such as fried chicken and watermelon. She hated fried chicken.

"Yes, I like jazz. But — it's not my favorite music." She folded her arms in ladylike confrontation, warm with flirtation.

"What's your favorite, then?"

"I like classical. You know, orchestra music. Even opera." Opera was a stretch.

"Ok," he said. "Change of plans. I have an idea. Do you trust me?"

"Yes?" *Do I?* she thought, too late to change her answer. The truth was, she didn't exactly distrust him, but resisted the urge to feel too comfortable. After Martin, well, she should keep her guard up.

He drove to a small corner grocery store. She watched as he ran in and wiggled in her seat where she'd been practically frozen, like if she moved her dream bubble would pop. He emerged with a paper sack jammed full. They drove through the city, past the White House and museums. As the lights from the gas lamps zipped past, she imagined she was flying through another world, a place where no one would recognize her. But when the car stopped in front of Constitution Hall, Maryanne shrank down into her seat.

"I — I can't go — we can't go in there," she said, anxiety crawling up her spine. There were some places regular Black folk were not welcome, despite public declarations of integration.

"Why not?"

"Well — you know — they don't like to let — "

"We don't have to ask permission."

But then he explained that his company had a contract to fix various construction issues in Constitutional Hall, and that one day he heard the National Symphony Orchestra performing. So, he'd found out their schedule and started eavesdropping on their practices from a quiet location above the stage. It just so happened, he said triumphantly, that he knew there was a rehearsal that night.

Maryanne shook her head. "You're *spying* on the orchestra?" she said. "Isn't that illegal?" She took a slight step back.

"No-no- not spying! The schedule is posted. Besides, I have a key, and can come any time work needs to be done. It's ok, follow me," he said, reaching out his hand.

Maryanne's eyes darted from his face to the dark alley in

front of them and shuddered. Alleys were dangerous places, and here she was about to dive into one with a man she didn't really know. But his eyes were cool and sincere, and her took her hands gently.

"I promise, we won't get in trouble," he said confidently. "I will not let anything happen to you."

Suspicion, which had been nipping at her spine, suddenly melted away, like once an aspirin kicks in. That night in the park, Martin's demeanor, his tightness and hunger, was palatable. With Michael, she felt safe. His hands were rough but warm, and she squeezed in acquiescence. "Yes, let's go," she said.

He walked just ahead of her, and she pressed in closely, her face nestled into his shoulder, as he unlocked the side door to the building. They climbed the creaky stairs and emerged into what looked like an abandoned control room, now apparently used for piano storage, softly lit through the symphony hall window. It was oddly romantic, she thought, and her cheeks burned. Familiar music surrounded them, vibrating off every wall and throughout her body. He father had an impressive classical music record collection, which he'd play as she rested by his knee when she was a child, and she'd imagine she was drifting away on melody.

Michael looked over at her and smiled, and she nearly fell to pieces. Then he ripped a blanket from a piano like a matador and spread in on the floor with extra flourish, and she silently clapped when he bowed. Next, he prepared everything he'd picked up at the store — charcuterie, snacks, and poured two glasses of wine, and she felt unlike ever before. No one had ever treated her so romantically. Light from the stage shone through the cobweb frosted glass, almost like flickering candlelight. They kicked off their shoes, she sat on one hip with her legs folded under, he rested on an elbow, and they floated on the soft waves of Chopin.

He asked questions about her job, and she shared more about how she had come in as an intern but was now a key member of a team, how it was her dream to be a full-fledged radio-astronomer, learning the secrets of deep space. When the music ended, she looked at him and lingered, but just as they were both contemplating moving closer, they heard the orchestra packing up.

"Better go," he said softly. "They'll cut off all the lights soon and it'll be pitch black. We won't be able to see our way out!"

They quickly cleaned up the picnic and flew into the alley as silently as possible, voices nipping at their heels, waiting to collapse into laughter until safely back in the car. She felt light and free like a child who'd gotten away with something very naughty.

Neither spoke during the drive to her house, but she felt his eyes on her from time-to-time, and his gaze warmed her cheek like the sun. The music still coursed through Maryanne's body, and she felt loose and fluid.

He was careful to park under a burned-out streetlight on her street. "I'd like to walk you to the door, but . . ."

"I know," she replied, feeling like she was floating somewhere above, looking down at herself.

He quickly scanned the street, then got out to open her door. As she stood their eyes met, and he pulled her close. Once their lips met she was surprised by how her passion matched his, and lost herself in the moment without fear. Suddenly a wave of consciousness crashed over her psyche, and she remembered where she was. She quickly pulled away, her lips hot.

"I should go inside," she said, looking at her feet. "Nosy neighbors."

He gently placed a finger under her chin and she lifted her gaze to meet his smile. "Yes, I know — that was stupid."

"Unsafe."

"Yes."

His lips brushed her hand.

"You know where to find me," she said, her heart on fire, and left him standing in the shadows.

❋ ❋ ❋

Maryanne carefully unlocked the front door and tiptoed into the hallway. Her father was snoring in his chair but awoke with a start when she stepped on a creaky floorboard.

"Oh," he slurred. "I thought you wuz your mother." He swung his arm in her direction, knocking his glass to the floor. "Sh . .shee what you made me do? Pick that up, hushee." He pushed himself up out of the abused lounge chair, and she saw that his pants were looser than normal.

"You need to go to bed," she said, approaching as if he were a wild dog, offering her hand. He smacked it away, then fell backward in his chair and promptly began snoring.

Fine, she thought without emotion. *You won't kill my joy tonight.*

She went up to her room and locked the door behind her. Her mother had been working more hours since her father, an already underemployed engineer, was demoted two weeks ago, not in pay but in terms of work duties after too many instances of him committing major testing errors on missile components. As a result, he was coming home *and* drinking earlier, rendering him belligerent and intolerable by dinnertime. He was convinced her mother was running around on him, without evidence, of course. It was if every surface of the house was covered in broken glass, as if the air was poisoned. Every step, every breath was fraught with danger.

But tonight . . . tonight had been like she was a world away. He asked so many questions — so many more than anyone had ever asked, his eyes boring into hers. She probably said more about work than she should have, but he seemed so impressed. "Amazing," he'd said. "You must be brilliant." She asked him about his childhood, and why he decided to come to Washington. He described his love of the city's architecture and history, its real history, and unique culture. She was astounded by how observant he was, how curious. She wanted him in the worst possible way, to rip him over her, wanted to lay down and give away her innocence. It was stupid to neck like that in the open but, ironically, safe, because had they been alone, she wasn't sure how far she would have gone.

She heard the front door open and close, which meant her mother was home. She wished she could rush into her arms and giggle together over an incredible night, because even though Maryanne wasn't sure, she felt like she might be falling in love. She could keep, well, the details about Michael to herself. Her mother would serve up praise just like she did when she saw how much in love Gladys was with Eric, along with a cautionary side dish to 'never love a man more than he loves you'. Maryanne's heart dropped slightly at remembering that her mother had never met her true love. Suddenly she heard her father's voice booming with paranoid condemnation, and almost immediately, her mother's sobs. So familiar, the evening symphony of angst, but heartbreaking, nonetheless. It wasn't fair, to be sure, but there was no doubt that mother would be happy if Maryanne was. She'd wait until the right time to tell Mother everything about Michael, including his race. That is, if it even got to be that serious.

But she wanted it to.

Maryanne wrapped the pillow around her ears and closed her eyes, and as she breathed in and out remembered Michael's aura, letting her mind flood with possibility.

Chapter 18

MIKHAIL/MICHAEL

Stéphanie was at home and lonely, but for some reason Mikhail lost all desire as soon as he saw her. Perfectly coiffed, powdered, and perfumed, she looked at him with come hither eyes and he felt *nothing*. Truth was, she was acting as much as he was, though her objective was simply to drive him love crazy. The game was exhausting and stupid, but he had no choice. He closed his eyes and imagined he was with Maryanne, which helped him perform convincingly in bed, but he wanted nothing more than to take the world's longest shower. Stéphanie wanted him to stay the night, but he created an excuse, leaving her in theatrical tears.

The truth was, he really did have to leave to pick up a drop from Marlboro. The rendezvous with Stéphanie left little time to return to the warehouse and put on a disguise. That night he opted for a prosthetic chin covered in acne scars and knit cap with long, stringy hair attached. Lastly, he slipped out of his trousers and wrestled into a pair of jeans with flared bottoms. Maryanne twirled through his mind, and he gently pushed her off the dance floor. He needed to stay focused.

Meridian Hill Park was quiet but for the sobs and laughter

of those who had come to indulge in chemical romance. He'd
made sure to warn Marlboro about the dog feces that had been
spread around the drop site, which was extremely effective at
keeping away both humans and animals. Mikhail cursed under
his breath when he realized he had stepped right into one of his
own decoys, and quickly recovered the film canister from the
inside of a hollow boulder, stuffing it in his pocket. Then he did
his best to scrape the disgusting mess from his shoes.

To see such depravity in the land of plenty tickled him when
he first arrived in the U.S., though he found it interesting that
the media reported on all of it — civil unrest, drug abuse, home-
lessness — without any censorship. Americans seemed to enjoy
airing their dirty laundry, even to the world, their faults on full
display. The rest of the world was a utopian mirage. Things were
changing in the U.S., and it was messy and open, but apparently,
necessary. If asked by Roman or Moscow, however, he'd keep
such editorial musings to himself. He was in America to exploit
it, to study it, and to capitalize on its weaknesses, not admire its
strengths.

He returned to his warehouse, tossed his soiled shoes in
a dumpster, and put on the clothing that was familiar to his
neighbors. He popped open a hidden panel in the wall to reveal
a hidden locker and turned on his microdot film reader. Placing the small roll of film on the microdot reader he rested his
eye on the lens, taking notes while scrolling through the photos
of handwritten documents. He was unsure of what exactly he
was looking at — he'd never been strong with numbers — but
from the light, quick handwriting it looked like the analyst was
excited by what he saw. And he knew enough about astronomy to know it was complicated. Finally, Marlboro had finally
delivered something of real value. The documents were marked
TOP SECRET and included satellite imagery, radio graphs, and
handwritten calculations and analysis.

Suddenly Mikhail saw something that made his heart skip a
beat. Could it be? He squinted, then sharpened focus. There, in
an elegant script at the top of each handwritten document, was
Maryanne Freeman.

He shook his head, nearly bursting into laughter. "Are you kidding?" he said aloud. His target — his beautiful and intriguing target — was more than just technical. She was a maestro of numbers. A scientific whiz kid who was, apparently, a key member of this classified team. And she was frustrated at work. He'd hit the jackpot.

✳ ✳ ✳

The next day Mikhail summoned Roman to the lumber yards at an hour he knew was painfully early, but he couldn't wait. The yards were busy, teeming with construction managers procuring materials for projects up and down the Anacostia and Potomac rivers. Mikhail checked the front pocket of his jacket to make sure that the film was still there.

"So, what was so urgent?" said Roman as he joined Mikhail on a walk around the stacks of wood and steel beams.

"Our man finally may have come through," said Mikhail. "The information he provided," he looked carefully around, then back at the clipboard he was carrying in case he needed to look like a legitimate shopper. "Seems to show that they're trying to intercept our signals, but I am not sure how."

He handed the film, wrapped inside measuring tape, to Roman.

"That is interesting news," said Roman. "And what of the Negro girl? You said there was some news about her too?"

Mikhail drew in his breath. He didn't need to tell Roman everything — yet. He had expected her to have access to the program and information, but not a key player. "You will see that her name is signed to every piece of analysis. Only her name."

Roman stopped in his tracks.

"You mean to tell me that *she* is an expert on their program?"

Mikhail nodded his head. "Yes, she seems to be the one doing most of the work."

Roman suddenly slapped Mikhail on the back. He was frighteningly strong for an old man. "My boy!" he exclaimed under his breath. "What instinct! You knew there was something about her. I'll tell the Center that you were right to focus on her. And they thought you were wasting your time — maybe even getting too sweet on her."

Mikhail felt his neck getting hot. "Who would have given them that ridiculous idea?"

"Well, your colleague said he thought you turned into a real Vladimir Petrovitch when you described her." Mikhail wrinkled his brow. "You know, from Turgenev?" Roman's voice twinkled.

Mikhail furrowed his brow. So, Geoffrey *was* reporting on him. "She's a great asset," he said. Of course, I try to know everything about her."

"Don't be defensive," said Roman. "You are right to know her well." He winked, then walked away.

Back in his truck, Mikhail felt something he could not recall ever feeling before, an urgency, bordering on excitement. He had to get back home in time to clean up and meet Maryanne. In the passenger seat sat a gift-wrapped parcel, with a bow, which he had picked up from Woodward and Lorthrop department store that morning. He'd slipped a tiny listening device in the new leather valise's lining while the salesgirl had her back turned to search for the perfect wrapping paper. He wasn't sure how well it would transmit from the bowels of NASA's building, but it would record every other moment of her life, and that was enough for him.

Chapter 19

MARYANNE

February 29, 1968
Northwest, Washington, D.C.

Maryanne lay in bed, clutching the soft leather bag that had so surprised her she almost cried. It was probably the most thoughtful gift she had ever received. And Michael had been so bold as to kiss her right there on the street when he picked her up. She didn't recoil, instead, melted into his arms. He even held her hand as they walked through Georgetown — an area generally avoided by any Black person who wasn't a domestic worker — to Blues Alley jazz club.

"This is where I was going to take you on our first date," said Michael, smiling. "Though the first one wasn't terrible."

He kissed her hand and her head felt light as a feather.

The gregarious maître d' tucked them into a table hidden by shadows, not out of discrimination but for privacy. It was like she was a glamorous starlet in one of her favorite films, and he was her suave and debonair suitor. Thank God he didn't smoke.

She'd barely heard any of the music, deep in conversation about the state of things in the world.

"It's still unbelievable to me that our country sells the American dream, but in reality, it means only for White people," said Michael.

"Well, my family is doing well," said Maryanne. "In fact, we are living better than most, but not as well as we should be."

"Because you're being held back. What if you were a White family? I mean," he leaned in, "your father would be the head of his department. And you'd be more than — what is your job again?"

Maryanne blinked. Had she told him? She couldn't remember. She could tell him just her basic title, that would be fine.

"I'm an analyst. But I'm going to get my PhD," she said. "In Astrophysics. But Dr. Atk — I mean — my boss says he is still looking for a graduate program that will take me." She twisted the words in her mouth, like it was rubber.

"Why wouldn't they — oh, never mind," said Mikhail, feeling a bit foolish.

"Black and a woman," she said feebly. "Double-whammy."

"It's ridiculous. Just ridiculous. Your talent is being squandered." His expression shifted from dark to light, as if he'd flipped a switch. "But it's amazing what you are doing. I mean — space! You're so lucky to have this job." His hands enveloped hers and she felt herself melting. His touch always seemed to peel her from the ceiling. "You should be proud."

She shifted in her seat, a sudden warmth below taking her by surprise. The urge to lunge across the table and kiss him was even more surprising. She swallowed hard to stop her heart from tap dancing in her throat.

"Most men are put off by my — interests," she said. "In fact, most of them want nothing to do with a girl who has aspirations to be anything other than a wife and mother." She pursed her lips. "Even my father wants me to just be married and give up my dreams."

"Well," said Michael. "I would not find you nearly as beautiful without your beautiful brain. Now, tell me more about how to find — what are they called again — Quaaludes?"

"Quasars!" Maryanne let out a laugh that made at least a few heads turn. She didn't care.

They were the last patrons in the club, the manager gently sending them on their way, but imploring that they return soon.

They walked silently in the warmly lit alley, until just about to crest onto the sidewalk he stopped and pulled her in close. She closed her eyes and folded herself into his embrace. She felt seen, truly seen, and adored. Not precious, needing protection, or rebellious needing control. It was the feeling of being fully materialized — whole.

It seemed too good to be true. A man so fully engaged, who hung on every word she said? A man who found her intellect attractive? And the compliments — while they made her feel radiant and light — they were also as intoxicating as liquor. Yes, she was letting herself fall for him. *You have a choice.* The little voice in the back of her mind, the one holding on by a thread, telling her to proceed with caution, well, it was slipping away.

Chapter 20

MIKHAIL/MICHAEL

March 1, 1968
Northwest Washington, D.C.

Mikhail felt like jumping as if he were a Cossack dancing the *Kalinka*. Maryanne had fallen for his ruse. Trusted him completely. She'd even descended into full waterworks when he gave her the new valise — you'd think he'd proposed marriage. Mustn't lose momentum now. The machine was in motion and all he needed to continue to stoke the engine. He made plans with her for the following Friday, and the Monday after that.

After dropping her off, he rushed to his warehouse to see if the listening device was working. All he heard was rustling at first, but then it got quiet, and he swore he could hear her breathing. An unfamiliar feeling flooded his body like molten lava and he shuddered. As he walked home, his mind raced. Her soft lips. Musky freesia and peony aura. Those dangerously genius and sparkling eyes.

Ugh, this was no good.

What's you with you? he scolded himself. *Stop thinking about her like that. She's just a job. She's the enemy.*

Geoffrey had seen right through him. So had Roman. His judgment was clearly being compromised. If he wasn't careful, it was just a matter of time before he made a major mistake. He had to figure out how to get everything he needed from her as quickly as possible. Then he'd walk away and not look back.

It was nearly midnight, but Leroy's lights were on and Nina Simone's voice crooned on the other side of his door. It sounded like he was alone — plus, Mikhail had never seen a woman down there. Should he invite him up for a beer? Mindless chit-chat might be a good way to get his mind off Maryanne. Plus, he could continue to establish trust — he was almost ready to test the waters and give Leroy a task. Ask him for a small personal favor, like taking a package to an unmarked location, and offer a bit of money.

Luckily, as soon as he stepped into the small entryway, Leroy's door swung open.

"Hey brother," said Leroy, smiling.

"Hey," said Mikhail, returning the smile. "Wanna grab a beer and talk about the latest *Mission Impossible*?" said Mikhail. They'd recently had a brief conversation dissecting the show's imperialistic messaging. American spy shows were a nonsensical but totally enjoyable indulgence.

"That'd be cool but I gotta go to work," said Leroy, looking down at his feet. "Night shift at a warehouse, hauling crates of random shit. Boring, but gotta pay the bills, man."

Mikhail's mind moved quickly. Perhaps Leroy was having money trouble. Maybe even embarrassed about it. He'd mentioned before that he had a sick mother and was paying her bills, plus every other extra dollar went to 'the revolution.' Marlboro was making a drop on Friday night at the National Arboretum, but Mikhail's date with Maryanne would make a pickup logistically difficult. It was worth a shot.

"Hey, remember I told you I use my resources to stick it to the man?" said Mikhail. "Well, I may have a small job for you, you know, for the cause. I'll pay you $500 to pick up something for me. That is, if you're interested."

Leroy knit his brow so tightly it looked like he could crush a pecan. "That's a pretty penny," he said. "But I ain't making no smack runs. That poison kills my people."

"No, no — nothing like that. It's something small. You just go get it from the spot I tell you, bring it to me, and that's it. It'll fit in your pocket."

Leroy's eyebrows crept up.

"It's for the cause," Mikhail continued. *Have I made a mistake?* he thought. Maybe he wasn't the right one. "Things are moving and I'm just trying to nudge them in the right direction," he continued. "Like you are."

Leroy's brow relaxed. "All right man. I'll do it."

Mikhail felt a pinch of relief. He said he'd get Leroy the specifics on Friday morning and to stand by. He'd pay him half in advance.

After Leroy left, Mikhail mounted the stairs to his apartment, and after double-locking the door behind him, went to his freezer to retrieve an unlabeled bottle of Stolichnaya vodka Roman had gifted him. It was the only object in the apartment that could give him away, so keeping it in a plain bottle concealed its Soviet origin. He poured a double shot and raised a glass to the Motherland. The crisp, herbal elixir was instantly soothing, cooling the fire in his belly enough so he could sort his thoughts. Orion. Marlboro. Leroy. Stephanie. And Maryanne. He wondered if Geoffrey was managing as many assets as he was. Probably not. Roman would tell him that more than three assets at one time was too many. But it was all under control, and Mikhail would prove to Moscow that he was one of the most valuable agents in America. Then he could write his own ticket. Maybe.

He wished he could tell his mother about his job. About how well he was doing. She would be so proud. But she had no idea where he was or what he was up to. Like his father, he'd selflessly put his life in the hands of the Motherland, and his mother was left in the dark. Such was the life of a Soviet woman. That made them the strongest on the planet. At least, that's what he'd thought until getting a front row seat to the travails of the Black American woman. And neither group seemed to have any agency — any choice about their plight.

He shook his head, willing his mind to think about the listening device in Maryanne's valise. Should he go to the warehouse and give a listen? Obviously, she wasn't at work, so there wouldn't be anything useful to hear. But for some reason, the idea of just listening to her talk, or even breathe, was intriguing. He poured another shot and drank without ceremony, his vision becoming as cloudy as his judgment.

Chapter 21

LEROY/DONOVAN

March 4, 1968
Takoma Park, Maryland

Donovan sat in the kitchen window with his third cup of instant coffee and watched the coral glow of the sun rise over the quiet street. Shirley, his wife, would be up soon, then the girls would then emerge, sleepy, hungry, and frizzy. Somehow, she always managed to make them breakfast and hot press their hair before the school bus arrived. He was usually on his way out the door by then.

He hadn't noticed his wife until she was standing right over him.

"Didn't bother to make a pot, huh?" she said, her foot tapping.

"Uh, oh, sorry," he said standing up abruptly, like a corporal at attention. "I'll make one right now."

"Never mind," she said, her head already stuck in the fridge. "I'm not too tired. Slept fine enough. Eventually."

The dig annoyed him. He hated not being able to sleep, and it had been another long night. He'd tossed and turned for only fifteen minutes before Shirley banished him to the couch. He'd been sleeping there more often, either because of his snoring or restless legs. He couldn't remember the last time they made love or even just flirted. It was like they were two blind goldfish, swimming around in a crowded bowl but unaware of the others' existence. It didn't help that lately his mind was elsewhere.

He must have looked dejected because she suddenly swooped over and wrapped her arms around his neck.

"I'm sorry," she said in a near whisper. "I know work must be giving you a hard time."

"Yeah," he said, surprised by her affection but bracing for the sting. She liked to give him a bit of honey before striking. "I'm sorry I've been away so much."

"And all your travelling?" she cooed. "I mean, these two- and three- day trips seem to be more often." She unwound her arms and looked him in the eyes, like an inquisitor. Hello, Dr. Jeckel and Dr. Hyde. "You're travelling alone?"

He knew where she was going. Again. "I've told you before, sweetie. I'm not stepping out on you. I'm working, and that's all I can say."

"I'm sure you are," she snorted, as the girls bustled in.

He placed his head in his hands and signed. Her jealousy was exhausting. He'd never strayed. Never even crossed his mind. Hell, he'd never even flirted with another woman. At least, not in front of her.

After giving his daughters hugs, he hustled out to his car before Shirley could throw another dagger. He didn't have time for her nonsense. There was too much at stake. Plus, he had to brief O'Connell as soon as he got to headquarters.

He couldn't let O'Connell know about his arrangement with Michael — not yet. O'Connell would tell the other division and they'd swarm the area with agents, waiting for Michael to make the drop. Donovan wouldn't get any credit. Plus, better that he get a look at what he was picking up, if possible. Would it be microfilm? Tapes? Michael said it would fit in his pocket. Whatever it was, it had to be highly sensitive.

Donovan started to salivate, his imagination bursting with vivid imagery of him stalking the drop site and getting pictures of the courier, then retrieving and inspecting the package. The grand finale, leading the charge to arrest Michael, or whatever his name was, and uncover his deception. It would be just the grand achievement to get him out of COINTELPRO and with the legit counterintelligence operations group.

He hadn't seen that girl again, and hoped Michael was leaving her alone. Donovan didn't need the distraction of having to save some naïve little thing from making a destructive mistake. Then again, might teach her a lesson not to mess with White men. Even if Michael wasn't a criminal or spy, no good could ever come from such a relationship. They all saw Black women as sexual commodities for them to chew up and spit out. Hopefully she'd got her head right and moved on.

If not, he'd have to do something. But what?

Chapter 22

MARYANNE

March 8, 1968
Northwest, Washington, D.C.

Maryanne's head sagged like a deflating balloon. She'd risen well before dawn to catch the first bus of the day and met Atkins and Roger for the car ride to Bolling Air Force Base, where they were going to present her analysis. Maybe they had a change of heart and would let her come into the meeting to present her own data. Instead, they peppered her with questions for the entire drive, which she answered with precision, making it painfully ludicrous that she was not allowed to brief the findings herself. How could she change their minds? Logically speaking, she was still new to the job, and it was way too early to demand anything. So, she bit her tongue, kept her head down, and worked flawlessly. Put on airs to be happy coming early or staying late — whatever it took to get the job done. It wasn't enough that she was already the most relied upon, most trusted analyst on her program. Wasn't enough that her findings were clear, cogent, and without mistake. How long would she have to toil, how long would she have to demonstrate excellence, to overcome prejudice? It was like trying to climb Kilimanjaro barefoot.

Thank God Michael was taking her out that night. She

needed to get out of her frustration and just have fun. And she certainly didn't want to go home.

Maryanne's stomach would turn the minute she walked through her front door, as if entering a haunted house or a morgue. Every night her father stumbled around the house slobbering and swinging his arms like a reanimated corpse, fueled by resentment and despondence. She could barely look at him, her emotions a tangle of pity and disgust. He represented her nightmare, that of squandered brilliance, driven into a bitter spiral that seemed to worsen every day. It was truly unfair how he'd been sold a pipe dream, because for every successful Black engineer on the pages of Ebony, there were 100 that couldn't get work worthy of their education. That couldn't be her. She was sustained by promise — the promise of the life she wanted — which now, perhaps unreasonably, included Michael.

She found herself fantasizing about a life with him, but a secret one if they were to stay in Washington. D.C., which, despite its cosmopolitan façade, was still below the Mason-Dixon line. Though the races were cordial, Blacks and Whites still retreated to their red-lined communities at night. They ate separately, worshipped separately, and loved separately. Those who dared cross the racial lines were often ostracized from their communities, floating on an island unto themselves, in the middle of a whirlpool surrounded by sharks. Her older cousin Veronica, a vivacious *bonne vivante* who'd married a French man she met while travelling in Paris, suffered for two months back in New York before they high tailed it back over the Atlantic. But that was almost 10 years ago, and Maryanne wouldn't let such rules define her happiness. Plus, something about breaking those rules would tickle her belly and spark her joy.

"Maryanne," said Atkins suddenly, waking her from her daydream. She often zoned out during the car ride from Bolling back to NASA. Sitting next to Roger was the only reason she stayed awake. She hated being so close to him that their legs almost touched. "I've been thinking about your request for information about graduate studies. Given your performance so far, I think you'd be a good candidate for a couple of programs."

"Really?" Maryanne sat up so straight her head hit the roof of the car. Roger, aka Marlboro, chuckled.

"No astrophysics program will take a woman," Marlboro chuffed. "Much less a colored girl."

"Black woman," she barked back before she could stop herself, her head still smarting. She braced for Atkins' reprimand, but instead he said, "Pipe down, Roger."

Maryanne felt a smug smile expanding in her chest..

Marlboro folded his arms and glared at her, sending a shiver down her spine. He was caustic and short with the other junior analysts in the office but went out of his way every day to remind her she didn't belong.

"I have pull with a few schools around the country," Atkins said. "Just keep up the good work," he said. "And you'll be rewarded."

They didn't get back until 5 o'clock and Maryanne felt like she might explode with anticipation. She couldn't wait to see Michael, but for some reason the idea of telling him she might leave D.C. piqued her anxiety. *I won't say anything yet*, she thought.

He was taking her to a poetry reading at a bookstore near his place, which was on 16th Street near Meridian Hill Park. It was a curious neighborhood, because unlike other areas of D.C. that had bright racial lines, its lines were a bit porous. She knew the area well. Wealthy Blacks shopped and banked along U Street, the less fortunate hung out on corners, and Black-curious Whites patronized places like Bohemian Caverns. It was less than three miles from her home and a stone's throw from Howard, but a world away.

There was always a chance, albeit remote, that she'd run into someone she knew. Someone who would run to Gladys or her mother and rat her out. But, so what? No, no, it was too soon. She wasn't ready to tell them, well, the details about Michael. Would she ever be? It was killing her not to share everything with Gladys. But would she react like so many others? They already endured stares, whispers, even giggles when they were out together. And she hated being so conspicuous. But when she was with him, it didn't matter. The only gaze that mattered was his.

She could feel eyes burning into the back of her skull as Michael led her by the hand to a small table near the door. It was a feeling she was now accustomed to, the looks of curiosity, amusement, anger, no matter the setting. Tonight, though it was a multi-racial environment, she was clearly fish-out-of-water amongst the dashikis, afros, love beads, and suede fringe. The air was heavy with the smell of tobacco, cloves, and bergamot. He greeted a couple of people as they came in, slapping hands and the occasional pat on the back, and introduced her to a skinny, copper-colored man named Leroy who looked her up and down. Michael put his arm around her waist, and she felt like she might burst into flames.

Michael slipped away to use the restroom as soon as they found a couple of seats, and the side where he'd held her suddenly felt cool. She wrapped her cardigan around her shoulders and took a sly look around the room. People were smiling and laid back, a kaleidoscope of hues, everyone comfortably integrated. Her heart skipped as she saw Michael weaving his way through the room, and gripped his arm once he sat down. Despite his easy grin, his forearm was tensed.

"Everything alright?" she whispered.

He looked at her with a gentle smile and kissed her head. "Everything's perfect," he said.

The room grew quiet as waifish woman with a gravity-defying afro and café-au-lait skin took the small stage. The performer's eye narrowed and she pursed her lips as if they were wrapped around a straw, drinking the world's most delicious milkshake. *I breathe you*, she sang, and the room swooned. Maryanne closed her eyes and swam in the unctuous lyrics, and when she opened them, Michael was looking at her, and she couldn't contain effusive yearning that consumed her entire body.

"Where do you live?" she whispered. It was wrong, her being so forward. But if she didn't take the leap, she'd drop dead on the spot.

Their swift flight from the club was a blur. He seemed surprised at first, but before she knew it, they were practically sprinting down the street. Every moment until they were inside his apartment was surreal, when she felt the warmth of his arm under the back of her sweater, and she pressed her hips into him, hungrily. She wanted nothing more than to be out of her clothes, and they tripped over discarded garments on the way to his bedroom. His skin was hot and musky, and she buried into his neck until their mouths met again. But the cool air grazed her bare back and she felt suddenly embarrassed. Her cheeks burned as he looked at her adoringly, his hands moving smoothly all over her, his face buried into her chest, then down to her belly. It was if he was worshiping her, and her knees started to buckle as she lost herself in sensation.

"Want to stop?" he asked, pained but sincere.

She climbed into the bed. "No," she replied, her voice shaking.

He held her gaze as he slid under the cover next to her, and she wanted to fold herself all the way into his musky warmth. He gently took her hand and guided it down, and she surprised herself by first touching, then exploring further.

"Are you sure," he gasped.

"Just be gentle," she said.

"I will."

His hips descended between her legs, and the pain was momentary. She quickly synchronized with his rhythm, which was slow and rolling, and dissolved into pleasure that she had only experienced once, alone. But this time she felt it everywhere and could not stifle her release. Suddenly he pulled away and she felt warmth all over her belly. She froze.

"Don't move," he said, jumping up and running to the bathroom. He returned with a towel and gently cleaned her off, then laid down again. She wiggled over to his side, and he wrapped in his arms stroking her hair.

"It got curly," he said gently. "I love it."

She giggled in slight embarrassment, but the urge to smooth her hair down never surfaced.

"And, I love you," he whispered.

Everything inside her shattered into a million pieces and fear tickled her spine. She had wanted to say something so badly it was killing her, but she didn't want him to run away. "Never tell a boy you love him," Gladys had said, "unless he says it first. And never believe him if he's trying to get something from you, *um hmm?* 'Cause sometimes they lie to get what they want. But you'll know when it's real."

Maryanne raised her head to look at him. He was gazing at her softly, eyes glistening in anticipation of her response.

"I love you too," she said, and drifted into sleep, smiling.

Chapter 23

MIKHAIL/MICHAEL

Mikhail looked at Maryanne, who was sleeping soundly, and suppressed a smile. *No good*, he thought. It was ok to enjoy the physical act, but he'd let himself feel, which was a problem. Still, his heart melted when her warm breath rolled across his chest. He wished he could magically make her disappear, send her back home, and exorcise his apartment. But he had to care, just a little bit, just enough to make it real for her.

He'd told women he loved them before. Women like Stéphanie, who were eager to spread their legs and give him as much information as he wanted. But Maryanne hadn't given him anything directly, at least not yet, though the info he got from her valise recordings was good. He was right, he could only pick up conversations here and there, and not for most of the day. But she took that valise everywhere. Unfortunately, Roman had been quick to remind Mikhail that he got nearly identical information from Orion and classified technical information from Marlboro. But he couldn't cut her loose. Not yet. She had value — to him.

He *did* love her. Now what?

Mikhail carefully slipped out from under her spell and walked quietly to the living room. There was nothing in there that would give him away. Most of his tools were in the warehouse, but he also had a small storage area behind a hidden panel in his closet. That's where he'd stash the microfilm after Leroy dropped it off in the morning. Mikhail gave him his payment and the instructions, including a detailed description of the drop site, when they met at the poetry slam. Leroy had a look in his eye like a jealous lover but agreed to go to the drop site at 4:00 am and meet Mikhail in their hallway at 5:00 am to deliver the item. Marlboro had sent the signal that he had something "big" and would drop the item at the site overnight. If Leroy pulled this off and didn't tamper with the item, Michael would indirectly recruit him. And if Leroy in any way, shape or form questioned him, or opened the item, Michael would reluctantly put a bullet in his brain and blame it on the Panthers.

A rustling and whiff of freesia and body heat awoke him from dark thoughts. Maryanne appeared, wrapped in a blanket, radiating warmth as light from the street danced across her nose.

"I need to go home," she said. "Can you take me?"

"Yes, but not yet," he said. He swept her up and carried her back to the bedroom.

Chapter 24

DONOVAN/LEROY

March 9, 1968, 4:00 am
Northeast, Washington, D.C.
National Arboretum

Donovan crept through the grove of bare-limbed tulip, oak, and beech trees, feeling exposed under the bright moonlight. He was still seething from the sight of Michael's hand around that girl's waist, a smug look on his face. *Son-of-a-bitch*, he thought, as icy branches smacked him in his face. Just a few more paces to the tree Michael described with a hollow space at the base of the trunk. "Get this shit and nail the bastard", he whispered to himself.

What was her name again? Maryanne. They weren't there for more than 30 minutes before Michael sleazed her into going home with him. Donovan's jaw clenched tight as a bear trap at the memory of his smarmy grin. And the thought of her in Michael's bed made Donovan's blood boil. It was like Michael was showing her off, like "look-y — I got one of your women," just like slave masters used to do on the plantation.

A sudden rustling made Donovan hit the deck, face down in the wet leaves. What if someone else was out here too? What if Michael had set him up? He slowly tilted his head and saw a young, 4-point buck trotting away.

Stupid girl got me off my game, he thought.

But then he was face-to-face with an ancient, craggy oak tree surrounded by muted green moss and a cross so tiny it was barely noticeable. Oak trees had always spooked him, especially when their crooked branches were silhouetted in the moonlight. By the age of 8 he knew every oak tree that had been used to lynch Black folks around his hometown of Wiggins, Mississippi, including his great uncle in 1918, after he'd returned from serving in the U.S. Army during World War I. A postcard from the murder that was passed out as a souvenir showed him dangling, naked, beaten, and bloody, surrounded by smiling White faces. His uniform lay unceremoniously in a pile on the ground under his feet.

Donovan's heart pounded loudly in his ears as he crouched down, draping his coat over the area to hide the camera's flash.

This is it, he thought, his mouth moist in anticipation. No one would go through the trouble of hiding something in the middle of the woods unless it was classified. Whatever he was picking up would provide enough probable cause to wiretap Michael's apartment, open a full investigation. Donovan had documented everything, from his first conversation with Michael to every interaction since then. Plus, he was so close to Michael, they'd have to put him on the investigation team. He hungrily dug through the wet, frosty leaves. Shirley would have a fit when she saw the state of his shearling gloves, but he'd stupidly forgotten his plastic ones. Couldn't leave fingerprints though, so expensive gloves be damned.

Finding the hidden compartment's seam, he carefully opened it, and snapped away. Feeling like a kid on Christmas morning, Donovan flung the coat aside and shined his pen light on the box.

"Gotcha!" he said aloud.

But the compartment was empty.

Donovan picked it up, turned it over, and felt around inside. Nothing. He dropped back down to his knees and dug around, just in case the bag man had dropped the item. Again, he found nothing. The anger in his chest started as a slow burn, which quickly burst into a forest fire. "That motherfucker," he cursed under his breath, rising.

Suddenly, he heard another, different sound in the distance. No, it was nearer. His ears stood up like cornered prey and he trained his hearing toward the sound. Oh no. It was a good click away but make no mistake — those were footsteps. Then, glow from a flashlight danced between the trees like the Northern Lights. Donovan slowly crouched back down, place the box back in the compartment, and recovered it with the leaves and moss. He looked over his shoulder one more time to mark the location of the approaching flashlight, then bolted in the opposite direction. He'd make it out of the park eventually.

But, empty-handed.

Chapter 25

MARYANNE

March 9, 1968
Northwest Washington, D.C.

Maryanne woke up to the aroma of warm butter and sage, which meant her mother was in the kitchen creating something amazing. She could still feel Michael in every cell of her body, and a lingering soreness was a delicious reminder. She'd gotten home close to midnight, tiptoeing up the stairs like a deviant teenager, and giggled herself to sleep. A morning shower would give her enough time to scrounge up a decent explanation for why she got in so late. She descended the stairs as casually as possible, a towel wrapped around her wet hair.

"Yum," she said, kissing her mother on the cheek. "What's the occasion?"

"Just leftovers," she said. "I made this big 'ole turkey breast and no one was here to eat it. So, pot pie it is." She put her hands on her hips and leaned back, peering at Maryanne over her nose. "So, where were you last night?"

"Did I wake you up? I'm so sorry — I lost track of time and before I knew it, I fell asleep."

"Where?"

"At — um — Gladys's house?"

"We're here!" Gladys crashed into the kitchen like a tsunami. Eric, loaded down with grocery bags, tumbled in behind her. "What's for lunch? I brought you some — ooh! Pot pie!" She breathlessly looked at Maryanne who'd made instant eye contact. "What'cha talking about?"

"Last night," said Maryanne, winking. "You know, how I fell asleep at your house?"

Gladys' face could not conceal her excitement at being complicit in Maryanne's ruse. "Oh, yes — we played Spades. And it got late so she flopped on the couch again."

Eric started to open his mouth, but Gladys shot him a look.

"Well," said Mother, looking at Maryanne, "you've been coming home later and later the past couple of weeks, and I've been worried."

"Mother — I," she started, but Gladys jumped in.

"Mary just works so late, you know, she just doesn't want to bother you when she gets home, so she stays over sometimes."

"Even on weekends?"

"On weekends we play Pinochle," said Maryanne, blinking.

"Oh yes, or even sometimes we go, uh, to the movies. You know that theatre on Connecticut Avenue?"

Their mother looked at the two women and smiled. "It tickles me how the two of you think you are so grown but still act like devious little girls when you're together." She pointed at Maryanne. "And I don't know what is going on with you. I just hope it's worth whatever risk you're taking."

Suddenly their mother's eyes rolled around like marbles and her head swayed, barely catching herself on the kitchen counter. The women rushed to her side.

"Are you ok?" asked Maryanne, helping her to sit down.

"I'm fine. Just got a little dizzy there," she said, rubbing her left arm. "Means I'm tired, is all." Her words sounded slower and buzzy, like she'd just woken up.

"You work too hard," said Maryanne, her heart piqued with guilt. "We — I should help more."

"Stop fussing." She shooed at them with her elegant hands, which Maryanne noticed looked older than she remembered.

Had they always been so fragile looking, blue veins pulsing under thin onion skin? "I don't need to be taken care of," her mother continued. "Go on now."

Gladys followed Maryanne up to what was once their shared room and turned to face her sister. "I'm worried about Mommy."

"So am I," said Maryanne. "I haven't been around much lately."

"Mmm hmm," said Gladys. "So, why did I have to cover for you this time? Home later than usual?"

Maryanne blushed. "Well, it's — more serious now."

"Serious how? Clearly serious enough that you've been with him late into the night. What've you been doing? Wait. Never mind. Are you at least being careful?"

Maryanne nodded, though it wasn't entirely true. They weren't prepared, but he pulled out before *it* happened. Plus, it was right after her cycle. She'd be fine.

"Well, if you're giving it up, where's the ring?"

Maryanne wrinkled her nose. Sure, they'd talked about the future, but in vague terms. She didn't want to push him. But she knew she felt good around him, that he made her laugh and paid keen attention to doing — and saying — anything to make her happy. And that he supported her dreams and applauded her achievements. He made her feel seen. She was, totally, definitely, and positively head over heels in love. But was she in love with him, or how he made her feel?

She was in love with *him*. The way he made her feel, well, that was only part of why she was in love. But she couldn't put her finger on anything else.

"We haven't talked about that yet." Her imagination began to swirl.

Gladys' face grew long. "Oh no, girl. Oh no, no, no. You're in deep. I mean, don't get me wrong — I am happy for you. But I'm worried. I'm worried that you're being taken advantage of."

"He loves me, Gladys. He said so."

"But . . ."

"I know what I'm doing."

She looked at Gladys and forced a smile, inside feeling as if she'd been knocked off her cloud, landing on cold, hard concrete. Of course, Gladys had reason to worry — Maryanne knew she was being reckless and could sense danger, but the euphoria of possibility drowned out any fear. Plus, she deserved to be happy. Right?

Chapter 26

MIKHAIL/MICHAEL

Mikhail was still furious, even though it had been over a week since Marlboro had failed, yet again, to make a drop when he said he would. Leroy, who looked like he'd been sleeping in a pile of muddy leaves, told Mikhail nothing was at the drop site and *what the hell man?* Mikhail nonchalantly shook his head, expressionless but for a slight smile. "Sorry man," he said and paid Leroy the balance anyway, calling it a 'deposit' for future jobs. But once Mikhail closed the door, it was nearly impossible to keep from punching a hole in the wall. F-ing Marlboro. In training, Mikhail was warned that assets could be difficult, cagey, whiny, demanding, and childish. Marlboro ticked every box and took it to the next level. He was impossible. But, dammit, the information that slimeball provided was good often enough to keep him around. At least, for a while.

Once Marlboro outlived his usefulness, he'd have to take him out. It'd be the first kill he didn't feel terrible about. He decided to float the idea with Roman immediately, just to get pre-approval.

Mikhail liked to walk the two miles uphill from his apartment on U Street to Roman's neighborhood, so long as it wasn't raining. Kept him fit, enough exercise to clear his head. He walked north for a bit, cutting through the leafy the Adams Morgan neighborhood until reaching Connecticut Avenue and continuing upward. Northwest Washington, D.C. was pleasantly residential, with tidy row houses, Art Deco apartment buildings, and tony single-family homes. It was a nice Monday morning, pleasant with a slight nip in the air. He approached Roman's door just as the fur-stole clad and fragrantly-powdered widow — Roman's occasional girlfriend — slinked out of another older gentleman's apartment. Upon seeing Mikhail, she blushed and pranced in the other direction.

Roman greeted Mikhail with a warm hug and hearty pat on the back, as if he'd just received the Order of Lenin.

"Your girlfriend seems to get around," said Mikhail, cautiously. He felt he needed to give Roman a heads up, even though he was a seasoned veteran. You just never knew who worked for whom in D.C. The entire city was crawling with spies.

"Yes, yes, she's hard to keep happy," said Roman. "But, hey, free love, right?"

Mikhail chuckled, eyeing his handler curiously. Roman, though by the book, was always considerably more relaxed than anyone else he'd met in the KGB. For some reason, Mikhail trusted him implicitly. As least, as much as possible.

Roman winked and continued, "The Center is very impressed by your work." He went to the kitchen and emerged with a platter of liver piroshki and various pickles. "Your girl is quite the — what is the word — whiz kid. And the work they're doing at NASA — my goodness. You seem to have hit the jackpot."

"It's convenient that Marlboro and Bunny are in the same office," said Mikhail, a tight, proud smile spreading across his face at his chosen code name for her. It was cute and innocent, but totally out of character. Maryanne was more like a lioness. Smart, seductive, but not to be messed with. "That's why my reports are so thorough." He took a bite of pastry. "Helps put it all together."

"Yes, yes" said Roman. "The Americans are working even

faster, making smarter decisions. And it seems like it is all because of your girl."

Mikhail nodded his head in agreement.

"My boy, I do worry though. Are you being careful enough?"

It was true that there had been a close call, just the day before. He and Maryanne were walking back to his car from the Smithsonian Museum of Natural History when he saw Marlboro ambling toward them, enveloped in a tobacco cloud. They were totally exposed, standing at the bottom of the museum's wide steps. Mikhail immediately switched into tactical mode, quickly assessing the situation, possibilities scrolling in front of his eyes like on a computer screen. Seeing a dark corner just off the stairs, he gripped Maryanne's hand and made a beeline, pulling her in for a passionate kiss. His eyes followed the melancholy engineer as he slumped past.

"Your heart's racing," she'd said breathlessly. She was none the wiser, but he had to be careful not to get careless. No more walks together on the National Mall during the day.

"Yes," said Mikhail to Roman. "I've started meeting her in other parts of the city, wherever it is safe for us."

"What about the recordings? Are you getting enough from them?"

"Just the recordings aren't enough. I get more from her when we are together, and I don't want to lose — lose her as a source." Mikhail took a deep breath. "I'm spending as much time with her as I can."

And things were going swimmingly, though he felt pulled in too many directions. It was true there was some convenience to having several assets in one place, yet, it was risky. Very risky. He had to rotate his drop spots for Orion and Marlboro, and make sure none of them were close to where he picked up Maryanne. He obviously couldn't call her at home or at work, so every meeting was carefully pre-arranged, and he could never be late. But now that he was sleeping with both her and Stépha-nie, he could never be with them both on the same day. That would be totally impractical. He'd just as soon drop Stéphanie. She was grating and clingy, clearly in love with her boss, but using Mikhail to get back at him. He didn't care for her at all. But her information was good, and there was no one to pass her off onto. He felt like a library card file, with each area of his life in its own little compartment that seemed infinitely deep.

"Well, keep her happy," said Roman. "She may not be pro-viding as much information as your other assets, but I have a feeling," he tapped his temple, "I have a feeling she will have more value than either of us had imagined."

Mikhail leaned in, his heart lifting. "How?"

"You know how Moscow values intellect, skill. We're always on the lookout for talent, be it in art, science, or technology. I wouldn't be surprised if the Center has other ideas for her."

This time, Mikhail couldn't suppress the thin smile that tugged at the corners of his mouth. He wasn't sure exactly, but Moscow was never coy about attracting and recruiting brilliant minds from around the globe. Dominance would be achieved both through knowing what the enemy was up to and techni-cal superiority. What a prize she would be for Mother Russia's space program! He felt pride swell in his chest, but then it hit him. She'd be taken away from him. Or she could say no and be taken from him just the same. Moscow always got what it wanted, one way or the other.

Roman looked at Mikhail quizzically. "You seem pleased by this idea."

"Yes. I am happy that they see her value. She would be a great prize." He touched his tongue to roof of his mouth, as if to excise what he just said. He hated speaking of her as if she were a commodity.

"Well, just keep up the good work," said Roman, slapping him on the back, then walking away.

"Yes. The good work," said Mikhail under his breath. Problem was, it just didn't feel so good anymore.

Chapter 27

MARYANNE

t had been two blissful weeks of full-on romance. Twilight walks along the Potomac, quiet dinners at Michael's house, laying under the stars on his roof. Maryanne felt as if she was being lifted and swaddled by a cloud, and her mind would drift no matter how hard she tried to focus on her analysis. It was her hunger to tumble back into Michael's cocoon that motivated her to finish work so she could leave on time. Then it was nearly impossible to pry herself from his arms in the morning.

Atkins was perched on the edge of Maryanne's desk when she arrived.

"Good morning, Maryanne," he said.

"Good morning," she said, her upper lip quickly glistening with perspiration. "Am I in trouble?" She checked her watch — she was on time. Why would she think . . . oh yes. Despite how happy she was with Michael, something was constantly tugging at her psyche, like she was doing something nefarious. Maybe it was because she was lying to her mother. Or maybe it was because all those years of Catholic mass had seeped into her self-conscious. Whatever the reason, she couldn't shake the deep itchiness of guilt no matter how hard she scratched.

"No, no, absolutely not!" said Atkins. He hopped down. "Follow me."

She exhaled loudly, but he didn't seem to notice.

She followed him to his office near the back of the section, past Roger's desk. He looked at her with a little sneer, which filled her with dread. She was grateful when Atkins shut the door.

"So," he said. "I've spoken to folks at a few universities with astronomy programs, like Wisconsin and Case Western. Even Cal Tech. Told them about your work. You should be able to apply to at least one." He folded his arms in victory.

Maryanne stood up, though it felt like she might take flight. "Oh, thank you — thank you so much! When can I start applying?"

"Not for a couple of months. I need you to keep giving it your all here. Hell," he snorted. "Even Roger says you're our secret weapon. I know he's hard on you, but in truth he wants to steal you over to the other side of the river, but I won't let'em."

Hard on me? thought Maryanne, her heart settling back into its cavity. *He's one breath short of straight out calling me a . . .*

Now," said Atkins, clapping his hands. "Let's get back to work beating them damn Russians."

Thank God Michael was out of town, otherwise she would have called him before thinking things through. He was going to be in the Midwest for a few days and travelling from city-to-city, which was for the best. What would she say? She closed her eyes and a movie played, where he promised to follow her wherever she goes. *Wake up, girl!* she scolded herself. No man follows a woman — ever. Plus, she'd mentioned the thought of leaving D.C. for school once, and he gripped her hand like she was about to tumble off a cliff. But this was different from her musings. Now she might actually have the opportunity of a lifetime — a dream come true. What she had worked so hard for. And if she was accepted — whoa — everything would change. She would have to go.

Or would she?

Because my God, she thought, fighting the urge to cross herself, *Michael, well, he was also a dream come true.* Though falling in love was never her dream, just a musing. Her heart started racing, like when sitting in the dentist's chair before getting her wisdom teeth removed.

She wanted desperately to talk to Gladys, but she'd been so coy about her relationship. And she still hadn't said anything about Michael's race.

Her life was both coming together and falling apart.

The bus stop was quiet, though there were more NASA employees and neighborhood residents lingering in the cool sunshine of early Spring and strolling under the budding Myrtle trees. How she wished that she were there with Michael, walking hand-in-hand, like a normal couple in love. Their relationship was opaque — not quite open, but not totally clandestine either. They kept their heads low and stuck to safe public places, like the speakeasy on U, but mostly tucked into his apartment, his bed, where she'd spent so much time her aroma melded with his. But what if only they could live somewhere and not have to hide? If only they could be in the sunshine instead of slinky around in the shadows. She looked at the sky and blinked, wishing she could take flight. But then she remembered that first meeting, Michael's easy gait, the electric jolt of excitement, the feeling of getting lost in his eyes. No doubt he wanted to live in the sunshine too, and maybe this opportunity would be just what they needed.

Just maybe.

Chapter 28

MIKHAIL/MICHAEL

Mikhail knew he'd need a full day to decompress from his trip to Texas before seeing Maryanne. It was the third time he had to travel under a completely different identity in the U.S., this time as an oil spectator in a big'ole Texas hat, frontier jeans, and paunchy belly, looking for business prospects in Houston. He knew from Orion that the NASA bigwigs were headed there for Space Task Group secret meetings, and what hotel they were all staying in. The D.C. stiffs got liquored up and chatty at the hotel bar and were easy to make friends with. He congratulated himself for getting so much information on the next phase of the U.S. manned space flight program.

Maryanne's self-professed favorite food was crab cakes, so as soon as Mikhail got back to D.C. he drove up to Maryland where Crisfield's prepared and packaged a complete meal for two. He'd just finished setting the table, complete with wine and flowers, when he heard her feminine knock on the door. She had taken the bus — he apologized for not picking her up because he needed to "prepare" dinner, so she looked at him sideways when she saw the discarded aluminum containers in the trash.

"I can see that you put a lot of work into this meal," she said mockingly, as they embraced.

"Ok now, look, I know you like my cooking, but I have zero skills when it comes to local cuisine. I want you to keep liking me, so I went to that place you told me about."

"Oh — I didn't know you were paying attention — I just talk and talk and talk."

"Especially when you've had a bit of wine," he said, handing her a glass. It felt so easy, so normal. Mikhail liked teasing her, making her smile, a flash of blush across her nose. He was so good at playfully pushing her buttons that she was sharing more and more about her job, including her now almost daily trips to Langley. Even better, she'd more than once complained about the U.S.'s focus on defeating the Russians.

"We all know," she said, "the real enemy of the people is right here."

Maybe, he thought excitedly, *he wouldn't have to keep secretly listening in on her. Maybe she'd turn willingly.* Then he wouldn't have to lie to her anymore. Hell, he could even get her some money.

But that evening, for such a talker, she was awfully quiet while they ate. She seemed to hesitate between each bite, like she was about to say something important, but then made an airy comment. Something was clearly on her mind, and it felt like his insides were twisting into knots.

She couldn't know about him, could she? Or, what if she was starting to have some doubts about their relationship? He needed to know, his stomach sinking.

"What's wrong?" he said.

"Wrong?" she replied, brows raised. "Nothing. Nothing's wrong. I'm fine. Just a lot going on at work." She looked away.

He reached out for her hands and leaned in closer. "You know I'm here to listen."

She squeezed gently. "I'm just so deep into analysis of signals that I'm almost forgetting that I want to do something else. I mean, I don't really want to listen for what humans are doing

— I want to listen to actual space."

He felt his pulse start to quicken, so he released her hands and pretended to check on the dinner. He was losing it.

Get focused, he said to himself.

"The food is going to get cold, we should eat now," he said casually. "But humans? Are there humans in space we don't know about?" He smiled and guided her to the table.

"What? No, no." She eagerly reached for the wine bottle. "Anyway, I can't really talk about it. Let's eat — I'm starving!"

Two glasses in, she relaxed, and he turned the conversation to the Apollo 6 launch, about which she knew little. No surprise to him, because thanks to his listening device, and Marlboro, he knew exactly what she was working on. It was much more interesting that putting a man on the moon. But if he could get her to start spilling more details about her work, he could possibly get rid of Marlboro, and even keep her — as his asset — even longer.

She's just a mission, he reminded himself, his heart feeling tight.

They made short work of dinner. Mikhail carried their glasses to the coffee table, and she sat on the couch, kicking off her shoes and tucking her feet under her backside, as per her custom. He'd bought the new record player and latest release from Miles Davis right before leaving town and was eager to give it a spin. The sun was setting, and the candles cast a gentle glow.

Once the music flowed it took mere seconds for them to fall into each other's arms. He buried his face in her neck, an aroma that instantly soothed him, and carefully slipped his hand up the back of her sweater, pressing his palm against the slope of her lower back. She arched toward him and swept her leg out from under, giving a roundhouse kick to the bottle and wine glasses on the coffee table.

"I'm sorry!" she said, and blushed across the bridge of her nose, which was irresistible, so he picked her up and carried her to the bedroom, careful not to step on the broken glass. Then he characteristically tripped, sending them both flying toward the bed, where she lightly hit her forehead on the headboard.

"Oh my God," he said, pride at his feet. "Are you alright?"

She nodded and snorted, holding back a chuckle. With all formalities a total bust, they dissolved into uproarious laughter while shamelessly ripping their clothes off.

They'd just dozed off when the sound of shattering glass and tormented voices rose from the street below. The distinct smell of burning rubber invaded the bedroom. Every nerve in his body went on high alert — he knew this energy well. He'd had a front seat to at least one violent uprising.

"Michael?" Maryanne sat up and gathered the sheet around her, clutching it tightly to her neck. "What's happening?"

The clock on his nightstand flipped to 10:28pm. He rummaged to find his clothes and dressed quickly. "Stay here," he said, and running toward the front door, "lock the door behind me." The hairs on his neck were standing up. He could feel it was more than just a typical street skirmish.

He stepped on the street into a war zone. The air pulsed with outrage, desperation. "They killed him!" someone wailed over the sound of breaking glass. "He's dead!"

Mikhail blinked hard and spun around, grabbing the arm of a boy, not older than 15, clutching his jacket to his chest. His face was glazed with furious tears.

"What happened? Who's dead?" Mikhail asked as gently as he could muster.

"Dr. King," said the boy, starting to sob. "He was murdered." The boy angrily wrenched out of Mikhail's grasp and ran off. Mikhail stood momentarily stunned, like he'd been caught in a flood light. The worst had happened. He flew back up the stairs and banged on his door.

"Mary, it's me."

He caught himself. Only Gladys called her Mary, and he only knew that because of his eavesdropping. Even though he was in the middle of a maelstrom, he could not make mistakes like that again.

Luckily because of the circumstances, she didn't notice. She flung open the door, flushed and breathless, and he took her face in her hands. It was a gesture his mother always bestowed when he got hurt that always given him instant comfort. But there was no soothing this gaping wound. He silently grabbed Maryanne's hand and led her to the television, switching it on. The screen flickered to life.

"Dan Rather reporting for CBS News from New York. The Reverend Martin Luther King Jr. was shot to death by an assassin late today, as he stood on a balcony in Memphis, Tennessee. Dr. King had planned to lead another civil rights march in Memphis next Monday. We've got the latest on the story now from Russ Hodge, News Director of W-REC in Memphis."

His eyes switched between the screen and Maryanne, who was swaying like she was on the deck of a ship. He wrapped her in his arms, feeling shocks ripple through her body. The voices outside grew louder and angrier. It sounded like glass was breaking everywhere.

"It's total chaos out there," he said, as calmly as he could manage. "I was only outside for a minute, and it seemed like more and more people were in the streets." He closed the curtains. "They're smashing all the store windows and even smashing up cars."

"I feel like smashing something right now," she said feebly.

"No one can believe what's happened. It has just been a little over an hour since Dr. King died from an assassin's bullet. For the first half hour the police were busy trying to find — to track down the young white man who it is believed fired the fatal shot."

"Of course, it was a damn cracker," she spat.

He knew enough that the word stung. But he continued to hold her, as if that would be enough to keep an atomic bomb from exploding.

Suddenly his thoughts shifted. What if it was the KGB? His mind raced. It was possible. They'd never carried out an assassination of someone so prominent on U.S. soil — not that he knew of, at least. But King? That would be one of the most disruptive actions they could take. He turned over options in his head, his stomach tightening.

It's not like he cared about the man — no — but King reminded him of a more perfect version of the Bolshevik heroes that toppled the Romanoff Empire and freed the Russian people. Though his words were powerful and sometimes fiery, he was a peaceful man, which was an anomaly. Perhaps Moscow was concerned that King was a role model to those countries that had been pushed behind the iron curtain of Communism and would inspire the next wave of revolution. Or maybe they just wanted to pour gasoline on an already raging fire in America.

Marianne was shaking, her teeth chattering though her cheeks were flushed with heat.

"My family . . ." she squeaked. "I have to call them."

Mikhail felt a surge of panic — where would she say she was calling from? And his number — well — he wouldn't want it connected to his. He stroked her hair as gently as he could, wishing he could just whisk her away. Of course she wanted to call home, but he'd have to delay until maybe, possibly, he could just get here there.

To his immediate relief, the phone in the kitchen started to ring.

"I have to get this," he said. "Darling, please sit down." He wrapped the blanket tighter around her. Then he walked into the kitchen, picked up the phone, and receded to the far corner. "Yes?"

It was Roman.

"Ah, Michael, my boy! How are you? Are you safe? What's going on?" Roman only addressed him by his alias.

"Oh, hi, yes, I'm fine — just fine. I — we're stuck in the apartment. It sure is a crazy scene on the street." He peeked around to the corner to look at Maryanne. She was as rigid as a marble statue. He wanted to go to her but Roman was still talking.

"Word is there's a curfew and that the police are just letting everything in the Black neighborhoods burn but guarding white areas. Beating back the Negroes whenever and wherever they can. And King — well, can't say I'm surprised."

"That's what she said," sniffed Mikhail.

"She's there?"

"Yes."

Mikhail gripped the phone tighter and tighter with each passing second, waiting for Roman to say *something.*

"So, what is the situation?"

"She's upset, of course, but quiet." He lowered his voice. "I just don't know how I'm going to get her home."

"That was not what I meant."

Mikhail's tongue felt as if were twisting, his mind tumbling to figure out what Roman was getting at. *Don't wait too long,* he said to himself. *Say something. Anything.*

"Do you mean on the street right now?"

"Of course."

Mikhail took a deep breath. *Ok,* he thought. He stretched the phone cord as long as he could to look out the window, taking a moment to look at Maryanne first. She was still sitting in a tight ball, her head between her knees. His heart started to ache, he didn't want to be working right now. He just wanted to sit with her and promise that he'd keep her safe. Not an empty promise, because he couldn't guarantee anything, but it was certainly his wish.

"Still chaos," he said into the receiver. "But funny, it seems the police have stepped back." Two men were running down the uneven brick alley, pushing a shopping cart filled with what appeared to be liquor bottles. If the circumstances were different and Maryanne wasn't there, he would have chuckled, maybe even cheered them on. Because in in the Soviet Union the military would have been called, and the streets would run with the blood of anyone daring to challenge the State.

"Good. I need you to meet me in Arlington. I have something I need you to and its best to discuss in person."

Mikhail cleared his throat. "Do you think it was -?"

"Don't know yet."

Mikhail looked over at Maryanne, who had uncurled and was sitting upright, a cloud of anger across her brow. "I need to get her home first," he whispered into the receiver. "And my car is in the alley, which is currently blocked. It might take some . . " he paused, because he'd never pushed back on Roman. "I will monitor and get moving as soon as there is an opening."

"I need you immediately. Find another way to get her home."

Mikhail turned to see Maryanne standing at the entrance to the kitchen, chewing a thumbnail. "I need — I — need to go," she said.

"I know. I'm trying to figure out what to do." He took a deep breath. He had to figure something out. This feeling of — of helplessness. *C'mon, get it together,* he scolded himself. *Don't lose it. Think.*

"You still there?" he heard Roman bark.

"Yes, sorry. I'm just wrapping things up and I'll be on my way."

"Good." Roman hung up.

"Who was that?" Maryanne demanded.

"It was just work, I have to get to one of our construction sites to make sure it's not affected. But don't worry, I'll get you home first." *But how?*

Outside shots rang out, followed by screams. The walls were a kaleidoscope of flashing red and blue lights. A sudden banging on the door, made them both jump.

"Hey, Michael, hey brother." The voice was muffled through the door, but he recognized it. "It's Leroy."

Mikhail opened the door and his friend — no, his asset — walked in and whistled. A momentary twinge of relief.

"Was just a matter of time," said Leroy, his eyes landing on Maryanne, then back to Mikhail. "It's crazy out there and everyone on the block is scared. Just came up to see how you're doing."

"Thanks, man. I'm — we're fine. Just a little shell shocked is all."

"I need to go home," said Maryanne again, every syllable dripping with angst. "My mother — she'll be worried."

Mikhail looked at Leroy and an idea sparked. He hadn't asked Leroy to do anything since the Arboretum fiasco. But he'd recently seen Leroy driving two different cars, and neither were parked anywhere near their building. Clearly, the man had resources, which meant he had either clout in the revolutionary community or exceptional skills. This could be another chance for Mikhail to see how useful he was.

"Got any ideas?" Mikhail asked Leroy, deliberately handing him the reins.

Leroy stepped over to the window and peeked from behind the curtain to surveille the action. "Yeah, I got an idea. Getting around chaos is my specialty." He looked at Maryanne. "But you're gonna have to follow me and do exactly what I say, ok?"

Mikhail stood taller and pulled Maryanne closer. "What do you want to do?" he asked her. "It's your decision." He'd remind Leroy who was in charge later. She buried her face in his chest and let go, her body shuddering with each sob until she fell still.

Leroy looked at the beleaguered couple and his eyes softened. "I'll give ya'll just a minute but then we have to go."

He gently wiped her tears with his thumbs.

"I can't believe this is happening," he said. "I don't want to you to go, but you should be with your family."

"Yes," she said quietly. "Will you be ok?"

She's concerned about my safety? he thought, suppressing a smile. "I'll be fine," he said, kissing the tears on her cheeks. "As soon as it's safe, I'll find you, don't worry."

It felt as if the walls of the room were shrinking, and he craved fresh air. Never in his life had he felt so helpless, so incapable. He didn't want her to leave his side, but it was best to get her home and away from him. He had no idea what Roman would ask of him next.

Chapter 29

MARYANNE

Maryanne clutched her bag and followed Leroy down the hallway to the rear stairwell, then down to the basement which stank from urine and dead rats. He flicked on the dim lights, which illuminated the dismal space. She felt almost like a robot, unable to feel anything, so numb that she didn't notice her keys and NASA employee badge tumble onto the floor.

"You dropped something," said Leroy, picking everything up and handing it back to her. "NASA, huh?" he said, eyebrows raised.

She looked at him and nodded.

He motioned for her to follow, grabbing her hand and placing it on the hem of his jacket.

"Don't let go," he whispered. It was so dark she could barely see, and the ceiling got lower and lower as they walked silently, for what seemed like an eternity. Finally, they came to a locked door, for which he quickly produced a key. They entered what seemed to be an underground garage in which was parked a faded black Mustang, police cruiser, and several other cars. He opened the passenger door of the Mustang.

"My lady."

How can he be so nonchalant after what just happened? she thought, panic turning to frustration. *Where are we? How will we get away?* she thought, again looking around the garage and pointed to the cruiser.

"Is that yours?" she said.

"Don't worry, we're a good clip away from the chaos," he said completely ignoring her question. She shuddered.

He got out and opened the garage door then got back in the car. As they pulled out onto the street, she realized that she had been in such a daze she didn't realize how far they'd walked — almost a mile to Florida Avenue. A couple of police cars zipped by, and people, mostly young men, filled the street. "Guess everyone's hungry for action," Leroy snickered. "Where to?"

She gave him the address, though she considered bailing. There was something about this man that didn't sit right. She hadn't missed the way he looked at her and Michael, the fire in his eyes, which betrayed his otherwise cool demeanor. Of course he didn't approve. But Michael trusted him and she had to get home.

"Oh, you're from that part of Northwest," he said, sucking his teeth. "You from one of those bougie Negro families, huh? Figures."

"What's *that* supposed to mean?" she snapped, suddenly no longer numb.

"Oh, just that you're too good for a Black man, you know, had to add a little cream to your coffee. Don't like it black."

"It's not like that at all." Her anger bounced around the narrow cabin. "That has nothing to do with it."

"Really now." He carefully rolled to a complete stop at a red light and looked over both shoulders. "'Cause seems to me like you've done everything you can to stay away from your own people."

Why are we talking about this now? she thought. *Dr. King's been shot, and the world is on fire!*

"Oh please," she said. "You don't' know anything about me. Just because I'm with someone White doesn't mean I'm no longer Black. I was Black when I was born, I am Black as I live, and I'll be Black when I die. And I'm proud of that. Plus," she sat up even straighter, "I went to Howard."

"Well," he said as he turned onto Georgia Avenue and hit the gas hard, "that explains everything."

They flew North in stony silence, her arms tightly wrapped around her chest. *The nerve!* she thought. *What gives him the right to say anything?* She held herself tighter. No one had come out and said anything so direct, so venomous to her about her relationship with Michael. And today of all days! It was why she still hadn't told Gladys, her mother, or even her father. God forbid anyone in the community found out. Surely strangers who saw them together would have the same or similar feelings. She was surprised that no one had said anything yet. But defending herself to Leroy, and thus all the strangers in her head, didn't leave her weary. She felt energized. Righteous. She loved Michael and he loved her. So what if the world was against them? She was happy. A happy Black woman living in a world on fire.

Leroy took a tight turn and screeched to a stop in front of Maryanne's house. She grabbed her valise and flung the car door open.

"Thank you for the ride," she said through clenched teeth. She started to close the door, then paused, leaned down, and looked him straight in the eye. She had one last thing to say, to call him out on his hypocrisy.

"So, if you got something against White men, why're you friends with Michael?"

Leroy looked at her with amusement, and her fury boiled. "One, I ain't got nothin' against White men, not in general," he said. "I just don't trust most of them — no matter where they come from." He cleared his throat. "I mean, no matter who they are. But Michael, well, he's one of the decent ones. Second, I ain't got no problem with them until they start taking our women. Distracting them. Treating them like their commodities — property. Just like Massa. So," he revved the engine and leaned over to look at her. "Did you scream 'Massa' tonight?"

She threw her entire body into slamming the door, praying

she'd clocked him in the face. But he just looked at her with condemnation, and her fury became an inferno.

The next morning, the city looked like it had been hit by a million little bombs. Smoke still rose above the roofs and hung in the air. It was a miracle she made it to work.

"You're late," said Atkins, as she rounded the corner to her desk. It was 10:00am, almost two hours later than her expected arrival time, even though she left her house at 6:30am.

"I am so sorry," she said with unfiltered frustration. "My bus never showed up, and I learned that it wasn't coming down Georgia because of — the situation — and so I had to take a bus across town and then transfer to another one, which was re-routed and . . ."

"Fine," he snapped. "Just make sure you figure how you're going to get here on time until things get back to . . ." He paused and wrinkled his brow. "Normal. Look, what happened is — ter-rible. I'm sorry." He took off his glasses and rubbed the perma-nently dented bridge of his nose. "But we still have a job to do. Our nation is depending on us."

She nodded. *Our nation — how rich*, she thought, sitting down. *Uncle Sam doesn't give a damn about people like me.*

Slumping into her chair, she carefully looked around the office. No one looked at her. No one asked if she was ok. She was expected to get right to work as if nothing had happened. Still, she wasn't surprised by Atkins' tone. That's how he was — hot and cold. As long she was a human machine, producing without complaint, meeting his arbitrary deadlines, everything was roses. But the minute she showed any sign of humanity or vulnerability, out came the fangs. "Don't you realize how I stick my neck out for you?" he would say if she made a small error or didn't have an immediate answer to a question. But then not even thirty minutes later he would tell her that the program would fail without her. It was exhausting.

Gladys and Eric had come to the house before dawn, look-ing shellshocked. Soon after the assassination was reported Eric had gathered with the growing crowd of grievers in front of People's Drug, before things went sideways, and decided to answer Stokely's call for all Blacks to boycott work in protest to Dr. King's assassination. Gladys reminded him that they had rent to pay and he relented, though clearly pained by the decision. To Maryanne, protests meant nothing. Did nothing. Nothing, nothing changed.

The bus she eventually found to take her toward Southwest was on the other side of Connecticut Avenue, the side where few, if any Black folk lived or spent any time, save for the herds of domestics following the same path as generations before, in service to wealthy Whites. It was so full she was forced to stand, though right in front of two younger and quite able-bodied White men for whom politeness would dictate that they cede their seat for a lady. One looked right through her, as if she were a wraith, and the other glared at her with lustful rage. She looked down and met his gaze, the vein in her temple throbbing and her eyes aflame, and he jerked his head away.

Smoke littered the horizon before them, in every direction. While some passengers demonstratively stared straight ahead, the majority strained to get a closer look.

"Can't understand why they would burn down their own neighborhood," said one man. "Probably gonna be lookin' for another handout to fix their mess," said another. "You burn it, you own it" and "Goddamn niggers," said someone in the back. She gathered her sweater tightly around her neck, but quickly released as it felt like a noose tightening. The few Black people around her sat stone faced, staring at their laps, as did a handful of Whites, and she wanted to rouse them to all collective wailing such that their pain would pierce the frozen hearts that surrounded them.

Her thoughts stumbled around, unable to keep balance, like a Saturday night drunk. Mother's crying was still ringing in her ears. Father just sat in his chair, fists digging into his thighs, whiskey at his side, fixated on the television. The night was shredded by helicopter blades and metallic sirens, and Cedric from four doors down called to perpetuate the rumor that the rioters were coming to their neighborhood. No one slept, not even the children. She blinked hard and tried to focus, knowing that Atkins would expect her to complete her work on time, her "personal problems" be damned.

As noon approached, she wrestled over whether to make her usual call to Michael on her lunch break, from the pay phone down the street. Given how late she had gotten to work, she would probably be stuck at her desk. She'd briefly entertained jumping off the bus and running to Michael's apartment, but the bus sped past the edge of chaos before she could do anything stupid. There was no phone at her desk, the only ones being on the desks of the secretary and in offices. She might have a chance, maybe just a minute or two, to call him from the reception desk phone when everyone left for lunch.

"Want anything from upstairs?" Maryanne looked up to see Mrs. Wilkins, the receptionist. Her normally gentle curls were frizzy, and her deep chocolate face had a gray pallor. There was a large, visible run in her stockings.

"Mrs. Wilkins?" Maryanne stood and the two women embraced as if long lost friends reunited after many years, silently shaking. It felt as if nothing, nothing would ever change. She had to talk to Michael.

Once the office was quiet, Maryanne casually rose from her work and walked toward Mrs. Wilkins' desk. She looked around just to make sure she was alone, and picked up the receiver, pushing one of the clear, unlit buttons for an open line. She pressed '9' and dialed Michael's number. It rang for what seemed like an eternity before she hung up, her heart in pieces.

Chapter 30

MIKHAIL/MICHAEL

April 4, 1968
Northwest Washington, D.C.

After Leroy left with Maryanne, Mikhail stood in his empty apartment and looked around. Echoes of her were still everywhere, from the indentation in the couch where she'd laid, to the lingering scent of her skin in the air. If he didn't get out soon, he'd drown. Plus, Roman made it clear he needed Mikhail immediately, riots be damned.

Stepping out into the night, his nostrils burned from the smoke and his eyes began to water. The horizon glowed like a hellscape. *She'll be ok*, he told himself, though there was something about Leroy that nagged at him. It was the way Leroy looked at him, out of the side of his eye, like a chameleon. Maybe he was just paranoid. Maybe the stress of managing multiple assets and missions was getting to him. Of course, Leroy was suspicious of him, a White man. But there was something else . . .

Mikhail put Leroy in a mental file to deal with later. So far, he'd proved his reliability, and if he got Maryanne home safely, Mikhail would use him more.

Maryanne.

Now was not the time to let his emotions take over. *Empty,* he thought. *Empty yourself. Do your job.* He slipped out into the night and walked to Roman's, every one of his senses on high alert. The night horizon glowed with smoke and fire like an eerie hellscape, and Mikhail proceeded quickly and carefully, occasionally ducking behind a tree, or pressed into a dark corner, his heart in his throat.

"You look like you just stepped out of the trenches," Roman teased once he arrived. "Come in and have some tea."

"I'll take a drink, thank you," said Mikhail. "And it is a war zone out there."

Roman poured two whiskies and they sat in his living room.

"Never thought I'd enjoy this drink," said Roman, after a hearty swig. "So smoky and syrup, but it's almost medicinal."

Mikhail nodded. "So, what do you have to tell me?"

"It wasn't us."

Mikhail's shoulders, which he hadn't noticed crept all the way up to his ears, dropped and he let out a big exhale. Roman looked at him curiously.

"Were you worried?"

Mikhail looked at his handler and knew there was no use in skirting the truth.

"Yes. Because I thought it would undermine my — our work."

"Well, remember we are but only one component in a massive machine. They are not thinking about us — they are only thinking about the big picture. Never forget that."

Mikhail nodded, though a pit formed in his stomach. Here he was, living and breathing only for the Soviet Union, running around D.C. and the whole damn country to get information, even killing. And they didn't care? No, he couldn't believe that. He was making a difference.

And they would surely care if he made a mistake.

"Michael, you in there?"

Roman was standing over him, and he hadn't even noticed. His handler looked at him with a hint of sympathy in his eyes.

"I'm sorry," said Mikhail, embarrassment flooding his brain. "I'm just tired."

"Yes, you need rest. But make sure you tie up any loose ends first. President Johnson has announced he's bringing out the National Guard close to where you live — by that park you seem to spend time in. That, plus the news crews with their cameras . . ."

Mikhail sprung to his feet. Marlboro had left a drop in the Meridian Park the night before, and he had planned to retrieve it once Maryanne was soundly asleep. In all the chaos, he'd forgotten.

"I'm on it," he said. His head suddenly felt like a snow globe, and he swayed.

"Careful," said Roman, guiding him to the couch. "Get some rest. Close your eyes for a couple of hours and leave at the crack of dawn. Things will be calmer by then."

"I hope so," said Mikhail, his eyes fluttering open and shut. He'd never been so exhausted, and Roman's paternal grace put him at ease.

✳ ✳ ✳

Mikhail awoke with a start and looked at his watch. *Pizdets!* He'd been out for five hours, and there was much to do. He had to get to the park. And he had to find out if Maryanne made it home safely. He blinked and shook his head, suddenly overcome by a longing for her to be by his side, in his embrace. It tugged at him, wanting her to be safe, imaging he would be her protector. And he would, he could protect her, as much as he could.

He carefully slipped out of Roman's apartment and looked over the horizon. Smoke as far as the eyes could see. He considered going into the park on the way back, but police were swarming the entire area and creating barricades. It was like being trapped on an island in the middle of a burning sea. He had to get to the park, collect the drop, then make his way to his warehouse. He'd never make it past the police on foot and if he got to his car, he'd have to craft an award-winning story to explain why he was driving around. Journalist, maybe? No, they beat them up too. His stomach turned at the thought of telling Roman he couldn't complete a mission.

He breathed a sigh of relief once he stepped into the vestibule of his building and knocked on Leroy's door. It swung open immediately.

"Hey brother," said Leroy, reaching out to shake Mikhail's hand. "Whoa, you look like shit."

"Yeah, I know, hey, about . . ."

"She's home safe. Delivered right to her front door."

"Thanks, man. I appreciate it." Mikhail looked at Leroy, who had a smug look on his face. *Must be proud for coming through,* he thought. Then another idea hit him.

"Think you're up for another favor?" Mikhail said. "I'll give you — $1000."

Leroy's face lit up like a kid who'd just met the real Santa. "That's a lot of money. What's the job?"

"I need to get inside Meridian Hill Park. But it's surrounded by police and possibly the military. I can't just walk in."

His fingers tingled, waiting for Leroy's reply. What if he showed his cards too soon?

"I got you, man," Leroy finally said. "And that's a good chunk of dough. But please — before I get in a car with you, you have *got* to take a shower."

✳ ✳ ✳

Just as he closed his apartment door, Mikhail heard the phone ring and paused.

"You need to get that, man?" said Leroy.

"I'm not expecting anyone," he replied, as casually as possible. He resisted the urge to bolt back inside, pick up the phone, and hear Maryanne's voice. She floated in and out of his consciousness, and he had to push her the margins. She was home, she was safe, and that was enough for now.

Leroy took him to an underground garage, where he had a truly remarkable collection of vehicles, including a police cruiser. Mikhail could not believe his eyes.

"How'd you get all of these cars?" Mikhail asked sounding impressed, though suspicion sat like a rock in his gut.

"Side business," said Leroy, sounding cool in a way that

only people like him could pull off. Mikhail felt a pang of envy. "Boosting is how we finance the movement."

"And quite lucrative to boot!" said Mikhail, pulling an envelope from his pocket. "Guess you don't really need this."

Leroy snatched the money with a half-smile. "The cars are for the movement. This cash," he peeked into the envelope and smiled. "The cash is for yours truly."

"Do this job for me today brother, and I'll see to it you get paid even more," said Mikhail.

Leroy's eyes lit up. "Well, have I got something for you then," he said, directing Mikhail to the police cruiser and tossing him the keys. "You've got a role to play. I can't just drive you up 16th street."

"Why?"

"Because ain't but a handful of Black cops in the Metropolitan Police Department. And they all know each other." Leroy reached into the cruiser and pulled out a uniform. "If you impersonate a pig it'll be convincing. No one looks sideways at a White cop but a Black one? Shit. I'd be lynched on the spot."

Mikhail held the stiff material in his hands and held it up for inspection. It was, indeed, a real uniform, badged and all. But how had Leroy gotten his hands on this? He pretended to conduct quality control to allow more time to digest the fact he was truly putting his well-being in Leroy's hands, and he suddenly felt he didn't know enough about him. He would seem to be the best connected, most industrious revolutionary he'd ever encountered. Was someone else paying him?

"I'm just gonna put this on over my clothes — so long as I don't get out of the car no one should notice," he said, turning around. "Hey, I get how you could boost these other cars, but how'd you land a cruiser? Who would buy this?" He tried to sound like he was ribbing him a bit but watched Leroy out of the corner of his eye. His benefactor's eyes narrowed, and his lips drew in, the kind of face men make before they're about to swing a punch. Or shoot to kill. Mikhail quickly sent his last leg into the pants and turned around. Leroy's face instantly relaxed.

"Oh, yeah, tried to sell this, you know, on the regular

market. No takers. And a good thing, 'cause it's perfect for your current problem."

"Got it," said Mikhail, making a mental note to check out Leroy's story later. This was not the time to second guess, and though he was suspicious, he didn't sense danger. *Just a bit shady*, he thought. *Like all aspiring revolutionary heroes.*

The two men stood looking at each other for a what felt like a heavy moment. Then Leroy said,

"Looking good, Comrade," and clicked his heels together.

Mikhail smirked, though hearing that word set him back on edge. He hadn't heard that term since the day he left Moscow three years ago, on the hottest day of the year. That day the only things on his mind were hunger to start his assignment, and mild excitement about experiencing a technology called "air conditioning" which was rumored to be in every U.S. building. On that day, he was fully consumed with patriotic zeal. Why did the term hit him so hard right now? Nothing had changed about the way he felt. Nothing. He still hadn't revealed his identity, but he and Leroy had discussed the evils of capitalism over beer, and how communism was a false enemy of the people and could be what Black folks needed to right the ship. But it was downright dangerous to be labeled a Communist — the feds would be down his neck for sure.

"Hey man, I don't think we should say that in public," said Mikhail. "Never know who's listening."

Leroy backed up. "Hey, sorry man. Just joking. Lettin' you know I'm down." He slid into the back seat of the cruiser.

"I know you're down. I know," said Mikhail, getting into the driver's seat. "Anyway, I really appreciate the help. I'd never make it through this chaos on foot."

He could feel Leroy's eyes boring into the back of his neck and he gripped the steering wheel so hard his knuckles turned white. *Breathe*, he thought.

Mikhail blinked then pulled out onto the street, authoritatively driving the cruiser toward chaos. It was nearly impossible to navigate through the heavy smoke, even in daytime, and he nearly hit two young men who ran directly in front of the car. Storefront windows were smashed, residents stood either in tears or stunned silence, and glass littered the sidewalks. His eyes started to water, and his lungs felt as if they were burning.

"Tear gas," said Leroy, holding his shirt up to his nose and mouth. "They stopped poppin' it off late last night and must've run out. Strong shit though — still in the air."

Mikhail blinked his eyes to produce tears. He'd learned how to navigate tear gas in training, though it was much stronger than this, so much so that Ilya Stepanovich, a young, vibrant man, had a heart attack and died on the spot. "We'll get through this," he said, coughing up an abundance of phlegm and spitting on the passenger side floor.

They crossed U Street and headed up the hill toward the park entrance, approaching a police blockade.

"Put your arms behind your back," said Mikhail as he drove straight toward them and rolled to a stop. Leroy complied but gave him a look like he might launch daggers from his eyes. *What's his problem?* he thought, but he'd have to worry about that later. He pulled the cruiser up to the blockade and rolled down the windows.

"Where're you taking this nigger?" said the frighteningly pink, shell-shocked officer, leaning into the passenger side window, which Mikhail had reached over to roll down.

"Gotta get'em up — I mean, down to the jail," he said with a throaty Chesapeake drawl. "But can't get south by my normal route, so I'm gonna deposit him for a spell at holding on Indiana."

"Yeah, but you still have to get across town. So why in the hell are you going North?"

"I'm gonna cut across up Missouri Ave." said Mikhail sounding assuredly relaxed but still on high alert. *This can go sideways fast,* he thought. "Then down North Capitol, you know, away from the action."

"But your cruiser is marked for this precinct." The officer stroked his thick, blond mustache and narrowed his eyes to get a better look at Mikhail's name tag. "So how — wait — what is your name — ok," he stood upright and shouted over the cruiser "Hey! Dick! We got one of yours over here! His name is — Anderson?"

Mikhail rested casually on one elbow, but his stomach was burning. He molded his face into a look of nonchalant annoyance, actively fighting the tightness expanding across his chest. *Be ready for anything*, he thought. *Save the mission.* Leroy squirmed.

The officer leaned back into the window. "That's your Sergeant over there. I'm going to let him sort this out. Just sit tight."

Shit, thought Mikhail. *Time to do something. Think fast.* He looked at Leroy, who looked like he'd been frozen in a hungry lion's cage.

A wraith in blue uniform walked toward their cruiser with his hands on his hips. Mikhail weighed his options. He considered shouting "Gun!" and shooting Leroy in the head, thank you, Comrade. Or, continuing with the ruse, improvising his story just enough to get through. *Save the mission.*

Suddenly, *POP-POP-POP*. Every officer sprung to action, including their interrogator, who flew toward the sound like a kamikaze pilot. Cruisers sped away, officers barked into radios. Mikhail looked around and saw that the road in front of them was totally clear. No one was paying attention to them anymore.

"Go!" shouted Leroy.

"Music to my ears," Mikhail shouted to the back seat. He put the cruiser in gear and took off like a joyrider, enjoying the sensation of being able to breathe again. Damn, he'd gotten lucky again. He felt a mild pang of guilt at considering killing his neighbor, but quickly stuffed the feeling down deep. He was, however, glad that it hadn't come to that. Because no matter how well he had been trained, or how indoctrinated he was, every time he had to kill, it took a piece of his soul. And this was the first assignment he'd been on where he cared a little about his assets. Well, more Maryanne than Leroy. He was starting to believe that maybe, he could actually trust her. His stomach started to hurt again.

He thanked a flustered and sweaty Leroy for the car and dropped him off near Howard University's off-campus dormitory, where students had gathered outside with banners and bull horns, then turned onto a side street. He abandoned the cruiser in a spot where it was sure to be vandalized, wiping down every inch of the interior, as well as the inside and outside door handles. Then he scaled a low wall to enter the park, which was eerily quiet, tossed the cruiser keys in trash can, and walked toward the drop spot with his hand on the Billy club. If he came across any National Guardsmen, he'd say that he was pursuing a suspect. He found the low cluster of rocks he'd arranged the week before and turned one over, revealing a compartment in which Marlboro had deposited the film. He placed the film in his pocket and stood up when he heard a crunching sound behind him, his heart in his throat.

"So, what do we have here?" said a wiry young Black man who looked as if he had just run a marathon in the desert. "A pig, all alone?"

Dammit, thought Mikhail. *Just kids.*

A younger boy, likely no more than fifteen, slightly shorter but significantly more muscular, appeared at his side. "Must be our lucky day," he sneered.

Another young man, about Mikhail's height and weight, wearing a smart leather jacket, stepped from behind a tree. Mikhail kept his club holstered.

"Why don't you just run along now," he said, this time with a flat, Jimmy Dean accent. "I don't want you to get in any trou-ble. You shouldn't be out. It's dangerous."

"It's always dangerous for us, pig," said the beefy one. "Dan-gerous for us every day because of pigs like you." Mikhail saw the glint of a short blade in the hand of one the boy with large hair.

"You need to go home — now," said Mikhail. "Before you get into trouble."

Mikhail's eyes darted from opponent to opponent, taking snapshot inventory of their gait, height, weight, and clothing. Just the one appeared to have a weapon, no, wait, the skinny one removed his belt with a heavy buckle. His pants sagged. The stocky boy stood with his fists in front, like he might know how to box. They formed an arc — the rocks were behind him and there was no easy way to run away, which, in training, he learned was always preferable to fighting.

Mikhail unsheathed his club and held it in his left hand and steadied his gait, feet hip width distance apart, the right slightly in front of the left.

"Get'em!" shouted the sweaty one, and the belt buckle came flying toward Mikhail's head. He raised the Billy club to catch it and yanked the boy toward the rocks. The boy tripped over his falling pants and his head landed with a thud on the large grey boulder. Then the stocky boy managed to land a punch to Mikhail's kidney, causing his knees to buckle. Mikhail used his lower position to spin in the direction of the boy with the knife, swooping up to grab his wrist and redirect the assault toward the groin of the amateur boxer just as he attempted to land a cross hook into Mikhail's jaw. The boy's agonizing cries were sure to draw attention, so Mikhail landed a kick to his voice box while holding the knife bearer in a sleeper hold until his body went limp.

Mikhail looked around. Two boys were still knocked out, and all that was heard from the other was a low, raspy groan. He checked his pocket — the film was still there. He exchanged pants and shoes with the larger boy and took his jacket. Then he put the film in his new pants, balled up the police shirt and his other clothes, and stuffed everything into the hat. Finding the sewer, he sent the bundle on its way to the Anacostia River, scolding himself for wishing things could have been easier. At least he was a far enough from the madness that he could avoid the police. As he jogged away, he realized that he'd left the hol-low rock back at the site, but it was turned over and wouldn't raise any suspicion. He could go back for it later.

Maryanne must be a mess, he thought, his ribs starting to ache. He turned north to look in the direction of her house. Had she kept trying to call? Could she be so mad about what happened, she'd never again see him as anything but a White man?

Maybe he could call her at home, pretending he was from NASA. He couldn't let this tragedy destroy all the work he'd put in.

He found the stop for the bus that would take him to his apartment in Southwest and waited with the other passengers, who looked as if they'd just crawled from the trenches in 1916. Smoke again began to rise on the horizon and the sounds of torment and fury filled the air.

Chapter 31

MARYANNE

Maryanne tried calling Michael again but hung up after the tenth ring. She looked down and winced at the sight of her bloody, chewed up thumbnail. The pain didn't even register anymore.

"What're you doing?"

She spun around. It was Roger, aka Marlboro, in the same starched shirt that he seemed to wear every day. His tobacco-stained fingers moved nervously as if playing a guitar. Her stomach turned.

"I — I'm just trying to call my mother," she said. "I'm not sure how — how long it will take me to get home tonight."

"Oh, I see," he said flatly. "Well, it sure is a sad thing that happened. You know, I'm just so sorry for your people and all, but I just don't understand how you can turn on your own neighborhoods."

Her cheeks burned. Normally, she would bite her tongue, like she had to every day, armor up, ready for the next verbal assault on her dignity, intellect, value. But she was too tired today to put on airs, too numb to worry about consequences.

"Dr. King wasn't for just our people," she declared, looking him directly in the eye. "He was for all people. That all people should be treated equally." She took a deep breath. "AND we are not destroying our own neighborhoods. People are just fed up, and tired of not being listened to, treated like second-class citizens." Her body sizzled with fearlessness, like when she'd mastered riding her bike without training wheels.

Roger looked amused. "Feeling a little sour toward the great US of A? Not surprising given your associations." He turned on his heel and slithered toward his office, whistling Dixie.

Her cheeks stung, like she'd been slapped. What did he mean by "associations?" Then her stomach dropped. *How dare he accuse me?* she thought, scolding herself for mouthing off. It was routine for Blacks who dared to speak up about injustice to be labeled Communist. Red. Unpatriotic. Her heart twisted as she remembered how certain lawmakers talked about Dr. King. All it took was for one person to make the accusation, and you were finished.

Roger would be that person.

Oh God, I hope he doesn't tell Atkins what I said, she thought.

He was showing increasing hostility toward her, which until now she thought was because she'd turned down his offer to work for him at NRO. But this was the first time he'd been that aggressive. Nasty. She decided to do her best to watch her tongue and avoid him. It was graduate school or bust.

At home, Maryanne set the table for dinner, recoiling at the sight of her ravaged fingernails. Hopefully her mother and Gladys wouldn't notice. Where was Michael? She cursed herself that she had told him never to call her at home, though she didn't tell him that it was because they'd know instantly that he was white. She would try one more time before dinner, if she could.

The entire house was filled with the savory, honeyed aroma of Spam and her mother's famous dirty rice. It was the meal reserved for busy nights and a lean budget, but that night it was because every market on their side of Georgia Avenue was still closed, and no one Black dared venture across D.C.'s normally invisible redline that was now patrolled by predatory cops. D.C. was now occupied territory. Mother would have to rely on whatever was in the freezer or pantry for who knew how long.

"Are you alright?" Gladys asked, placing a covered casserole on the table. "You look so tired."

"I'm fine," said Maryanne. "You know, work, the riots."

"Don't you give me that nonsense. I know lovesick when I see it." She put her arm around her sister. "What's going on?"

"It's Michael. I haven't been able to reach him."

"Oh no! Where do you think he might be?"

"I don't know. He hasn't been home, I don't think. Maybe he left D.C."

"And not tell you?" Gladys shook her head. "Do you know any of his friends? Family?"

"No — we — we come from different worlds."

Gladys looked at her sister with narrow eyes. "What does that mean?"

Maryanne closed her eyes and took a deep breath. It had been eating at her to the point she could barely look her sister in the eye.

"Can we go into the back room?" she said. "I don't want," she jerked her head toward the kitchen, "them to hear."

Gladys' brow twisted into curious concern. "Of course."

The two sisters unceremoniously strolled through the dining room toward the small covered porch, Maryanne holding her breath until they closed the door behind them.

"He's White," she exhaled, and braced for Gladys' reaction.

On cue, her older sister's face drained of blood.

"What?!" Gladys' voice jumped up and down like a prepubescent boy's. "No wonder you've avoided introducing me. Mary, what were you thinking?"

"I wasn't."

"And you say he lives by U Street?"

Maryanne nodded her head, her eyes swelling with tears.

"Well, maybe his lines are down, you know, it's been crazy down there. I mean, anyway, do you really think he left town or something?"

"I don't know. Maybe he's just using all of this as an excuse to ditch me or something."

"Well, if he did, then he's a scoundrel. Just like all of them. Every single one. Doesn't matter where they come from, or what color."

Gladys never missed a beat. And yet, she never judged. Never. She always listened, and only offered encouragement. Maryanne always knew she was safe to tell her sister anything. Why had she waited so long?

"Mary, why didn't you tell me?" said Gladys, breaking Maryanne's heart even more.

"I didn't think you'd approve."

"Mary, I don't care who you love. I really don't. I just want you to be fully loved. And you seemed so happy."

"I was happy," said Maryanne, "but now . . . I- I just don't know. I mean, you found a good one, Gladys. A really good one." Maryanne started to sob. "What's wrong with me?"

Gladys grabbed her by both quivering shoulders. "Nothing. There is nothing wrong with you. What's happening now — it has nothing to do with you, so get that out of your head."

Maryanne nodded weakly. "What if something happened to him?"

"Mary, you're going out of your head. Listen — I'm not saying you shouldn't be worried. And if he's really using this whole situation as an excuse, to Hades with him. But you're smart, and I can't believe anyone would be able to get past you, pull the wool over your eyes. You dig him too much and it's gone on for too long. Give it a few more days — he might turn up."

Maryanne wiped her tears and hugged his sister. "Thank you."

"Yes," said Gladys. "Listen, I'm fine with whatever, but Mommy? Daddy? Well, you know this would not go over with them, uh-uh. Or anyone else in our neighborhood. They cannot find out. It would kill them. You need to think this through. If you choose to be with him, well, you'd have to basically disappear from their lives."

"Yours too?" Maryanne felt herself say, her heart pressing painfully inside her chest. Lose her family? She'd never even considered it. No, it just wasn't an option, her mother, her sister would never shun her.

Would they?

Their mother walked in carrying a peach cobbler, her head high with culinary pride. "Who's ready to — what's wrong?"

"Nothing," said Maryanne, her voice cracking. Just the sight of her mother was enough for her fall apart. "It's just been a hard week."

"Yes," said Gladys, gripping Maryanne's hand. "I'll never leave you," she whispered and Maryanne's eyes filled with tears.

"Oh girls," said their mother. She set down the pie and embraced them both. "Yes, it has been hard. But we're going to survive. We always do."

Maryanne loved Michael. But she loved her family too. What would she do?

Chapter 32

MIKHAIL/MICHAEL

Mikhail sat at his desk and looked at his staff. They were much less busy than he expected. How was it that so much of the city had burned to the ground or had been damaged, and yet there were no new construction bookings? Then, he remembered what Leroy had told him as they travelled across town — Black businesses and homeowners would never get the capital or loans to rebuild, and those White businesses that had preyed on the community for so long? Well, they would just cut their losses and never come back.

The Center could float the business for a while, but eventually any money coming in would be suspect. He actually spent as much time at the company as he did executing operations and managing his assets, because full time work was the best cover. But the last thing he wanted to spend his time right now on was rainmaking, especially with thoughts of Maryanne running amok. It had been four days, and his only connection to her was via the listening device in her valise. She wasn't doing well. Her nighttime sobs rattled every molecule in his soul, and he wanted to rush to her side.

He hadn't been back to the U Street apartment since the

night King was killed. Too dangerous. Maryanne must be beside herself, he thought. But he couldn't go back yet. Too many police, national guardsmen, and even perhaps, FBI crawling around. Best to stay in Southwest where things were eerily quiet. But he had to figure out how to contact Maryanne in the next 24 hours. He knew she wasn't well, listening to her sobs at night when the valise must have been close to her headboard. It seemed she worked silently, and he noted that she had not attended a single meeting that week. It was if she was a mournful wraith, unnoticed by survivors, while the world burned.

Geoffrey stepped into the office, covered with brick dust. "What a waste," he said. "We should be rolling in new contracts." He sat down with a thud and turned to face Mikhail. "I mean, if this were anywhere else in the world, they would have already cleared the damage and started pouring concrete."

"Did you see the signs in some of the windows?" said Mikhail.

"Yeah — *Soul Brother.* Like, 'I'm Black too, don't smash my windows.'" He waved his hands. "Didn't work half the time. Certainly didn't protect them from fires next door."

Mikhail had been unable to completely avoid the unrest as he walked back toward the waterfront the day after the assassination. He felt as his he was swimming through the river Styx, emerging saturated with the wrathful anguish of tortured people. He thought back to the boys in the park — the boys for whom he had risked his own safety not to kill. Just a few months ago he wouldn't have hesitated, but being with Maryanne had somehow shifted his perspective, just a little. The boys had called him pig, but he understood that they were otherwise powerless, and that attacking him was their one shot at justice, no matter how futile.

Marlboro, on the other hand, was merely annoyed by the entire situation. "Not much to give you this week," he had included as a note with the drop. "Girl distracted and unproductive."

For now, it was better for him to stay away from her, at least until things settled down. The Black neighborhoods in Northwest were isolated and heavily policed, and racial tension was higher than he had ever experienced. He'd never given up the second apartment in Southwest, so there was still a place for them to meet quietly, away from the world. Still, he knew that if he didn't reach out soon, he could lose her, and her trust, and the entire mission would fall apart.

And then, there were her aspirations — advanced study in astrophysics, somewhere outside of D.C. It was a wrinkle, for sure, perhaps a new mission would evolve. The Center had already sent him to Texas, and he would soon head to Florida to surveille the Apollo launch sites, so perhaps they would see fit to keep him on Maryanne, especially as she moved through the U.S. space program. It would be exhausting, but he found himself excited by the idea. He decided to broach the subject with Roman who, as luck would have it, called for a meeting.

Mikhail met him at a diner in Bethesda, Maryland, a location they could both drive to without having to go through the city.

"She has dreams of getting a PhD," said Mikhail. "Or working at a NASA research site. Those places are impenetrable from what I know. She would be quite the asset at one of the sites."

"Perhaps, perhaps," said Roman. "But we have a few agents out there already. Plus, isn't it really her work here that is of the highest priority? If she leaves, what happens to their program?"

"Well, that remains to be seen. She really is the brain behind their progress."

"But Marlboro has made sure we see everything on the program, yes?"

"He has. But all he does is take pictures of her work."

"Yes, we're aware."

Mikhail suddenly felt as if he was in jeopardy, his mind dancing with the Soviet paranoia he'd almost abandoned. "They can see your heart," his mother had once said of the KGB, and he resisted the urge to grip his chest. Marlboro and Stephanie — they were nothing to him, gum on the sole of his shoe. But Maryanne — could they see her in there, nestled between the chambers? They were always watching, even in the Land of the

Free. *Don't let them see*, he thought. It would put both of them in danger. Well, mostly her.

"Is there a problem with my assets?" he said, keeping his voice steady.

"No, not at all. They have all provided very useful information. But it seems your girl is getting very close to a breakthrough, and we are concerned that will mean our own deep space program will be compromised."

"What do you want me to do?" asked Mikhail, afraid of the answer.

"I think you'll find this to be very interesting; not what you would expect. Even I was surprised. Normally, I would just tell you to terminate her. Someone that dangerous — well, we can't take any chances."

Mikhail felt his jaw turning to stone, then a cold, hard sensation pushing its way down his spine. "Is that my mission?"

"No, not yet. In fact, I hope it doesn't come to that. I can tell you like her."

Mikhail said nothing.

"Listen," continued Roman. "Our program at home — our deep space program has apparently hit a bit of a snag. Seems the senior scientist had a heart attack and would like to go on pension soon. He was showed some of your girl's work and was very impressed."

"Go on." Mikhail leaned forward in anticipation.

"Apparently, she has exactly the skill set — the brilliance our program needs. He thinks she could be the key pushing our program forward."

Mikhail felt the blood flowing back into his heart. "They want her?"

"Yes. They want her to come to us. Defect. Come work in Russia. And you, my dear boy, are going to convince her to do so."

"But I'd have to blow my cover," said Mikhail, said without skipping a beat, though his head was spinning. "She'll be livid."

"Livid?"

"It means, very, very angry."

"I see. You don't know that. Besides, haven't you said she's fed up with America?"

"I mean, yes, but, not enough to leave."

"How do you know? Have you ever asked her?"

"No, but, I guess California may as well be another planet."

"And she's in love with you?"

Mikhail felt completely exposed, like a recurring dream where he was standing naked and undefended in the middle of his Arbat. Nowhere to go.

"Are you alright?" asked Roman.

"Yes, sorry, just a headache," said Mikhail. "Yes, she's in love with me."

"Good. Look, you know that in the U.S. she can only go so far in her career." Roman wrinkled his nose. "And her program won't let her go, no matter what they say. Our country has so much more to offer. Not until she's spent. Start exploring how she really feels — you know — about her work, her life. Plant the seed. See what takes root. But work quickly. You have two months."

Chapter 33

MARYANNE

April 9, 1968
Southwest Washington, DC

Maryanne was so tired she could barely keep her eyes open, though she knew better than to fall asleep on the bus. She wasn't sleeping well. It had been almost a week since the assassination and her last night with Mikhail, she hadn't made any more breakthroughs at work, and her father was sloshed 24/7. He was ornery and paranoid, and her mother's shoulders started to slouch, as if weighted down. Mother was also losing balance more often, which even her drunken father noticed, but just shrugged it off as fatigue. Maryanne felt heavy, like her soul was made of lead, unable to move.

But what could she do? Couldn't control her parents. Couldn't control Michael. The only thing, the only person she could control was herself. She needed to snap out of it and get back to knocking their socks off at work, because she was losing her shine. Atkins had not said that he was unhappy with her performance, but she was now frozen out of meetings and back to doing strictly transactional analysis in a vacuum.

Just as she was ready to succumb to sleep, she felt someone squeeze in next to her.

"Excuse me," she heard in Michael's intoxicating baritone.

Maryanne whipped her head and looked at him with fiery eyes.

"Where have you been?" she said in a breathless whisper. She was flooded with relief, but she could feel anger rising in her belly.

"Darling," he said. "I'm so sorry. It's just that since the fires we've been working day and night, without any breaks."

"You could have called. Or sent a letter or a note."

"But you said never to call you at home, and I didn't have your number — "

Are you kidding me? she thought. "Given the circumstances, you should have found a way to call anyway," she said, straining to keep her voice low. "I thought you were — hurt — or dead."

She looked deep into his eyes and for the first time noticed that despite what was happening on his face, be it joy, sorrow, or concern, they held a cool nothingness. She caught her breath.

He pulled the cord to request the next stop. "Let's go," he said. They stepped off — it was about two blocks from NASA. He looked around and then took her hand.

"Where are we going?" she said cautiously, as if she were meeting him for the first time.

"I am going to show you my new place," he said.

"But I have to go to work." She looked around nervously, Gladys' warning flashing before her eyes. Plus, how could he disappear, then just materialize out of nowhere? She fought for her brain to rule her internal conversation, but her heart swelled with joy at being next to him.

"You'll get there on time — I promise. It's really close by." He squeezed her hand. It was warm and strong, as always. As it had been that first night he led her into that dark alley at Constitution Hall, as asked her to trust him. When he led her into the bedroom that first time. He'd never done anything to betray her trust. Could she trust him again?

They walked together in silence, Maryanne's eyes fixed on her feet. She could feel him looking at her and suddenly felt like she was being studied.

✳ ✳ ✳

Maryanne stood in a strange place, in an apartment she didn't know existed. And Michael — how could he just slide back into her life, so casually? He had abandoned her, gone silent, and she'd started to exorcize him from her mind. Then, out of the blue, he ambushed her. On the bus, no less, where she had to sit captive to his entreaties. Where he sat so close that she could feel the warmth of his body next to hers, evoking memory of being held naked against his broad chest.

When did he have time to establish an entirely new life, just like that? She stood frozen, feeling awkward, taking in the well-appointed surroundings. His place on U Street was nice, but this one was filled with artwork, expensive-looking rugs, and the kind of furniture you protected with plastic. It didn't seem to suit him.

"How — where did you get all this — and this apartment?"

"A client owns the building," he said confidently, "and because of the — riots — I mean — unrest — he offered this apartment, which had been empty. Lucky me, huh?"

She furrowed her brow. "Lucky you, indeed. The rest of us, well, we have nowhere else to go."

"Oh, of course, I'm sorry. I didn't mean to be so insensitive."

She peered at him, and noticed the lines around his eyes, which were slightly darkened underneath, as if he hadn't slept well in days.

"I missed you," he continued. "I couldn't get to you and so I wanted to find a place — for us. So, when I could, I would swoop you up and we'd be together somewhere safe." He took a step toward her.

She closed her eyes and opened them, slowly. He was standing so close she could feel his breath. "You mean, you want me to — ?"

"Stay with me," he said, his cheeks flushed.

Marianne stepped back and stood with her arms folded protectively around her chest, like a shield to protect his words from piercing her heart.

"I can't," she said. The words felt spicy, biting. *This is too much, too much*, she thought. *I can't leave Mommy. I can't just up and leave for this man who disappeared once — what if he does it again? Mommy, Gladys, even Father, they are always there.*

"Why not?" he said gently. "Maryanne, I love you. I want us to be together."

He again stepped closer and she wrapped herself tighter, fighting not to dissolve into his broad arms.

"It's not about just love," she said, her voice getting stronger. "My family — society just isn't ready — for this — for us."

His eyes started to glisten. Was he — crying? She was suddenly struck by the fact that she'd never seen a grown man cry before — not even Eric after he was beaten. He was always so solid, so strong. Unwavering. Her arms slowly unfolded, and she started toward him, but he turned away.

"I'm -I'm sorry," he said, sounding embarrassed. "I don't know what's wrong with me."

She practically flew to his side, wrapping her arms around him. He turned and buried his face in her shoulder, his weight bearing down on her, but she knew she could support him.

"I'm sorry too," she said. "I want to be with you too, but . . ."

Ok, he'd been missing for a week, but it wasn't because he abandoned her — no — he couldn't go home and couldn't call her. Then, he gallantly went out of his way to see her in person. Plus, how lucky a client had this beautiful apartment for him? And he wanted to share it with her.

". . . but you disappeared!" she said, tears welling in the corners of her eyes. "And you sent me with that man and didn't even bother to check and see if I was ok." And what he'd said to her! Just more proof that no one would approve of their relationship.

But her family. Her family would never shun her, no matter what Gladys said. It would pain them, yes, but wasn't it time for Maryanne to make her own decisions and do what was best for her?

"Leroy is my friend," said Michael. "And he told me you made it home safely. I trust him." He stepped back to look at her, his face ruddy and tear stained, his eyes dripping with remorse.

"You stayed on my mind. I knew I'd get to you as soon as it was safe."

Michael had never lied to her. And what she felt when she was with him could not be put into words. He was her solace, her safe space. Her new home.

"I missed you," she finally said, and they embraced. She breathed him in, letting him populate every cell in her body, and relinquished her last shred of resistance.

✳ ✳ ✳

She had to pry herself from his arms to go to work, but he promised to be there when she returned. Luckily it was a quiet day — Atkins and most of the team were at a meeting somewhere off site. For once she didn't care that she'd been excluded. She could barely sit still as the hours ticked by and bolt from her desk at 5 o'clock. Despite the fear that nagged her, he was waiting, just as he'd promised.

Maryanne called Gladys to say that she needed cover for the night — that he had re-surfaced, and she was staying at his place for the night. Maybe even the next few nights.

"Mary," Gladys whisper shouted into the receiver, her voice breathy with concern. "What are you going to do? You aren't planning to actually live there with him. Are you?"

"Gladys, please, don't," she said quietly, feeling a tinge of anger. "I'm happy, really happy for the first and maybe last time ever." She turned and flashed a sweet smile toward Mikhail, who was buried in the latest issue of Life Magazine with a photo of Dr. King. The headline: *Week of Shock.* Her smile slightly dissolved. "He loves me so much he — *cried.*"

She knew Gladys eyes had widened to the size of saucers, like a cat who'd stuck its paw in a socket. It was her signature look whenever amazed. Maryanne waited for her to process.

"Well," Gladys finally said. "That is something. I mean, I have never in my life . . "

"I know," Maryanne said, a smile returning to her lips.

"What'd magic you put on him? What've you got down there?" Gladys giggled. Maryanne did too, and soon they were both laughing uncontrollably.

"Everything ok?" asked Michael from the other room.

"Yes, honey, it's just Gladys. You know, sister stuff."

He winked and got back to reading.

"Look, you play house as long as you need to," Gladys continued. "But you have a decision to make. Just know that I am always here for you, no matter what you decide."

Chapter 34

LEROY/DONOVAN

t had been an impulsive, borderline dumb, move, but it paid off. Donovan beamed with pride as O'Connell read his report. O'Connell then looked up at Donovan with his face scrunched up like he'd just stubbed his toe.

"This is — I can't believe you took it upon yourself to track this clown — on foot nonetheless — while the city zoo was crawling with cops and guardsman." He tapped two fingers on the report. "You get an A+ for initiative and a D- for common sense."

Donovan shrugged casually, though inside he was filled with jumping beans. "When I saw Michael expertly take down those cats and chuck his uniform in the sewer — I knew it was time to loop you in."

"And this?" O'Connell held up the hollowed-out rock Donovan retrieved from the site.

"Brought it to you instead of the suits down the hall."

"Good move." O'Connell's face relaxed. "We'll brief them soon, but not until you figure out exactly what he's up to. That means we need to know what he's dealing in. Information? Components? Plus, are you sure he's Russian?"

"75% sure." Donovan sat up in his seat. "Makes the most sense. Doesn't strike me as Cuban. Infinite resources at his fingertips." Donovan turned over the next question in his head before asking. "Hey -you said you learned something from down the hall?"

O'Connell looked at him quizzically. Donovan knew it was a gamble to try and punk O'Connell into giving up info, but also knew he was cozier with the Counterintel guys than he let on. O'Connell also often forgot what he'd said.

"Oh, yeah," O'Connell finally replied. "Turns out there's an investigation of a CIA spook assigned to NASA who's been living way outside of his means. His soon-to-be ex-wife turned him in after finding a pair of lacy women's underwear — not hers, mind you — in the back seat of his new Cadillac. So she'd been enjoying the high life, no questions asked, though she admitted she suspected what he was up to. It was his cheating — not treason — that changed her mind about turning a blind eye to his treachery. Gotta love it."

Donovan's heart began to sprint. "NASA?" He hadn't included Maryanne in his report to O'Connell, but at home he'd noted in his journal:

Girl's name is Maryanne and oh boy — this is a whopper. She's NASA. The S.O.B. is working her. Bet she don't even know it.

"Got a description of the spook?" said Donovan.

"Tall, sandy brown and greying hair, perpetual five o'clock shadow and a slight overbite. Chronic smoker. Frequents the colored — I mean — Black- working girls on Logan."

Donovan felt the acid crawling up his throat and coughed. "And they think he's passing secrets to the Soviets?" he said, giving his chest a single thump with his fist.

"You about to die?" said O'Connell, slapping him on the back. "Yeah. But there's no smoking gun — only the smell of gunpowder in the air. The boys down the hall got good eyes on him. Haven't seen him do anything lately but waiting to catch him red-handed. But seems they saw him with a man matching your description of Michael a few weeks ago."

"What?" Donovan's pulse was now at the speed of light. If

they saw Michael with this NASA cat, then maybe they'd seen Maryanne. "Did they follow him? Get any more information?"

"Nope. It was just the two agents watching, you know, and they had to stay on their guy."

Donovan's nose started to run, which it always did when he was nervous, or his temper was about to explode.

"Tell me again when they last saw him?"

"About a month ago. Do you have a cold or something?"

"No — just allergies." Donovan grabbed his jacket and started for the door.

"Whoa, where do you think you're going?"

"Listen to me." He wiped his nose with his sleeve. "I need to find out who else there is — who's in their network — their operation. This could be big."

"Ok, ok, I hear you. But listen. It bears reminding you that the boys down the hall don't like outsiders stepping on their turf."

Donovan shook his head. "This ain't *West Side Story*, man. This is my guy. I know him and he thinks he knows me. This could be big, but those gumshoes are so focused on that traitor they're missing the bigger fish."

"Fine. But keep it quiet for now. We don't want the cowboys over there sabotaging your operation."

"So, it's an operation now?"

"Give it a month. Maybe two."

A red veil descended over Donovan's eyes. Two months? The trail would go cold. "Why?" he finally managed to say.

"'Cause if you don't get me something good on the Panthers soon, we'll both be out of a job, and your little side project will be D.O.A."

Chapter 35

MIKHAIL/MICHAEL

May 15, 1968
Woodley Park, Northwest Washington, D.C.

For once, Mikhail was actually interested in what Stéphanie had to say. Sure, she'd always provided useful information. Useful, but uninteresting, just like she was. But she was now talking non-stop about the student riots in Paris, how the Socialists and Communists had taken over and that French democracy was "teetering on the precipice of demise" — she was always frustratingly melodramatic — and he sat in rapt attention as she spouted off the names of various known agitators.

"Are you serious?" he'd said, after leaving her near babbling after a series of little deaths. "Do you think the *Russians* are there? Do you know who they are?"

"Peut-être," she said while lighting a cigarette. "But our police, they are so dumb. They just grab all the topless girl protestors and then beat up the men. They have no idea who is who, its complete chaos, and our *Compagnies Républicaines de Sécurité* think everyone is a spy. Meanwhile, de Gaulle swears we are in the middle of a second revolution."

She handed him the cigarette and he took a drag. He hated

smoking, and it would take at least 24 hours and a ton of mint leaves and licorice whips to cleanse his breath before returning to Maryanne. Not to mention Stephanie's cloying powdery perfume, body lotion, and body powder, which got up his nose and into his lungs. It was almost as bad as having to kill someone.

"Well, I'm sure things will die down eventually," he said in a cloud of smoke. "Sounds like it's just kids and bored people. You French are so good at protesting."

"How do you know that?" she said stroking his chest. "You said you've never been to France. Are you lying to me?"

"Oh, I've been to France too many times after meeting you," he said playfully, rolling over to kiss her. She squealed in delight.

Shit, that was close, he thought as he went to work. *I've got to watch it, letting things slip.* He glanced at the clock. It was 9:15am, which gave him at least 8 hours before Maryanne would arrive at his apartment in Southwest. He'd promised to make her dinner.

✳ ✳ ✳

Later, after they'd polished off their meal and washed the dishes together, Maryanne had caught him by surprise with a question.

"So, you know how I've been wanting to shift my focus at work?" she said while drying a plate. "Well, it looks like it might finally happen."

She was beaming, but he could tell there was some hesitation in her voice.

"That sounds incredible darling," he gushed. "Tell me more!"

"Dr. Atkins said he's submitted my application to several graduate programs in radio astrophysics. The best programs, in fact. And he says there is actually a good chance I'll be admitted."

She'd already spilled Atkins's name and he'd checked him out. But the taut, middle-aged physicist was straight as an arrow, churchgoing, and not one hair ever out of place. The one-time Mikhail thought he might catch Atkins doing something deviant was when he followed his target into a seedy magazine shop, and he emerged with slim paper bag. But when Atkins found a secret place to consume his contraband it wasn't a girly magazine, but a journal on alien life. Embarrassing, perhaps, but not exploitable. Besides, he couldn't handle any more NASA assets.

"Where?"

She paused. "Uh, looks like nothing here. In D.C. I mean, most of the schools are in the Midwest or California — at least, the ones I'm interested in. I mean, there's a program in Maryland, but you know, Maryland isn't much better than Virginia."

"California, huh?" he said. Something in his heart started to rise, and for a moment he imagined a life in the sunshine with her. "That's awfully far, isn't it? Far from your family."

The corners of her mouth dropped slightly, and she sighed. He immediately regretted his question.

"I've already put some daylight between them and me by being with you," she said. "And even though I don't like being away from them, well, this is my dream."

"I'm your dream?" he said, feeling his cheeks get hot.

She sucked in, as if trying to catch her breath. "Yes, I mean, you're part of it — you and space and I have to live my life and be happy and . . ."

He circled his arm around her waist and drew her in for a kiss, his heart threatening to burst from his chest. "I want you to be happy. I will do everything I can to make you happy."

They stood holding each other, his heart breaking. Of course he couldn't — he hadn't — promised to follow her. But he knew she believed he would do anything for her. And he would, he would do anything he *could*.

Chapter 36

MARYANNE

May 21, 1968
Southwest Washington, D.C.

n early morning the sun would peak through the upper corner of the bedroom window, as if trying to pull back the curtain. She loved that time of day — Michael had the habit of rolling over and slipping his arm under her waist, drawing her close. One morning she awoke to see a parade of Ladybugs marching on the ceiling above them. He saw them too, and they quietly watched them make their elegant trek to the ceiling fan.

"I wonder how many of them are in there spying on us?" she said. He shuddered and she was mildly amused. "I didn't know you were afraid of bugs!" she teased.

"I'm not. Just caught a chill," he replied.

Maryanne had been practically living with Michael for a little over a month. Gladys covered for her when she told her mother that she was staying with a friend closer to work to cut down on her difficult commute, and that she was looking for a place of her own. She didn't bother to tell her father and didn't feel she needed to. At this point he was barely coherent, or around, anyway. She also mentioned graduate school, but since she'd been talking about it since her freshman year in college, neither mother nor sister batted an eye.

The apartment was a refuge, giving her the feeling of total freedom, protected from prying eyes. She felt unburdened by the weight of her existence the minute she walked through his door. Outside, the world unraveled, as if teetering on the edge of apocalypse. Black DC had been scorched and abandoned — stores and services were gone, neighbors no longer sat on the porch or waved hello. The National Mall had turned into a mass protest shantytown called Resurrection City calling attention to poverty. Anti-war protests erupted in every city across the country and children of privilege were dropping out of society in droves. American flags and bras burned in defiance of the status quo.

At night Maryanne would stare at the stars, imaging herself skipping across cosmic waves, or floating up close to the planets, like in *2001 A Space Odyssey*.

Re-energized by her domestic and romantic bliss with Michael, she threw herself back into the job. Atkins seemed happy with her work, seeing her with her head down in concentration, not depression. This was slow, careful work. There were many more analysts now on the team, as the project became more complicated and dimensional, but she was still Atkins' go-to girl when he wanted something done right. He was back to telling her the project would be lost without her. But he hadn't mentioned graduate school lately, which fueled her motivation to work extra hard.

Everything, in fact, was going to plan. They were only a few weeks from briefing the top brass. Maryanne stood over a stack of data, pushing yet another last-minute deadline imposed by Atkins, moving like a machine. But when Roger walked into the conference room, she immediately lost her focus, overwhelmed by the smell of stale tobacco and Bay Rum aftershave. She saw purple spots.

"I — I'll be right back," she said, trying to gracefully exit the conference room without drawing too much attention. She'd been mildly nauseated all morning and wondered if maybe she had picked up a stomach bug on the bus.

She made it to the Ladies' room in just enough time to

throw up in the sink, running water to wash away the evidence. In the mirror, her face looked green under the fluorescent lights. She'd missed her period for the past — few weeks? It was never very regular — she'd never bothered to track it — plus there was never any reason to worry.

Until now.

"It can't be that," she thought as she wiped her face with a towel. He always used prophylactics. Always. Except the first time. *Oh no.* She paced the bathroom, her stomach roiling, and her brain on fire. *Can't be, can't be!* She held her hand out in front and counted off the weeks on her fingers. Gasping, she wrapped her arms around her waist and felt a softness she didn't want to recognize.

She'd told herself it was just his cooking, wrapping herself in the soft blanket of denial.

I've been in here too long, she thought, and straightened her clothes. She went back to the conference room and powered through her project, then handed it to Atkins and asked to go home early. The queasiness lingered and she felt exhausted.

"Fine," he said. "Just be back bright and early tomorrow morning — we have a deadline!"

Maryanne wanted nothing more than to walk the short distance to Michael's apartment, her home away from home, and plop face down on the bed. But he was on yet another business trip and not back for the next three days. The small park across the street would still be a nice place to rest until her stomach settled. The confines of the bus would just make her nausea worse.

She sat on her favorite bench — the one where she used to wait for him to pick her up — and looked up toward his window. The curtains were always drawn nearly shut, just open enough so they would know when it was daytime. He never opened them more than few inches. "I don't want the sun to fade the rugs," he said. "Plus, it gets hot enough in here already." She never objected. She felt an ease in his home and under his gaze that she had never felt in her entire life, which both shocked and delighted her. Her hair wasn't always proper, her clothing sometimes askance, and makeup an afterthought. He never looked at her sideways, or wrinkled his nose, instead drew her closer and held her tighter, even as she started to get a little plump.

Maryanne looked back up at the window and squinted her eyes for a better look. Suddenly, what looked like the shadow of a man's figure floated across the far wall of the living room. She jumped to her feet and leaned forward, rubbing her eyes to zero in. The figure was gone, just a reflection of the setting sun. *Am I crazy?* she thought, sitting down again. *It's just because I'm dizzy.* She closed her eyes to refocus, then opened again. *What?!* The curtains, she swore, were now completely shut.

Chapter 37

MIKHAIL/MICHAEL

May 21, 1968
Southwest, Washington, D.C.

Mikhail could not believe what he was seeing. What was Maryanne doing outside his apartment so early? He always left in the late morning, after the last of the commuters settled into their offices, when the street was quiet and no one would notice him. But there she was, peering right into his apartment as he was about to walk out. Had she seen him? He jumped to hide next to the curtains as soon as he saw her curious eyes narrow, and when her eyes closed, he bolted for the door. To exit the building, he took the back stairs and hopped out onto the fire escape, climbing down into the alley.

Maryanne seemed happy lately, though she was prone to drifting away in thought, looking as if she was having a vision or observing something miraculous miles away. Then she'd scribble on a piece of paper, or napkin, or anything else she could find. Numbers. Indecipherable numbers and formulas. Sometimes she would beg him to go to the roof where she would lay on her back and stare so intently at the stars, he felt she might lift off.

So, maybe she was just outside to gather her thoughts, he thought. *No way she was looking for me.*

Why would she?

No, of course she wasn't.

Well, at least he got away. He was meeting Stéphanie for dinner to find out about an upcoming meeting her "asshole" boss was having with Czech dissidents at the White House. But first he had a meeting with Roman.

He walked the few short blocks to his storage facility, which was in a low, old brick building with "1883" at the cornerstone. It was double secured, as the neighborhood was prone to break-ins, but a family of rats had once managed to infiltrate and nest in his wig collection. He opted for some unsullied greying sideburns, thick glasses, and padded belly. He'd been mugged in this disguise before by a young, sweaty addict to whom he had given all his cash but had to kill him when he went after his camera watch. Suffocated him with his own shirt and left him propped up against a tree. No one would suspect foul play, as the kid's arms were riddled with needle marks and his eyes were already bloodshot. Mikhail generally felt annoyed that he had to dispatch the kid, but afterward his thoughts drifted to how Maryanne would be horrified to learn about his work, and what it entailed. Once she learned the truth, she might no longer trust him. No, he would never tell her that part, the killings, even if confronted. His head started to hurt.

Roman was waiting for him in a corner booth of an antiseptically cool dining room laced with the aroma of greasy burgers and fries. He looked like a rumpled Southern curmudgeon, which Mikhail suspected was one of his favorite disguises, especially the seer suckered pants he was so proud of.

"She's making progress again," said Roman in a polite Virginia drawl. "Moscow says she's close to locating the exact location of the signal." He took a sip of an ironically cheerful milkshake.

"She's in a better mood since I re-established contact," said Mikhail. "She's working very hard, often into the night. I know that she's expecting to get into graduate school and her bosses are very happy with her work."

"All the more reason to accelerate," said Roman. "Have you

been working her sensitivities?"

"Yes. She's fed up with the state of things in America, and her home life is a disaster. She also has no passion about the work she's doing right now — it's just a means to an end."

"So, clearly she wants to leave D.C."

"Yes. And she has already asked whether I would consider going with her." His heart lifted at the sound of his words, which he hoped Roman could not detect in his voice. There was no way they'd approve him to go with her — or would they?

Roman tented his fingers. "Not so surprising, yes? She seems to be completely smitten with you. The question is, is she so much in love that she would follow *you* anywhere?"

Mikhail felt a flutter in his chest. "Meaning?"

"Our space program needs talent. If she were one of ours, I mean, if she had been a numbers whiz in Beginning level school, the science academies would have snatched her up. And if she knows how to find our network, she could help us find theirs."

"I don't think that would be enough motivation," said Mikhail. "Why would she want to go all the way there just to do the same work?" *Maryanne in Moscow?* he thought, a smile blooming inside.

"She might think of it differently if she were given a research lead position our deep space program. And if she thought she would be with you." Roman leaned forward. "A place where she wouldn't be judged for her race. Where you could be together — openly."

Mikhail took a gulp of water. Getting Maryanne to defect, while it had seemed a mere possibility in the past, now seemed real. It would be such an achievement, monumental in fact, that he was sure to be rewarded. He'd never considered walking away from the life, certainly not so early in his career. But for some reason the idea didn't instantly turn him off and Roman's proposition sounded delicious. He could see them strolling arm in arm through Red Square, ice skating in Gorky Park, curled up together listening to the radio in a proletariat but cozy apartment. Warmth flooded his core. He searched for the right answer.

"I could meet her there," he said. "You know, finish up here and then go home until the next assignment."

Roman peered at his protégé over thick glasses. "You care for her."

"I only care that I complete the mission I've been given. And that is to do what it takes to get her to go to Russia."

Roman looked at Mikhail with amusement, then signaled for the check. "Then raise the stakes. Make it clear you'd do anything for her. And make it so she can't stand this country anymore."

Mikhail knit his brows. He had an idea, but the thought of it made him queasy. "I know what to do," he said. "I just need a couple more of our guys to help me out."

"Whatever you need," said Roman.

Mikhail watched Roman drive away, jaw clenched. The Center was using him as bait. And he was sending her to an uncertain future in a strange country that wouldn't understand her. A place where she would have to learn to hold her tongue because there was always a sickle nearby. And not judged for her race? Well, maybe not judged, but certainly stared at, ridiculed. That wouldn't matter if he were with her. He could protect her. And she would be doing the work she'd always dreamed of.

The problem was, no matter what Roman said, nothing was guaranteed. He couldn't just walk away from the job, and she couldn't just leave the U.S. He had to believe Roman would come through. There was no other option.

Chapter 38

MARYANNE

June 3, 1968
Southwest, Washington, D.C.

Maryanne looked at the report cover, then back at Atkins, then back at the document. There, in the byline, was her name after a string of others.

"How does it feel?" he said, taking the report from her hands and putting it in the classified carry bag. "We couldn't have gotten this far — this fast — without you."

She grinned so hard her cheeks felt they might burst. "I'm so happy that I was able to help," she said. "Thank you for the opportunity."

"Help?" he snorted. "You did more than help." He zipped up the bag and locked it, putting the key in his shoe. "You did great work, kiddo." He started toward the door.

A surge of confidence propelled her forward and before she could stop herself, she tugged Atkins' elbow. "Uh, sir?"

"Yes?" he said, somewhere between annoyed and amused.

"I'm sorry, but I was just wondering," she smoothed her skirt, "Can I come to the briefing too? Everyone else on the team is going." Even the junior analyst who did nothing other than check her reporting for typos, adding errors where there were none as if to make a point, was part of the posse.

"Well, they aren't ready for you — yet," said Atkins. "But don't worry. I'll remind them that you're the brain behind this incredible work. You're sure to get several admissions to school after this. Time to get you to doing real research!" He clicked his heels and strode toward the exit. She watched him walking away, her hands in tight fists, her jaw tight. Promises, promises, but so far, nothing had happened. She could quit, just walk away, get into school on her own. But she knew that was impossible without an advocate, and Atkins would be the best. She had to be patient, but she wouldn't stop pressing.

The office was suddenly empty, leaving her alone. At least, that's what she thought.

Roger slithered from an unseen corner and stood directly behind her. Her skin crawled and she had the urge to run but she turned and met his scowl.

"Ready to leave D.C., huh?" He pursed his lips and looked her up and down. "Good for you. But then, probably best for you to get out of town, anyway."

Maryanne took a step backwards, her neck hot. "Why is that?"

"Well, it seems like you might be running with the wrong crowd. And a good little colored girl like you. Tsk, tsk."

She took another step back, closer to the door, ready to make a break. He was dangerous, a venomous snake, primed to strike, and she filled with terror. *What should I do?* Just then the door clicked open, and Atkins popped his head in. "Roger! You coming or what?"

"Sure thing, Chief!" he shouted, then looked at Maryanne, his mouth twisted into a horrific smile. "Wish us luck!" he chirped as the door slammed the door behind him.

She sat down and exhaled, rubbing her right middle finger, which was thickly calloused from weeks of non-stop writing. She would have loved to shove it in his face, and in the face of the smug engineers who looked at her with unveiled resentment every time Atkins asked her to correct their work. That snake Roger, who had recently started wearing cowboy boots to the office, reserved a viper's venom for her, doling out salacious quips about her figure, or vile comments like "where can I find local color as pretty and loose as you?" And then there were the times he would brush against her backside under the ruse of taking a closer look at her work.

"Soon," she whispered under her breath. Yes, she was going to get admitted to graduate school and done with that place, done with D.C. She'd done an exceptional job, risen head and shoulders above the rest of the team. Deserved to follow her dream, and Atkins would come though.

"You have to work twice as hard as those White boys if you want to get ahead," her father told her during a rare moment of sober parenting. "And even then, they'll look for a reason to hold you back. Don't be too disappointed when things don't work out the way you want them to."

＊ ＊ ＊

It was nearly the end of the day when Atkins and the team returned. He walked right over to Maryanne, frowning.

"How did it go?" she asked nervously. What if she's gotten everything wrong?

"They were impressed," he said. "More than impressed. But they're taking over." He took off his glasses and rubbed the bridge of his nose. Her momentary elation instantly dissolved.

"What does that mean?"

"It means that our entire whole operation is being moved to NRO. The National Reconnaissance Office, remember? It's in Virginia — Chantilly — not too far from here."

"Oh, ok. Sorry. I know that's not what you wanted."

"Out of my hands now." He put his glasses back on and shrugged.

"When do you move?"

"What do you mean, *you*?"

"Well, I thought that now we've finished our assessment and made recommendations, it would be a good time for me to start interviewing with the graduate programs?" she said, on a razor's edge of hope.

Atkins frown morphed into its usual flat shape. "Sorry, kid.

That's gonna have to wait. You're too valuable and your country needs you here."

Maryanne could have screamed. *What?!* She wanted to holler. *Virginia? And you're keeping me here?!* The betrayal shook her to her core. All her hard work, and her dreams deferred. She felt her hands start to shake, angry building behind her eyes. She nodded quickly and muttered something about going to the bathroom.

What would Michael say? Something supportive, of course, but also that they didn't appreciate her. He'd knit his brows and tell her she was brilliant and deserved more. "But where would I go?" she'd say in frustration. She certainly didn't want to work anywhere Roger worked. And she'd never get anywhere in NASA so long as Atkins held her reins.

She sat down in the stall and cautious pulled down her underwear, hoping for a sign that at least her body was back to normal. But there was nothing there, and her heart sank even further. It was time she got a pregnancy test.

Everything was falling apart. All she had was Michael. *Please God, please, just don't let me be pregnant,* she prayed.

Chapter 39

MIKHAIL/MICHAEL

June 12, 1968
L Street, Northwest, Washington, D.C.

Mikhail was annoyed. He gave Marlboro explicit instructions on how to activate the signal, but, yet again, the self-important Onegin decided to call the shots. Even worse was his choice of venue this time.

The restaurant was a high-end, see and be seen place, where D.C.'s elite swigged noontime double-martinis and dined on bloody Chateaubriand. On any given day you could spot a congressman chatting up a Pulitzer Prize-winning Post reporter sitting next to a White House crony. If you dined at Duke Ziegert's, you'd made it. Apparently, Marlboro felt as if he had made it too.

Too many people, thought Mikhail. Eyes everywhere. Today everyone was chattering about the latest assassination — this time Robert F. Kennedy, brother of John, one of Moscow's most hated U.S. Presidents. Young Americans loved him. The Democratic Convention was sure to be a total circus, and he'd heard rumblings that massive protests were expected. Moscow would surely send him to observe. The U.S. was in utter turmoil and he had a front row seat.

Mikhail found Marlboro at the bar, dressed in a tailored

suit and considerably less crumpled than usual. And cowboy boots. Shiny, ridiculous cowboy boots.

What a clown, he thought to himself.

He took a seat and motioned for the bartender, who had a barber shop mustache that looked like it took hours to perfect. *Never can tell if they are one of ours or one of theirs*, Mikhail thought as he ordered a drink. Once he was handed his Bourbon on the rocks, he turned slightly toward his asset.

"What've you got?"

"Big news," said Marlboro aka Roger. "A big move, in fact." He took a long drag of his cigarette.

"So?"

"We knocked their socks off. Said it was a 'game-changer.' They're moving the whole program to some field in Virginia."

"What was in the report? You never shared the final version."

"It's right here." Marlboro reached inside his jacket and peaked out a corner of paper with blue edges.

"Put that away! You know better than bringing something to me like that!" Every nerve in his body was seizing.

"There was no time," Marlboro snorted in defiance. "I couldn't take pictures, so I was sure to get a copy before we packed them up to take to Langley."

Mikhail wanted to slap the smug, self-important look off his face.

"Tell me as much as you can now," said Mikhail, restraining his anger. "Then take that damn thing home and burn it."

Marlboro delivered neat talking points on the meeting, that they were close to having the funding to fully intercept the Soviet signal.

"Oh," he said. "One more thing. That colored girl I told you about? Well, she's going too. Boss wouldn't shut up about how brilliant she is, a crucial asset. And she is — good. Intelligent. I tried to recruit her to work for me, but I guess I'm not her type." He demonstratively slurped the olive from his martini and took a large swig. "Anyway, he told the brass the program would still be in the dark if it weren't for her. And they bought it — hook line and sinker. I swear," he took a drag of his cigarette. "She's smart and all, but I'm sure she's only in Atkins' good graces because, you know ... "

"Know what?"

"Well, she's a looker. A dark beauty if you will. And she spends a lot of time with the boss — alone."

Mikhail imagined putting Marlboro's face through the mirrored backbar but kept his composure.

"That doesn't seem like the reason he has interest in her. From what you've provided, she seems to have done most of the work."

"Defending her, eh? Well, that doesn't surprise me. I mean, you seem to — know her."

Mikhail's eyes began to blur. He knew that meant his heart rate was severely elevated, that his amygdala was enflamed and adrenaline surging. He tapped his thumb and index fingers together to reset his brain. "Yes — from your reports."

"I saw you chatting her up on the street one day. You looked friendly," said Marlboro with an oily grin.

Mikhail used the bar mirror to quickly scan the room, checking to see if any ears were burning, then leaned in close. "Now you listen and listen good." He felt like a raging bull trapped in a pen, nostrils flaring, murder on his mind. But couldn't lose control — not now. "Your opinion is unimportant. I do not want to report that you are dipping your nose in our ink. Don't forget who's paying you."

Marlboro snorted, but his face turned ashen.

"Fine. I'll get you photos of this thing." He tapped his breast pocket and put the bar tab in front of Mikhail. "Have a nice day."

Mikhail swirled the ice cubes in his glass, took a final swig and signaled to the bartender for another. That slimy weasel had tried to entrap him! He wanted to slap his own face for being so sloppy — of course he knew his own people were probably keeping tabs on him, but Marlboro? Mikhail blinked hard, clearing an impulse to chase him down, break his neck, and dump him in the Potomac.

Mikhail's thoughts moved to Maryanne — she'd mentioned

how much she couldn't stand him, but without too much detail. Marlboro was playing close to the edge again and Mikhail often felt as if he were deliberately trying to get him to react. But he'd come to them promising access to NASA's classified work, and he'd delivered. The man was awful, but Mikhail had to keep him happy, at least until it was time to let him go, perhaps with a suicide note and noose.

Staring at the mirror, he wasn't sure, but two men sure did seem to be walking rather close to Marlboro as he exited the restaurant. *Don't be paranoid*, he scolded himself, but quickly paid the bartender and rushed home, looking over his shoulder.

Chapter 40

MARYANNE

June 22, 1968
Southwest, Washington, D.C.

Michael looked fresh and clean despite the sultry, soupy afternoon air. By contrast, Maryanne felt sweaty, sticky, and shiny. Not even a cold shower could cool her down. Ironically, it felt cooler outside than inside, so when Michael suggested a drivethru movie, she agreed.

"What's on your mind?" she asked playfully, reaching over to tuck an errant wisp of hair behind his ear.

"Nothing, darling." He smiled, but seemed distant, like he was memorizing a sequence of numbers. "Excited to see *The Thomas Crown Affair*?"

Maybe he was nervous because the last time they tried to go to the movie theatre the ticket taker harassed them about sitting together. He'd taken the smarmy wisp of a man aside and whispered something in his ear, and they enjoyed the movie but practically ran out before the credits finished rolling.

"Are you worried it's not safe?" she asked, chewing on her thumbnail.

"Not at all," he said confidently. "Totally integrated, no race problems."

"I've heard that before."

"I'm serious. I checked. It'll be fun!" He swept her up in a tight embrace and planted a kiss on her forehead.

"Ok. But after the movie — can we come back here? I want — I need to tell you something."

"What's wrong?"

"Nothing. I just have some — news to share. Work and stuff like that."

Work was one thing. He'd probably be happy she was staying in D.C., though he already said more than once he'd be happy to follow her wherever she went, if he could.

But the other thing — the other thing was different. She missed three periods, her nipples were sore, and she could barely keep any food down before 10:00am. She'd finally gone to the doctor — a clinic on the other side of town and not the family physician and accepted the truth. She was pregnant.

"3-4 months," said the disinterested doctor. "Do you know who the father is?"

"What kind of girl do you think I am!" she barked, storming out of his office. She was in her most pulled together professional outfit, hair neatly styled, and spoke immaculately. Of course, this man, like so many others, instantly judged her just because of her race. It still stung, no matter how many times she'd been insulted. But this time there was no denying it, she *was* a walking stereotype, knocked up and single, like so many other Black women, just none that she knew. And it was a White man's.

But not just any man. It was Michael's, the love of her life. This was — had to be — different. And they didn't have to worry about his parents, because he said they had died five years ago back on Long Island, where he was from. He was 27 years old and had been living on his own for years. No siblings and no contact with family except an uncle that would visit from time-to-time who he swore had not one racist bone in his body.

Michael said he wanted to be with her forever. Did that mean *really* forever? There was only one way to find out. She gathered her courage and told Gladys.

"He'll show his true colors then," she said when Maryanne

told her she was going to tell him about the pregnancy.

"Don't say that — he — he loves me. He'll be fine, I know it."

"Oh, please. He's a *White* man. They don't want to have anything to do with little brown babies — even when they make them. Been like that since the dawn of this nation Mary, you know that. Plus, it's not like you can get married."

"Yes, we can. You know — the court just said that even in Virginia they can't — "

"And you think that you can just walk into any church and have them say "Amen'?"

"No, but — "

"And that he would even want to give up his life for you? Oh, Mary, I didn't mean to -"

Maryanne was shaking, her fists clenched, tears streaming down her cheeks. "That White man in Virginia — you know-Loving? I read about it in *Life* Magazine. He went all the way to the Supreme Court to stay with his Black wife." She wiped her face with an open palm. "And he told that lawyer to tell the court 'he loves his wife.' So, just because he is — who he is — does not mean that he can't love me."

"Of course, sweetie, of course." Gladys embraced her sister. "I'm sorry."

❋ ❋ ❋

The drive-in was a revelation. All they had to do was go get the tickets, then they drove to a spot well away from curious and judgmental eyes. When the car became too stuffy, they spread the blanket on the hood of the car and reclined under the stars. His shoulders were relaxed, and he said 'oh' and 'wow' at all the right moments, but his mind was clearly elsewhere. On the other hand, she was completely caught up in the dizzying cat and mouse plot.

"Nuts," she said at the film's end.

"What?"

"I said nuts. I don't like how she got played in the end."

"Yeah. I kinda wanted her to nab Crown too." He took a deep breath, started the car, and followed the caravan out of the parking lot.

"Good!" she chucked. "Still, I would have rather seen 2001 again."

"Not me," said Michael. "I didn't get it. Plus, don't you remember everyone booing?"

"Well, I loved it. Especially the close -up shots of planets. But yes, it was different."

"I preferred Kubrick's earlier movie — *Dr. Strangelove?*" he said, wincing.

"Never saw it," she said.

"It was funny. Not an acid trip, like *2001.*"

"What do you know about tripping on acid?" she said, leaning onto one hip and kissing him on the neck. "Keeping secrets from me?"

"Careful now . . ." he said, giving one of his signature, delicious smiles.

He turned onto the long, dark road through Rock Creek Park which bisected wealthy from middle-class. Maryanne grew rigid as the memory of her last night ride through the feral park crept back into her mind, forcing her to shift focus. No more playing — she had to tell him. She felt a pang of nausea.

Michael looked over and saw the discomfort on her face. "You alright?" he asked.

"There's something I need to tell you," she said.

"Yes?"

"I — I'm . . ."

The moment she opened her mouth to speak, the sudden flashing of red, white and blue lights silently exploded into the darkness. She looked over her shoulder, then their eyes met. She was terrified, but he was as cool as ever.

He pulled the car over onto the narrow shoulder and turned off the engine. She felt her entire body shaking, uncontrollably, and she needed to steady herself. She reached for Michael desperately, like a drowning woman, longing for the safety of his arms.

"Don't worry," he said, hugging her briefly. Then he reached for the door handle.

"What are you doing?" she cried, buried in his chest. His heart was steady, compared to hers which was racing like a scared mouse. "Don't get out of the car!"

"It'll be fine," he said, and kissed her moist forehead.

Why is he so calm? she thought as he got out of the car with his hands up.

Maryanne turned again to look through the rear window. Two police officers emerged from the patrol car. Each of the men was holding a flashlight in one hand and the other on their waist. She knew what that meant, but Michael strode toward them with his chin up.

"Good evening officers! Can I help you?" she heard him say. One of the officers peeked around Michael's shoulder at her in the car. She quickly turned to sit forward, her heart screaming. *Oh no — they saw us together,* she thought, shaking.

Suddenly, Michael cried out in pain. She surged with electricity and grabbed the door handle to get out, but the curious officer appeared at the passenger side of the car and shined the light directly in her face. She could see nothing but white-hot light.

"Well, look what we have here!" he shouted to his partner. "Out of the car. NOW."

She opened the door carefully, but just as she set one foot on the earth, she felt herself lifted and then dragged across the pavement. Dragged toward the other officer, who was standing over Michael, who lay crumpled on the ground. She tried to wiggle but he held her in an iron grip. All she managed to shake loose was a shoe. He propped her up like a grotesque puppet. Every movement was excruciatingly painful, and tears flooded her eyes.

Not a single car passed.

"Who's this pretty nigger?" said her assailant. Then he looked at Michael. "You got one of them well dressed whores, huh? When we pulled you over, we thought you'd just picked up a junkie, but no — looks like you got one of them fancy hookers." He reached over to grab a lock of her hair. "Nice one too."

"I'm not a prostitute!" she said, jerking her head away. She could feel her dress ripping where she was held in his tight grip.

"Leave her alone!" Michael sat up, only to be smacked down again, hard. It looked as if he was knocked out. Maryanne started to scream, but a sweaty calloused palm clamped over her mouth.

"Look at that, and uppity too."

"Think we should do a search? You know, some of them hide their smack in — unseen places."

"Oh yeah."

Her legs faltered but she was still being held up, her dress strap now fully ripped. The other officer strode toward her, pelvis forward, with a sick smile. He unsheathed his Billy club and slipped it under the hem of her dress.

"Let's take a look . . ." he was licking his lips. Then he reached under her skirt with the other hand and pulled at her underwear.

"No-no-no," she whimpered, clamping her legs tightly together. Her neck was itchy and hot, her chest burned. She would have clawed his eyes if her arms weren't held behind her back. Suddenly, Michael scrambled to his feet, a look on his face she'd never seen before.

Without warning, she unleashed a volcano of popcorn-laced vomit directly in the officer's face.

"Nasty bitch!"

She was thrown to the ground, right at Michael's feet, and she felt him kneel next to her.

"I'm so sorry, so sorry" he said, gathering her hands in his. "We're going to be ok . . . I promise." She saw blood trickling from the corner of his mouth and felt a scream crawling up her spine.

Then, CLICK. The barrel of the gun leered at her, mouth open.

"Michael!" she heard herself say.

"I'm gonna kill that bitch," said the vomit drenched officer, his uniform glistening with the contents of Maryanne's stomach.

"Go ahead," said the other one.

Michael jumped up and stood directly in front of them. He looked the officer directly in the eye.

"Put the gun down."

"Get out of the way, man. This doesn't concern you anymore."

"Yes, it does. This has gone too far," he growled. "She is my girlfriend — my fiancé."

Maryanne watched her body stand up, heard Michael shout at her to stay back.

The two officers looked at the spectacle before them, then each other. "Right. Sure, she is."

Michael stepped closer to the gun. Landing back in her body, Maryanne's feet were heavy as anvils.

Please God, oh please, she cried in her brain. It felt as if she were frozen in time while events swirled around her, getting dangerously close. She wanted to run, to grab Michael and fly to the stars, to go where no one could menace or threaten them.

And their baby. What if she told them she was pregnant? No, this was no way for Michael to find out. Plus, it might make them angrier.

"I said back off," said Michael with even more ferocity. It felt as if her heart might explode.

The officer narrowed his eyes, then sheathed the pistol, his murderous designs dissolving into mocking laughter. "We were just teaching you a lesson, nigger lover. Havin' a little fun." He turned on his heel and walked back to the patrol car. "I don't want to see the abomination of the two of you in *my* park ever again."

The two policemen got into their car and drove off.

❋ ❋ ❋

Ice coursed through Maryanne's veins, and she still couldn't move. It wasn't until she felt Michael's hot palms on her cheeks that she began to thaw. He looked at her, and his eyes were flooded with warmth and movement, unlike that day on the bus. This man — the man who her sister said would never stick by her side — had put himself in front of a gun to protect her.

Her heart raged with love.

He helped her to the car, swung her feet in and closed the door. It was as if she were invalid, incapable of doing anything for herself. It wasn't until they broke free of the dense foliage of the park that she felt herself exhale. She'd never go in there again.

Michael held her hand as they drove through the city, the streets quiet, unrecognizable. Streetlights whizzed by like comets, and she closed her eyes to steady her stomach. They were already pulling into an alley — it must have been behind his apartment — when she blinked them open again. The sour taste lingered in her mouth and torn dress scratched her skin. He silently parked the car and drew her close. His shirt was damp and smelled of musk, blood, and tar.

"I thought that you fell asleep," he said.

The lines in his face were drawn deeper and she noticed that the color of his eyes darkened to the color of a sorrowful ocean. He looked like a guilty man on his way to the electric chair — helpless and remorseful.

"I'm so sorry," he said, choking back tears.

"Don't be sorry — no — no — you saved me. They were going to shoot, but you stopped them," she said.

"You got them good." He cracked a weak smile.

"No, *you* saved me." Her eyes filled with tears. "Why would you put yourself in front of a gun like that?"

"Because I love you," he said.

She looked at him, eyes wide. Her heart leapt, the words dancing throughout her body. "Did you mean what you said back there?" she said, her voice trembling. "I mean, that you think of me as your . . ."

"Yes."

She felt dizzy and drew in a breath, her ribs aching, "I'm pregnant." She was too tired — too spent to hold back.

"What?" He pulled back from her and stared at her midsection. "Are you sure? I mean, how do you know?"

"I hadn't had my cycle. I mean, didn't get it for the last three months, since the first time we were — together. So, I went to the doctor."

His eyes met hers and she felt like she was unraveling. What if he took back everything he said? What if this now meant he'd leave her? She hadn't let herself consider that before, but now it seemed real.

"I'm sorry," she said desperately. "I should have said something sooner. But I wasn't sure."

He blinked silently, his chest rising and falling rhythmically. How could he be so calm? It felt like an eternity before he said anything.

"Oh, Maryanne, don't be sorry," he finally said. "I mean, this is incredible." He took her hands and a single tear rolled down his cheek. "It's going to be ok. I've got you."

✳ ✳ ✳

The steam did not conceal their injuries. Washed away dirt and gravel revealed a kaleidoscope of bruises, abrasions, and lacerations, the kind that are almost impossible to explain away. He carefully cleaned her as if she were a frail child. She could not stop shivering despite the heavy air in the apartment.

"I hate it here," she said suddenly. "I hate this Goddam place. I hate not being safe anywhere I go. I hate not being able to get free."

She continued. "I am scared to bring a child — our child — into this hateful country."

Her shaking intensified and she pressed her nails into her palms. "What is this place to me? Why am I working to the bone on something I don't even care about? And now — now — they went back on their promise, and I'm trapped."

"Maryanne, what do you mean?" he asked.

"I mean I'm not going to school. They took it back. I have to stay here — no, even worse — I have to go to Virginia. Goddamn Virginia. Lynching and cross-burning Virginia." The tears burned the abrasion on her cheek. "If we are seen down there . . . my God. . ."

He looked down at her, the corners of his mouth slightly upturned, like he'd just found a twenty-dollar bill on the sidewalk.

"We — you don't have to go to Virginia."

"Yes, I do. Where else am I going to get a job? And doing what? A schoolteacher? A typist? That's the only life for Black girls with a degree. I'm never going to do the work I want to do. Never. All I want to do is look at the stars and listen — listen in hopes that there is a place better than this, a planet where color or skin doesn't matter. But instead, all they have me do is look for what the Russians are doing. And I say, who cares? As far as I am concerned no one owns space. It's infinite, way beyond our solar system." She wiped away a tear. "There is no future for me here. I'm trapped. And now," she waved a hand over her abdomen, "this."

"Look at me, Maryanne," said Michael. "You — we are not trapped. You have a choice. You have a choice to decide if you want to be with me, to be a family. And you have a choice over where you want to be."

What on earth can he mean? she thought. It was hopeless. She looked at him quizzically.

"I don't understand," she said.

"I mean, what if you could find your dream job? A job where you are truly valued, where you will be seen as the leader — the genius you are. Not just used up and strung along. And — we could be together. Free to be together somewhere without racism."

"If you mean the North or California, I already said it's not happening. Nowhere is perfect, anyway. Some places are just better."

"I'm not talking about anywhere in the U.S. I'm talking about where I come from."

In an instant, her heart stopped.

"I thought — you said you were from New York?" she said.

"No." He swallowed hard and took her hands. "I'm from Moscow. Moscow, Russia."

All the air was sucked out of the room. It was as if a 10-ton elephant was squeezing her throat with his trunk while sitting on her chest. She reached back to find the counter but only found nothing. He sprung forward and caught her. Her rage erupted in the flurry of clenched fists.

"That can't be true." she cried, pounding on his chest. "You're lying. Michael, please, please tell me you're lying."

"I'm really sorry." Tears welled in his eyes. "I'm here — in the U.S. to do a job. I never expected to fall in love. Never."

"What job?" she asked, petrified of the answer.

"KGB."

"You're a spy?" The words stung her tongue, like old vinegar. Even as the words left his mouth, she couldn't believe what she was saying. *KGB? He lied, oh my God, he lied.* Her mind felt like it was filled with buzzing, angry hornets. And what a lie. Such a disgusting, awful lie. It couldn't be true.

"Tell me you're kidding," she said through her tears. "It can't be true."

"I'm so sorry, Maryanne." Another tear streamed down his now ruddy cheeks. "It's true."

"Don't you dare cry," she spat. "That may have worked once, but not again. Not ever again."

She seethed with anger, but more with herself than Michael. How could she have been so stupid? It felt as if there were a million tiny balloons in her body, exploding all at once. No, she wasn't brilliant, or promising, or intelligent. She was stupid, stupid, stupid. How could she have been so damn stupid?

"And you were assigned to spy — on me?" she gasped.

"Not exactly," he said, wiping his cheek.

"What does that mean?"

"I was assigned to spy on NASA. Your program. But you — well — I picked you."

"Why? Did I seem like an idiot? Did I look easy or something?" Her face was hot with rage.

"No."

"Then why?"

"It was love at first sight."

"You're lying *again*," she said. "You're just working me. And the things I told you! Did you record me or take pictures or anything?"

"No."

She studied his face. His lips were pouty, his eyes sincere. "Why should I believe you?"

"Because I can't live without you. I just can't. I've even found you a job at home, a real peach of a position, taking over for one of our most respected scientists. They don't care that you're a woman; they don't care that you're Black. All they care about is that you're brilliant. And I all I care about is being with you. We'd be together somewhere safe for us."

Maryanne wished she could escape. Wished she could jump from the window and get free of the lies, broken promises, and deception. She looked at the man she'd fallen in love with and wanted to get as far away from him as possible. She couldn't believe she'd been so gullible. But why should she expect anything different? Almost every man she knew had let her down. But what was this choice her was giving her? Didn't seem like much of one given the circumstances. She didn't think she could feel any more trapped than after Atkins told her they were going to Virginia. And now, this. Everyone was making decisions for her, and not one was in her best interest. Even Mother Nature. She looked at him, her heart unravelling.

"What's your real name?"

"Mikhail. It's just the Russian version of 'Michael'.

"That's creative." *Stupid me*, she thought.

"You can call me 'Misha'. But only here, never in public."

"I'll stick to Michael."

He smiled.

"I don't know why you're smiling," she said, on the verge of rage again. "You betrayed me. How can I believe anything you tell me?"

"You don't have to. Listen, Maryanne, I mean it. I love you. I want you to have the life you want."

"I don't know what I want anymore," she slurred, suddenly overcome with fatigue. "I just need to sleep."

Chapter 41

MIKHAIL/MICHAEL

Early morning, June 23, 1968
Southwest, Washington, D.C.

Mikhail got up and went to the window to pull the curtains back, ever so slightly, so that the soft glow of moonlight bathed the bed. She lay on her side, still wrapped in his robe, her shoulders expanding and contracting with each breath, as if she would sprout wings. He was filled with guilt for what happened to her, but it moved him closer to completing his mission.

He should have been pleased. The plan worked flawlessly; he felt she could be close to saying 'yes' to him. His compatriots had given their best Dragnet impressions, though a bit southern fried, and exuded pitch perfect menace. But they took it too far, and he detected true malice behind their behavior. The one with the Billy club he recognized as Alexei, who at the institute used to sexually torment and assault female recruits, to toughen them up he said. He shuddered at the memory of Alexei's hand up her dress. Maybe there'd be a chance to deal with him, later.

He'd had no idea that she was pregnant. Shame on him for not following protocol the first time when it came to prophylactics with her, though he did with every other conquest. They'd made love with abandon, the specter of pregnancy a fleeting concern. *That's what women do when they're in love,* he thought, *and what men do when they plan to split after the first missed period.* He should have known better. At home there would have been no pause, no hesitation for her to make her own decision. Abortions were cheap and easy, more available than even a decent dentist. In America it was nearly impossible, criminal in fact. No choice. *How ironic,* he thought.

But even if she had a choice, this — this was different. Mikhail's mind swam with possibilities. Of course, he had no choice but to be supportive. To pretend that he was happy about the pregnancy. The truth was, he wasn't unhappy about the news, which was why he couldn't mask his excitement when she broke the news. It would bind them together forever. He let his imagination wander, fast forwarding to them cooing together over a baby. Then he shook his head to clear the slate, frivolous thoughts swirling then settling to stillness like the particles in a snow globe.

Maryanne rolled over and moaned. No doubt she was having a dream about the night, the gun in her face. Being violated. Lied to. Helplessness. He felt a pang of guilt, and tried not to think of the worst that could have happened. He'd experienced such trauma before too, only it was in a controlled environment and part of his training. She wasn't prepared, like he was. Then again, he knew enough about her life, and he finally, truly understood the daily trauma of being Black in America. She was tougher than any woman he knew.

Shit, he thought. *I'm in big trouble.*

Mikhail learned about the type of emotional crisis he was suffering in training. "You will think that you are in love, that you care," said his instructor. "But it is just a fantasy, an illusion. Don't let yourself be caught in the moment and forget that your true love is the mission."

But she was the mission.

He thought of informing Roman about the pregnancy immediately but decided to wait. There was no telling what Moscow's reaction would be if they found out she was pregnant. They would want their star acquisition to go right to work and not be burdened with a child. They might even want him to cause her to abort before bringing her over. What would he do then? But if she made it to Russia before anyone else found out, she could get so near to the end of the pregnancy that the baby would have a chance.

He wanted their baby to have a chance.

The first order of business was to check on the arrangements to get her safely out of the country. He could go after passing Marlboro off to some other agent and Stéphanie, well, he'd break up with her in dramatic fashion, which he knew she'd appreciate. He'd be a hero for poaching Maryanne, who was such an incredible brain power, from the adversary. *Like our own Oppenheimer,* he thought, again, blinking his eyes to exorcize any vision of what might have happened if things had gone sideways in the park.

All he needed was for Roman to come through.

Chapter 42

MARYANNE

July 3, 1968
Maryanne's House, Northwest, Washington, D.C.

Maryanne blinked her eyes open and remembered she was back home. Home for a holiday she, and now a good chunk of the country, had no interest in celebrating. She rolled over in her bed and reached over to smooth the cool spot where Michael would be if she were in his room. She hated that she missed him. But no matter how hard she'd tried, how much she'd prayed and prayed, she just couldn't hate him. He risked his life to save hers, and unknowingly that of their baby. She loved him. She just couldn't trust him.

Sure, he said the Soviet Union was free of American-style racism. No history of slavery, no Jim Crow. No segregation. She just shrugged at him. She didn't believe racism was a uniquely American affliction. People were people, after all.

Then he pledged his commitment. They would be together, *a family*, he said. Then he doubled down. Said she would finally be in a place where she would not have to worry about the daily trauma of being Black. And, he'd promised, "they" were ecstatic about her genius. "In the Soviet Union genius is genius," he said. "They don't care if genius comes in the form of a man or a woman. Black or White. Young or old. All they care about is what you can do."

Too good to be true, she thought. Then again, wasn't he a professional liar?

Plus, the Soviet Union? She'd be a traitor.

But traitor to a country who preached democracy to the world while stepping on the neck of Black people. A country that enforced fealty with the lash, noose, and police baton. Assassination of heroes who dared call the nation's endemic racism a stain on the shine of democracy. No freedom in the U.S. — no freedom in the U.S.S.R.

"What do I want?" she said aloud. It had always been to go to graduate school, but that was just a means to an end. She wanted to do research. Make discoveries. And get recognized for it. Going to get her PhD was the only way she could think of to get there, but the door kept moving farther and farther afield, no matter how fast she ran to burst through.

Space belonged to no one — it had no nationality. What would it matter if she did her work for the NASA or in Russia? And it didn't look like NASA would ever let her follow her dream.

Michael — Mikhail — was offering both himself and her dream job. *Mary, stop crying again,* she scolded herself.

Suddenly there was a knock on her door. It was her mother.

"Mary? You're home!" She ran over to embrace her daughter, then recoiled. "Oh my Goodness, what happened?"

Maryanne sat up and grabbed her hand mirror. The large scrape across her cheek was healing, but still quite visible.

"I'm fine. I just tripped, that's all."

"And then dragged your face across the pavement?"

"No. It was a very bad fall."

Her mother wrinkled her nose like an exasperated rabbit. "Don't you lie to me. You may be grown, but I'm still your mother." Two weeks ago, Maryanne had let Gladys tell her mother, who was pressing her for information, that she was going steady. She shared every detail she knew except, of course, his race and that Maryanne was pregnant. And Maryanne had made her visits infrequent and extremely short to avoid any more questions.

Maryanne buried her face in her hands and took a deep breath.

"It was the police."

Her mother's face blanched. "Where? What happened?"

"Rock Creek Park. I was with — my boyfriend."

"The boy Gladys told me about?"

Maryanne nodded.

"What did they do to you?"

Maryanne felt her skin grow cold as she walked through the events. She could still feel the officer's sour breath on her face, the ugly expression of hatred as he molested her.

"Oh my goodness, oh my goodness, Mary, how did he get them to leave?"

"He said I was his fiancé."

Maryanne's mother looked as if she'd just been told she was the next Queen of England.

"You're engaged?"

"No, I'm not engaged. He — he just said that to get them to back off. But he wants us to be together. He wants me to — to leave D.C. with him."

Her mother froze for just a moment, then stood up to fuss around the room.

"You know, I've been a bit worried about you, but I was happy to see you finally having fun. I wanted you to have some freedom. I know it's been hard — Daddy is, um, not in his best health."

"If you mean that it's because he's always drunk . . ."

"He's under a lot of stress."

"Which means he's always drunk."

"And I made a vow to stay with him through sickness and health. Whether I love him or not."

Maryanne felt the pull of despair, letting it settle that her mother was tethered to her marriage, never able to rise. Was she ready to take that risk with Michael? He seemed to want her to soar.

But the lies.

"Mother?"

Her mother's voice and unsteady hands betrayed her stoic demeanor. She looked at Maryanne with red-rimmed eyes.

"You *should* leave — go to California or wherever, for good. It's what I never told you when you beamed about going to graduate school. I never wanted you to think you had to stay here — for *me*. For anyone."

Maryanne could not believe what she was hearing. "What are you talking about? I can't just leave you."

"Don't sass me. Listen. There's no future for you here. You are — grown. Beautiful, and smart. And you should not bring," she looked at Maryanne's midsection "a baby into this home."

Maryanne sat down, her heart jumping like a fluffle of rabbits. "How did you know?"

Her mother smiled. "I'm your mother, remember?" She looked her daughter up and down. "Plus, I've seen you hunched over the commode enough to figure it out. That is — the times you're actually here."

Maryanne was still surprised by her mother's candor about her immoral lifestyle. Of course, Gladys must have said something, her jealousy, perhaps, getting the best of her. She and Eric had been trying for almost a year and Maryanne was knocked up and unmarried, while Gladys was struggling to hold onto a pregnancy.

"Just tell me," her mother said. "Is he good to you?"

Maryanne paused. *Yes, except for deception and lying,* she thought. "He's really, really good to me," she said.

"But does he truly love you?"

"He says so."

"That isn't good enough. You should feel it. If he doesn't love you more than you love him, then stay here."

"I feel it. And he risked his life for me."

Her mother's face relaxed. "Well, then, I should like to meet this incredible man who's come to whisk my baby away."

"He's not what you'll expect."

"Perhaps, that's a good thing."

Maryanne embraced her mother and was blindsided by the

sudden pull on her soul, like she was in mourning.

"What's wrong?" Her mother's soft brown eyes, framed by delicate lines, broke her heart even more.

"I'm fine, I'm just so happy that you understand. I love you, Mommy." She stopped fighting the tears.

"I love you too, Sweetheart. And I will always be here for you."

Chapter 43

MIKHAIL/MICHAEL

July 11, 1968
Roman's Apartment, Northwest, Washington, D.C.

Roman was impossible to read, though there was always a hint of warmth behind his steel gray eyes. This time, that warmth was cloaked in paternal concern.

"You have news to share?" he said to Mikhail as he took his coat. As always, the aroma of something painfully comforting greeted his senses as he crossed the threshold. "Solyanka?" he asked. Roman nodded.

"Sit down." Roman ladled two bowls of the piquant stew and placed a plate of sliced bread, some rendered pig fat, and a frosty bottle of vodka between them. He took the opposite seat and settled his gaze on Mikhail. "So?"

"It worked perfectly. She's ready."

"And she wants to work for us?"

"What we — I did — was a lot. But I know she will say yes."

"That's good, good. She will not be disappointed in the work, that's for sure." Roman cocked his head, the way old men do when they pretend like they really want to hear what you have to say. "Do you still want to go with her?"

"Yes."

"I see."

"For her to be happy."

"Yes, her."

Roman's eyes sparkled, then paused. He swallowed hard, then said, "You know, I was married once."

Mikhail sat back. "I didn't know that."

"Yes, she was the love of my life. My only love. But this job, this life, came first." Roman pulled a handkerchief from the pocket of his sweater vest and dabbed his eye. "Allergies. I was not able to be there with her when she was dying. Dying while giving birth to our son."

It was as if a heavy curtain were opening between them, allowing them to truly see one another, unfiltered.

"And I carry that pain, that emptiness with me always. I love my country, our mission, but I should have loved my Natasha more." He stood up and Mikhail stood with him. "I see it in you, no matter how hard you try to hide it. I see it every time you speak of her. I can see when you're thinking of her."

Mikhail blinked his eyes. Not one sip of the vodka yet, but he felt as if he were unable to keep balance.

"I -" he started, the words tangling in his throat.

"I will ask that you be allowed to travel *with* her," said Roman. "She will need you to be with her to be happy, yes? No point in bringing her over if she is just going to mope about her *First Love*." Roman winked.

Mikhail's cheeks warmed. "I'm no Vladimir Petrovic," he said, his eyes smiling. So, she will go to Moscow then? To the Institute?"

"That is my understanding."

"Could we — would we be able to live together?"

"That's not up to me. What's the rush?"

Given the circumstances, the news about her pregnancy could wait. "No rush, I'm just curious."

"Very well, let's have a toast then." Roman poured them each shot.

"To the mission," said Roman, and they emptied their glasses.

Roman picked up the bottle to pour another round when

the kitchen phone rang.

"Give me a minute," he said. Mikhail sat down and resumed eating.

Roman returned, his face long. "I have some news." He sighed. "They want to wait."

"Wait? Wait for what?"

"Apparently, they want maximum value out of her being posted in Virginia, at least for a while. Marlboro too. They want to know more about the facility — this U.S. reconnaissance operation."

"That was not the plan. She can't — I won't ask her to spy for me. That's too much." He felt something swelling, burning his chest. It's what he felt when he got in a fight with that little shit Piotr when he called his mother a shlyuka. Outrage. Unfiltered. Don't show it, he told himself. But Moscow had pulled the wool over his eyes and the rug from under his feet.

Plus, he needed to get her there before she started to show.

"I'm sorry. If you want to keep her alive — if you want her to go to Moscow — you'd better get her prepped." Roman grabbed the bottle of vodka and poured two generous shots. "Or they will."

Chapter 44

MARYANNE

"I won't do it," said Maryanne. "You can't make me." She cradled her slightly rounded belly and looked up at him in desperation.

"I'm so sorry, but you — we have no choice. They're not ready for you yet and need everything to keep going normally until they are ready to extract us."

"Extract? I told you, I'm not a spy!" Her hands flew to her temples, a storm raging in her head.

"No, darling, I know, but . ."

"You put me in this situation. I didn't ask for it, I didn't wake up one morning and think, 'oh, I'm bored. I think I'll fall in love with a spy and maybe go to jail."

"Darling . . ."

"And now you want me to go back to work like everything's normal? I have to go to Virginia. Do you understand? Middle of nowhere Virginia. Into a facility where — I'm still not even sure where it is, that place no one is even supposed to know about. They'll take one look at me and know something isn't right." She would smack him if she could bring herself to do so. But she was still in control, just a bit. Sure, she was on fire, but she knew exactly what she was saying. She'd been holding it in too long.

"But you don't have to do anything," he said, peeking out the curtains of his apartment. "Just go to work, tell me a little bit about the site, that's all."

"How am I supposed to work? How'm I supposed to keep my head straight? I don't know, I don't know."

Maryanne felt a sudden, sharp pain in her abdomen and doubled over. Michael rushed to her side, and she gripped his arm in panic.

"What's wrong?" he asked.

"It's just, *Ahhhhhh!*" She bent over again, sweat springing forth and dripping from her brow. Nausea washed over her like a sickly wave, and the floor bounced like jello.

She felt herself lifted, painfully, the room swirled, and then she was on the couch. Her entire midsection twisted in pain, and stars danced before her eyes. He ran to the kitchen and returned with a damp dish towel, which felt wonderfully cool across her forehead.

Another tsunami of pain made her writhe in pain again, gritting her teeth. Suddenly, a warm trickle between her legs.

"Oh no," she said, and reached under her skirt, withdrawing fingertips moist with blood.

Michael rose. "I'm calling an ambulance," he said.

"No! Please, please don't call them."

"Why?"

"You know why," she through clenched teeth.

Michael fell to his knees and squeezed her hand. "I know someone who can help. Do you trust me?"

"That's the wrong thing to ask me right now," she moaned, her face feeling sweaty, but ice cold.

It wasn't clear how much time passed, she dozed in and out of consciousness, punctuated by pain which pulsed in and out like a raging tide. Suddenly, there was a knock on the door, and she woke to see Michael walking to it.

"Michael, my dear," someone crooned from the hallway. "Your Auntie Stella is here!"

Maryanne saw an older White woman with her gray hair

loosely wrapped in a kerchief, holding a picnic basket. The woman gave Michael a glare and she saw his shoulders drop, making him look smaller. Her face then softened, and she wad-dled to Maryanne's side. "How are you, my dear," she said in a soothing voice.

"I'm ok," she said, saturated with embarrassment. Who was this woman? Michael never mentioned an aunt. "The bleeding has stopped, I think."

"Come with me to the bathroom and let's get you cleaned up, ok?" the woman said.

Suddenly Maryanne filled with fear. Of course, this woman wasn't family. She was KGB.

✳ ✳ ✳

The woman started a warm bath and poured in Epsom salts she found under the sink. Maryanne undressed, trying to slyly look over her shoulder. The woman's eyes met hers, and a shud-der went down Maryanne's spine.

"Now don't worry, love," said the woman, gently. "I am here to help you. Really." Her demeanor was calm yet commanding — slightly unsettling, and she was very strong. She let the tub fill only to waist deep and effortlessly lifted Maryanne into the water. Maryanne looked away as the woman carefully inspected her underwear, which was coated with thick blood and other matter.

"I'm afraid that you've had a miscarriage, my dear," said the woman, unceremoniously shaking the underwear over the toi-let and flushing. "I'm so sorry."

Maryanne's hands started shaking. "Oh no, no, no."

"You wanted this child?"

Maryanne nodded. She'd accepted the pregnancy, just hadn't realized it until that moment that she wanted the baby.

The woman looked at her curiously, but with a shadow of concern across her brow.

"This was not the right time for a baby. You're young, and you have a bright future in our beautiful country ahead of you. There's work for you to do — to fulfill your potential."

The water was now a deep pink. The woman instructed her to stand, then drained the water and turned on the shower. "I'll be right here outside the shower curtain if you feel dizzy," said the woman.

Maryanne closed her eyes and let the hot water run down her face, her torso. She felt strangely at ease, as if she were in the right place at the right time. The woman was right — this was not the right time for a baby. But what about Michael? Would he still want her? What about them being a family?

And after what he'd asked of her, did she still want to go through with this?

As the woman turned off the water and wrapped her in a towel, Maryanne started to cry.

"What is it my dear?" she asked.

"I'm just worried that Michael — Mikhail — won't want me anymore. We were to be — together. To have a life together over there."

The woman shook her head. "Don't you worry about that my dear. I don't think you'll ever find a man as committed to your welfare as he is. You will be together. He wouldn't have it any other way."

The woman seemed sincere, so Maryanne let herself believe every word. She had no doubt this gentle, matronly woman was a killer. But she'd taken care of Maryanne and spoke with clear sincerity. Maryanne had to comply. She couldn't drown in distrust anymore. It wasn't safe. Dangerous to her heart. And maybe, even more dangerous to her life.

Chapter 45

MIKHAIL/MICHAEL

July 15, 1968
Mikhail's Southwest Apartment, Washington, D.C.

When they emerged from the bathroom, Maryanne was wrapped in his favorite bathrobe again, which made him smile, momentarily. But then his eyes moved back to the older woman, who was clearly Roman's counterpart. As her steel eyes pierced his heart, his nails pressed deeply into his palms. He mustn't lose it in front of that woman, who he knew was one of the KGB's stealthiest killers on U.S. soil. Her specialty was rogue agents, and given this situation, he wasn't sure she was on his side. When she took Maryanne to the bathroom, he'd positioned himself near the painting of a large seashell above his end table, behind which he kept a .22 Berretta, and slipped a retractable knife up his sleeve. He may not succeed in killing the woman but would be able to give Maryanne enough time to get away, if it came down to that.

Maryanne smiled weakly at him, and his insides fell to pieces. Then the woman gently escorted Maryanne to the bed and tucked her in like a child. The woman closed the bedroom door and returned to the living room, standing a breath's distance from Mikhail's face. She was a full head shorter than him, but he felt his tail tuck between his legs.

"She's had a miscarriage," she said with authority. "Next time, don't be so careless with," and she pointed to Mikhail's crotch.

"Yes," he said looking straight ahead. You never looked a senior officer in the eye unless commanded to do so.

"Very well. My work here is done." She packed up her picnic basket and pointed to the bloody couch. "Burn that," she said. "And take care of her. *She* is valuable." And with that, she waddled out and shut the door behind her. He peeked again through his curtains and saw her get into the passenger side of a car and take off. He was grateful she'd come to help, but his nerves were shot.

Mikhail went into the bedroom and lay down next to Maryanne. She rolled over and he gathered her in his arms.

"I'm so sorry," she said. Her tears soaked his shirt, right next to his heart.

"No, don't be sorry. It's my fault. I've asked too much." He caught himself but let the words flow. "If you want — if you need to walk away, I will understand." He swallowed a growing lump in his throat.

Maryanne pulled away and they gazed at each other. "I can't walk away. I'm with you — do you understand? We're in this together."

He kissed her softly and lingered for a moment. "I don't deserve you," he said.

"I know," she replied and rolled on her other side, her back to him. The air suddenly felt cold. Then he remembered he'd promised Stéphanie a trip to the beach that weekend and his soul sank. He'd have to lie to Maryanne — again.

✳ ✳ ✳

Roman, who had waited an excruciating three days to call, agreed to meet Mikhail at the beach. He was furious.

"Why didn't you tell me she was pregnant?" he growled. "That kind of information is critical, and you kept it from me. Do you know how that makes me look to the Center?"

"I'm sorry."

"Sorry isn't enough. Do you realize that if they found out before I did, they might have found cause to take both of you out?"

Mikhail shuddered. "That's why I said nothing. I didn't want anything to happen to her or the baby before she was extracted." He'd been stupid — should have known better. She was an asset. No matter what she meant to him, to them, she was valuable. The State was more important than his small, insignificant life. So much was at stake, and he'd almost blown everything up. *At this point, she may even be more valuable than me*, he thought.

Roman studied his face, then his shoulders softened. "I understand. But next time, never keep information from me."

Roman looked up and down the boardwalk and wiped the back of his neck with a cotton handkerchief.

"This is a nice beach," he said.

"Took forever to get here though." This was the last place on earth he wanted to be, but he needed an excuse to whisk Stéphanie out of town to follow up on what the U.S. may have told the French about their involvement in Czechoslovakia, plus the French had just successfully conducted their first hydrogen bomb test. She'd mentioned more than once how much she missed her annual trip to the Mediterranean — Ocean City, Maryland would have to suffice this year. He told Maryanne he was travelling, visiting steel and lumber producers in Appalachia.

"And how is the French girl?"

"Insufferable. She complains more than an old shrew. But her information is still good." Mikhail looked in the direction of the hotel where Stéphanie was characteristically sleeping off too much champagne. He wished he could just leave her there, walk away. It felt wrong, rolling around in bed with her, proclaiming his love, feigning passion. Not wrong toward Stéphanie — no — wrong toward Maryanne. He'd already layered lie upon lie, but he wanted to be open with Maryanne, his true self. He wanted to be fully exposed to her, all his faults, and be fully seen. She made him feel — *safe*. Like home. But for now, he still had a job to do.

"Yes, the mademoiselle's information has been very good. It was a good idea to bring her here for a couple of days. Keep her happy, if you can, for a while longer."

"That's the problem, she wants more of me."

"Keep being an asshole then."

"The more I'm an asshole, the more she seems to like me." Mikhail spotted an ice cream vendor and Roman nodded in agreement. They slowly walked over toward the bored teenaged vendor. "She's more in love with that boss of hers, who sounds like an even bigger jerk than I am."

"Well, she can be his problem when you leave."

Mikhail stopped. "So, it's been approved?"

"Yes. You and your girl will leave together."

"Thank you," he said, awash with relief, hope burning in his heart.

"Don't thank me. Thank the Iron Maiden. She apparently had a lovely talk with your girl while mothering her, which I would have killed to see, by the way. Anyway, she's the one that put in the good word, saying that you needed a smart woman like that to keep you straight."

Mikhail was not insulted. He cleared his throat. "So, when?"

"Soon. Arrangements are underway."

The two men walked in tandem, eating ice cream, like father and son on holiday.

"I still can't believe how insanely hot it gets here. How's the apartment?" said Roman.

"Stifling. That air conditioning device I bought barely keeps one corner of the room cool. I have fans everywhere and am forced to keep the windows cracked at night."

"Which means that you're not sleeping. I can see the dark under your eyes."

Mikhail noticed that he was feeling a bit slower lately, and his mind was not as quick.

"Yes, but I'm still committed to the mission, which is to get as much information from Marlboro as I can before going — home." He looked at his watch. "I need to get the embassy girl up so we can get back to D.C. Then I'm off to Chicago to meet

Geoffrey at the convention."

It was reassuring to hear Roman say that he could go home soon. He was starting to feel stretched thin, between Mary-anne, Stéphanie, Marlboro, and keeping on top of every political and social intrigue that the Center wanted him to investigate. Two days ago, Roman told him it was all hands-on-deck for the upcoming Democratic National Convention. Plus, the Center had assigned Mikhail a Chicago-based McDonnell Douglas engineer with missile schematics. The engineer would make the drop at the airport.

"We've got our press credentials and will stay at the margins. It's going to be chaos- no one will notice us. I'll pick up the package on my way out of Chicago. Soon as I get home I'm meeting up with Bunny to tell her I'll be gone for a couple of weeks in August."

"And how is she doing?"

"She's doing her job. Nothing more, nothing less."

"She has no idea what Marlboro is up to?"

"Doesn't seem to. She's mentioned him before though — apparently, he's true to form at work — a real jerk. She hates him. Says he makes her skin crawl." Mikhail paused. "He mentioned that he saw me talking to her once, though."

"When was that?" said Roman, sounding like an exasperated father who'd just learned his son crashed the car again.

"Just a few days ago," fibbed Mikhail. "I told him that it was none of his business and that he should be careful."

"Sounds like you should be the careful one. We're working on finding someone else on the inside there, so we can cut him loose soon, I hope. You never know quite what you're going to get with these volunteers. Most of them are completely unstable. And this one — well, he's as difficult as it gets. But the Center thinks he has value, so manage him the best you can."

"I don't know. Something tells me I need to put some daylight between us. I haven't met him in person in a few weeks, and I've changed up our drop locations."

"Fine. Follow your instincts. Just keep your girl close by for the next few weeks. Things are going to happen fast."

Chapter 46

MARYANNE

August 19, 1968
Chantilly, Virginia

Maryanne loosened her grip on the steering wheel and breathed. It was a new gate guard, a ramrod man with short blond hairs that stuck out from under his hat like he'd stuck his finger in a socket. He was, of course, inspecting her ID, and license, and license plate, and her face, and her ID, and license, and so on. She wanted to stick her head out the windows and smack the outside of the car door barking "I'm late!" like the car driver right before her, but she knew she didn't have the same clout.

Eventually the stiff young man mechanically walked back to her window, returned her documents, and waived her through. *All this trouble*, she thought, *for a place I can't stand.*

The daily drive to Virginia was like tiptoeing through a minefield while balancing a chicken on your head. It was only about a thirty-minute drive from D.C. in the car Michael had bought for her, a modest blue Chevelle that she had first protested until she calculated her commuting time via three buses, each way. Chantilly, Virginia felt like a world away, directly through redneck alley, an expanse of farms and new subdivisions. She almost missed the facility entrance on her first trip, as it was only an unmarked chain link fence with razor wire and generic "Do Not Enter" sign. She eventually found the guard stand and showed her badge to the skeptical officer, who after making at least two separate phone calls "just to check" finally waived her through. Then it was another long drive across the campus, and a long walk to the prefab building which housed her program. Fortunately, there was a Ladies' Room on site, despite it often feeling like she was the only woman there.

And now that Atkins was no longer in charge, he was always in a sour mood. She was put back in a purely support role, no longer asked for her opinion or expertise. No illusion of inclusion. The new set of bosses with starched collars seemed to have no idea who she was or what purpose she served, and Atkins was too busy advocating for himself to speak up for her. They'd hold closed door meetings and she'd be left waiting outside for orders. To make matters worse, that slimy ashtray Roger would hover nearby all day. She could feel his eyes boring into the back of her neck, and when she got up from her desk he would swoop in and look at everything. This is just temporary, she muttered to herself. *You'll be away from him soon enough*, she thought as she slid behind her tiny desk.

"How're you holding up?" Maryanne looked over her shoulder and was surprised to see Atkins. His eyes were red as if he'd been rubbing them and his shirt collar was shiny, as if it hadn't been laundered in weeks.

"I'm fine," she said politely, though her voice inflected up as if she was asking a question. "Lots to do — calculations and whatnot." She felt like bursting into tears. Calculations. She was nothing but a calculator.

Atkins grabbed an empty chair and sat close enough to her that she could see every pore on his face. She wrapped her arms protectively around her midsection, but he didn't seem to notice.

"This work is beneath you," he said.

Her mouth dropped open before she could stop it.

"What I mean," he continued. "Is that you don't belong here. Sure, I sold it as a great opportunity and all, but I can tell your heart's not in this work."

If only you knew, she thought. *My heart is with a KGB agent who wants me to spy, with a graduate degree that's never going to happen, and a lost pregnancy.* At least she wouldn't have to hide the pregnancy anymore.

"I know your life's dream is to be an astrophysicist. And that I promised to get you into graduate school. You know we made applications, and everyone has said you are a talent. You record is impressive. But no bites yet."

You mean no one's ready for a Black girl yet, she thought. "Thank you for trying," she said, half-heartedly. Of course, he couldn't come through. Wasn't his fault, really. This was America, after all. They'd never let someone like her follow her dreams.

"But there may be a work around."

She leaned in even closer, her heart suddenly racing. She didn't know what that meant, but it sounded positive. "What's a work around?" she asked.

"Well, out at Cal Tech they've got the Deep Space Network, you know?"

She nodded. Oh yes, she knew. The university had an entire program structured around deep space exploration and one of the best doctoral programs in astrophysics in the country. Not only was it on her list of top choices, but it was in central California and far, far away from the south. "Are they ready to admit me?" she asked hopefully.

"No — not exactly. But they could use someone like you to analyze data transmitted from NASA radio telescopes and satellites. You've already got a degree and stellar recommendations," he sat up proudly, "so they'd be happy to bring you on as an analyst. That is, if you are interested." He beamed.

Maryanne's heart swelled with joy. An actual astrophysics position? She would have hugged Atkins if she knew he wouldn't recoil. "That's just amazing," she said finally. "Of course, I'm interested!"

Then, her brain started to swim. What about Moscow? Michael? What would she do? It should be so simple, so easy.

She loved Michael, yes, but would she follow him to Moscow if it weren't for the promise of furthering her career? God, she needed to talk to him, but he was travelling — again. And travelling for what? He was KGB, and it wasn't lost on her that his country had nuclear warheads pointed at her city. What if they wanted her to work on systems or analyze information that would lead to war?

"Maryanne?" said Atkins, bringing her mind back to the present.

"Sorry, my mind was in the desert already."

"Yes, well, I need you to take these memos," he handed her a locked security bag, "back to headquarters and the Administrator's office. Can you go now? Then, go home and celebrate." He winked.

"Yes, celebrate," she said, her mind drifting yet again. "Sure, Dr. Atkins, I can go now."

Maryanne grabbed her valise and headed toward the door, hoping to avoid Roger. But there he was, leaning against the front desk, chewing on a toothpick, his lips curling into a sneer at the sight of her. Something inside her roiled, unfurled, and she stopped to face him. "Got anything to say?" she sneered back.

He looked like she'd just socked him in the gut. "Cheeky today, huh?" he said, breathlessly.

Maryanne gave him one last hard look in the eye and stomped out the door.

✳ ✳ ✳

Gladys was sitting on the front porch when she got home. She had a concerned look on her face.

"What's wrong?" said Maryanne, suddenly frightened. "Is everyone ok?"

"We need to talk. NOW," said Gladys.

"Oh," said Maryanne, her heart in her throat. "I think I know what we need to talk about."

It had been one month since the miscarriage, and yet Maryanne still felt a heaviness in her womb and was even plumper around her waist. She hadn't mentioned her symptoms to Michael. Her mother assured her that was normal, that the hormones stay with you for a while.

But something was off. Maryanne's breasts were still high and swollen, and she could smell everything, including Atkins's wife's lipstick that grazed his collar, from across the table. Cody Cardinal Red, she'd think to herself while scribbling a string of code.

She asked — no begged — Gladys to take a jar of her urine to the family doctor for a pregnancy test. "You don't have to blood test anymore," she'd said. "It'll be so easy." Gladys had protested that it was fraud, and well, disgusting. But Maryanne didn't want to deal with yet another smarmy, judgmental doctor.. So, Gladys relented and submitted the test under her name.

"You're still pregnant," said Gladys once they'd reached their bedroom and shut the door. She looked exasperated.

"But how?" said Maryanne.

"It's not unusual to go through all that you did and still be pregnant. I know at least two girls who swore they'd lost their babies but it was a false alarm."

"But there was so much blood!" Maryanne cried.

"Or, could've been twins." said Gladys her face in an inquisitive ball. "That happened to a girlfriend of mine. She lost one baby but the other hung on. Ended up giving birth to an 8-pound baby boy five months after she thought she miscarried."

"Oh no, I can't, I just can't . . ."

"Oh yes you can. Plus, did you even think how this would make me feel, all I've been through? Now I'll have to say I miscarried — again." Gladys looked completely deflated and Maryanne instantly felt treacherous. How could she have been so selfish? Gladys didn't deserve this, didn't deserve what she'd had to endure.

"I'm so sorry, Gladys. I've been so caught up in my own problems that I never considered how affecting you."

"That's right," said Gladys, swallowing her tears. "But that doesn't matter now. Right now, you've got a baby growing in you. And you're going to love it. You hear? Michael will be back soon. And of course, you've got me."

The women embraced and Maryanne instantly felt safer.

"Can't believe they think I'm pregnant again," said Gladys. "Ain't that rich?"

I can't believe this, Maryanne thought, her heart breaking for Gladys. She was devastated when she thought she lost the baby but reached a place of uneasy acceptance. Now what would she do? If Atkins found out, he'd probably say no to the California job. Well, maybe not, there were at least a couple of women at NASA that were mothers that she knew of by overhearing conversations in the Ladies Room. But the Russians, if they found out she was pregnant, they may not want her anymore. She just didn't know. She was pretty sure Michael would be happy, though it would certainly complicate her transition. What if they made her leave the baby here? Oh no, that would not do. But how would she say no?

"Sit down, Mary," said Gladys. "I know this is a lot, but you'll be ok. It's not that bad."

"Oh Gladys" said Maryanne, shaking her head. "You have no idea."

Chapter 47

LEROY/DONOVAN

August 27, 1968
Chicago, Illinois

onovan never liked Chicago. Next to the glittering Lake Shore he saw a thoroughly vexing city where the mob was as active as it had been during Prohibition and the color line was as bright as in rural Mississippi. Ironically, this was the city the Democrats chose for their convention, to put forth a nominee no one wanted. In response, the entire government establishment — from local law enforcement to the military, to the Bureau — was mobilized.

The Chicago FBI office was like a kennel of rabid dogs frothing at the jowls, hungry to take down the "militant commie bastards" who were planning to protest. It was all hands-on deck.

"You're looking fly," said O'Connell to Donovan.

"Thanks Chief" said Donovan, rubbing his shoulder, which finally no longer ached. "Also — breaking news — I've been promoted, of sorts. Gonna be right at Seale's side in Grant Park." *Waste of time*, he thought. Here J. Edgar is all bent out of shape about a group that made him uncomfortable because they spoke out against racism when the real enemy was slithering around, undetected.

"Well, be careful. Gonna be a powder keg. Don't get shot by

the police again. Or by one of us."

"Don't worry boss," he said, a shudder crawling up his spine. But he had to go.

Donovan had been so busy spying on Americans that his unofficial investigation of the Russian stalled. The scent had gone cold, and he hadn't received news from the other team that was investigating the spy's patsy. Well, not officially. He eavesdropped on their discussions and learned that it was expected the KGB would be in full force at the convention too. A love-in in for every foreign intelligence operation on U.S. soil. He convinced himself that he could keep one eye on Seale and the other looking for Michael, amid what was sure to be utter chaos.

"I have never seen so many damn hippies in one place in my life," said Donovan, scanning the Lincoln Park crowd. There had to be thousands of people. No one in his group smiled, no one chuckled. No small talk. One of the Panthers carried a speaker and microphone for Seale to use during his speech. Seale's plan was to drop into the park, give his speech, and get the fuck out. An hour or less if he could manage it. That'd give Donovan plenty of time to fulfill his undercover work with the Panthers, then look for Michael.

Donovan walked just ahead of Seale and his entourage, keeping his eyes trained straight ahead, his peripheral vision fully activated. The park was packed with humans, and he felt claustrophobic despite being outside. Electricity rocketed through his body, and he tried to ignore the incredible funk of thousands of angsty, unwashed bodies. The Chicago Police Department and National Guard surrounded the park and occupied every corner, hungry to escalate. Men with cameras sat at the ready, primed to swarm at the first drop of spilled blood. The atmosphere was electrified. Plus, it was insanely hot and sunny.

Bobby Seale stepped onto a slight rise, surrounded by his Panthers and one or two White folks, and grabbed the mic. He blinked hard, like he was trying to clear the sweat and dust from his eyes and scanned the crowd. Then he raised his arms, immediately catching the attention of those around him, and the crowd fell silent. Donovan stood off to the side in order to keep an eye on things but listened with intent to every word. Seale was a powerful speaker who pulled no punches. The mostly rapt crowd offered the loudest applause when he condemned racist oppression and urged resistance. Seale wrapped his short speech with some choice words and was surrounded by a crush of fans and reporters, as Donovan and the other men worked to create space around him. Suddenly, the crowd's mood shifted from jubilant to panic.

"Man, do you see what's happening?" said a young man to the left. It was difficult to get a clear view, but Donovan saw the glare of sunlight reflecting off the helmets of what seemed like infinite police pressing into the crowd. The day before, the Chicago Police took a heavy hand against the protestors, fighting like it was 1776 with bayonets and clubs against unarmed stoners, and their assaults were getting worse with each hour. He was unwilling to suffer, yet again, at the hands of the police.

"We need to move," said Donovan, loud enough for the group to hear. The mass of humanity shifted, as if the Earth had been tilted to the left. Donovan got separated from the group, his heart pounding in his ears, but knew he could meet them at the rendezvous. He ducked and weaved through the advancing crowd, able to gauge from which direction the police were coming. Finding an opening, he burst through, right before the sound of 'pops' and masculine screams, meaning tear gas was deployed somewhere. He continued outward and found himself at a corner, directly facing a bank of reporters who were standing on cars, light posts, and newspaper boxes, just to get a great shot of the chaos and bloodshed. Snipers hid in plain sight just above them on rooftops, ready to make a point.

Donovan pulled his shirt up around his face — could not risk his picture ending up in the paper — and froze.

It was Michael, M, the Russian.

His face emerged from behind a large camera, slightly sunburned and sweaty. He narrowed his eyes and scanned the horizon, as if looking for prey. Donovan was so close to where Michael was standing that he was looking almost right over his head. Realizing that none of the reporters were paying attention to anything right in front of them, Donovan moved closer then off to the side. Never taking his eyes off his subject.

Finding a new subject, Michael slipped back behind the camera. *Intelligence gathering*, Donovan thought. Looking for people to corrupt or black mail. He kept walking, shirt up around the lower half of his face, and took a wide berth to walk around the photographers. He found a spot behind his target and waited, sweat pouring down his brow, his mouth dry as cotton balls.

Then, movement. Michael packed up his equipment, put on a straw Bermuda hat, and walked away from the action, past the barricades that shut the rest of Chicago off from the war zone. Donovan stepped in line behind him, hands at his sides. *Walk easy,* he thought, suspicious eyes dancing all over his body, twice over. Damn this hair. His freshly-dyed, blown-out afro seemed to absorb every ray of light then concentrate it, so his head felt like a lit match. He couldn't afford a stop and frisk, so when a particularly curious police officer looked his way, he gave a vacant, minstrel smile. The officer looked away.

Michael, who was just 35 yards ahead of him, took a few tight turns then walked down Dickens Avenue until traffic was normal and it looked like any other summer day in Chicago. He stuck his arms out and waved to hail a taxi.

Shit, thought Donovan, as Michael easily stopped a cab, hopped in, and sped off. There was no chance in hell any cab would stop for a sweaty Black revolutionary -looking cat. Had he been home he probably would have cursed to the heavens, maybe even find a garbage can to kick. But not here, not today, in a town with cops thirsty for blood. He'd have to return to his motel on the Southside, an hour-long walk, then regroup with any remaining Panthers before returning to D.C on his own. At least he'd confirmed that Michael was an operator, but damn, he needed more. He'd go home and get back to work.

"Damn!" Donovan said aloud.

It was another three hours before he made it to Midway to catch a flight to D.C. He'd missed his earlier flight and knew there was just one more. At least he'd showered and was respectfully dressed. He hated flying, the smell of burning fuel and feeling like the plane was driving over a bumpy road made his stomach turn. But he wanted to get home to sleep in his own bed, even if his wife was frosty.

Unfortunately, the ticket agent informed him the last flight of the day was full. He sulked away, resigned to the fact he'd need to spend the night in the airport, his second most hated aspect of air travel. He checked his pockets for change then trudged over to the airport lockers to stash his suitcase, which also contained his FBI-issue Smith and Wesson. Better than risking someone nabbing it while he was sleeping, or the random airport cop shake down. Finding an empty locker, he stored his belongings, then closed the door and turned toward around to find a place for nap.

Are you kidding me? he shouted in his head when he saw Michael making a beeline for the lockers. Donovan maneuvered carefully behind a tour group that was filing past, ducking into the pay phone bank with a clear view of the locker where Michael stopped. The phones were just close enough for Donovan to get a good view of the locker numbers.

"You gonna call someone?" Donavan glanced over his shoulder and saw an alabaster powdered TWA flight attendant glaring at him.

"Yeah, um, just looking for the number." He fumbled around in his pocket and fished out a card, quicky returning his gaze to Michael. The locker was open!

"'Cause I need to make a call before my flight," she commanded, her patent leather toe tapping furiously.

"So do I," he practically shouted, mindful not to berate a White woman. And he did, because Michael had just pulled a briefcase out of the locker and put something else in it, then started to walk away. Donavan's renowned eagle eye looked down at the card, soggy with sweat.

"Dammit!" he shouted. The writing on the card was barely

legible, but he picked up the receiver, threw in a nickel and dialed.

"I beg your pardon — I'm — I'm getting security," she said pointing her finger in his nose, just as he heard on the receiver, "FBI Field Office Chicago."

"O'Connell! I need O'Connell!" shouted Donovan.

"Who is this?" said the nasal voice on the other end. Donovan saw Michael disappear into the crowd.

"Just tell'em that Fro Man called and that he needs to get eyes on locker 387 at O'Hare NOW and apprehend whoever opens it. He's sure to find something interesting. I'll call him when I get back to D.C."

He slammed down the receiver and gave a triumphant glare to the righteous pixie, who was trying to get the attention of a pair of police officers who were preoccupied with a group of Hare Krishnas. Donovan bolted in the direction he'd last seen Michael, exhaling when he saw him leave the ticket counter, briefcase in one hand and ticket in another. Then he confidently strode toward the departure lounge for the full flight to D.C. leaving in an hour.

I have to try, Donovan thought. He walked back to the ticket counter and THANK GOD it was a Black woman with a tight afro, because by that point he must have looked like a rebel who'd crawled out from the chaos.

"Can I help you?" she asked sassily when he flashed his signature smile.

"Thank you, sister, I really need to get on a flight. A ticket on the flight to D.C. leaving in 50 minutes. I was told it's full but if you could check again . . ."

She looked down at the flight ledger and her face grew long, as if she'd just realized she was one number short of winning the lottery. "Not full — there is one seat available, but it's — first class."

Of course, the agent earlier hadn't bothered to tell him there was a first class seat available.

"What, don't I look first class?" he said, leaning on one elbow and placing his FBI badge under her nose.

Her eyes grew wide, then she scowled.

"Why should I help you?" she snorted. "You're one of those brothers no better than the overseer on the plantation, huh?"

Her words stung more than those type of comments had in the past, but he wasn't surprised. "No, sister. I'm not after us. I'm after the real enemy — foreign. They target us. You know White folk, they're the same world over."

She studied his face and it burned.

"And if I don't get on that plane someone truly evil is going to get away. So please — please — can you issue me that ticket?"

Donovan made it to the gate just as he saw Michael disappear into the stairwell to the runway. *Don't see me, don't see me, don't see me*, he thought. He boarded, head down though anyone with eyes would be taken aback by a tall Black man with a shiny afro. If spotted, he'd just tell Michael that he was out with the Panthers. For all he knew, he'd gotten a picture of him next to Seale. But the target was already sitting, cozy and relaxed, hat over his face.

Donovan took his seat and seethed. The hubris. Not a care in the world. That's how it was with liars, manipulators. Soviets. It was their nature.

His uncle bought into the lie. A sharecropper from Alabama, he'd been the lead agricultural engineer on his parents' master's plantation, a genius at cultivating cotton. Except he wasn't called an engineer — just 'boy' or 'nigger' or 'you.' He took his talent and skill to the Tuskegee Institute to study under George Washington Carver. When the Soviets came calling, looking for talent to develop their nascent cotton-growing enterprise in Uzbekistan, promising a land free from racism and promising to treat Black men like dignitaries, Uncle Samuel "Sachmo" Donovan packed his bags and left. He joined other ambitious black American men who left under similar auspices, dined with Paul Robeson and Langston Hughes, and lived in an exceptionally well-appointed home with indoor plumbing, a luxury that he'd never before enjoyed. He even married a Russian woman and had a son he named "Yosef," which was ironic because it was life under Stalin that led him to abandon his family and high-tail it back to the U.S. Uncle remained tight-lipped about his experience there until he was on his deathbed, where he recounted tales of malnourished Uzbeks toiling in cotton fields under a sun that looked remarkably like the one that menaced African slaves and sharecroppers. Donovan held his uncle's story close to his heart, never sharing it with anyone other than his wife, but there was no question it stoked his hatred.

Donovan stayed close to Michael once they landed and followed him into the parking garage. Michael never set down the briefcase. The garage was full of cars but eerily quiet, so though he stayed light on his toes the sound of his feet seemed amplified. *Step in time,* Donovan told himself, watching Michael's feet while ducking behind cars and concrete poles to stay concealed. 100 feet. Get closer. Michael stopped at a black Plymouth GTX that Donovan had never seen before and unlocked the door. *New car?* he thought. He'd run the tags of Michael's other vehicle and it had come up clean, registered to a Michael Stevenson at the address of their building. And Michael Stevenson, well, there was nothing to report.

Suddenly Michael spun around to look in Donovan's direction. Donovan stiffened as the spy slowly started walking toward the pillar where he was hidden, hand in his pocket. *Dammit, he's got a gun,* Donovan cursed in his head, remembering the suitcase he'd abandoned in Chicago. *I can get the drop on him,* he thought. *I can take'em.* His heart was pounding in his ears.

Suddenly, screeching tires, and Donovan stopped in his tracks. A second later a sedan sped down the aisle, driven by a pissed off looking dad with a mother turned to scold two unruly children in the back seat. Michael jogged back to his car, slamming the door. He slowly pulled out and reversed course to back up to where Donavan was still hiding. *Shit!* Donovan hit the ground and rolled under a car just as Michael reached the pillar where he'd been hiding. Michael scanned the area like a hawk, his blue eyes flashing, then abruptly drove away. Donovan exhaled and let his face rest on the hot, oily pavement, muttering the license plate number.

Got you.

Chapter 48

MIKHAIL/MICHAEL

August 27, 1968
Southwest, Washington, D.C.

t was nighttime when Mikhail got home from the airport. He was surprised to see Roman sitting at his kitchen table.

"How was your trip to Chicago?" asked Roman.

"Good," said Mikhail, cautiously setting down his bag and retrieving the package. "I got what you wanted."

"Excellent work, as usual," said Roman, smiling. "Now I have some good news for you."

"Yes?"

"You and your girl are slated to go home next Monday," he said. "All of the arrangements have been made. I'll get you details in the next few days."

Mikhail let a smile spread from ear-to-ear. "That's great," he said. "Can I tell her?'

"Yes, but not yet. We don't want her changing her behavior — it could raise suspicion. Just tell her everything is still in the works."

"Thank you," said Mikhail, feeling like he was filled with light. "I'll make sure we're ready."

After Roman left, he wanted to call Maryanne so badly his head started to ache. But it was too late in the evening. He went to the freezer and downed two shots of vodka, letting joy seep through every bit of his soul. As his head hit the pillow, he drifted into an easy sleep.

✳ ✳ ✳

The next morning, he called.

"Can you come over, Sweetheart?" he said, elated to hear her voice. "I'm dying to see you, plus I have some updates." He couldn't be sure, but he sometimes thought he could hear a faint clicking when he was on the phone, like someone else was listening in. It was better not to share too much detail during calls.

"Yes, of course," she said. But though she sounded upbeat, she also seemed distant, as if being forced to say 'happy birthday' to an unfamiliar relative. "I'll come over tomorrow, after work."

His heart sank a bit. Why couldn't she come right away? "I'll be here," he said. "Can't wait."

"Me too."

He paused. "Love you," he said, for some reason afraid of her reply.

"Love you too," she said, her voice tinged with something. Was it sadness?

He hung up, feeling uneasy. Something was off and he needed to know what it was.

Chapter 49

DONOVAN

Donovan rubbed his eyes. His body was exhausted from Chicago, but his mind was flooded with adrenaline. Was it actually her? He'd driven by her home more than once but hadn't the time for an all-out surveillance. He'd even driven past NASA headquarters every few days or so, just hoping for a chance sighting. It was his only option. He didn't want to bring Bureau attention to her by poking around NASA. But there she was, cautiously navigating her front steps, a small suitcase and leather valise in hand. Her head hung low, and he could see the shadow of several sleepless nights under her eyes.

Maybe it was stupid of him coming here to confront her. But he had to know if she was an innocent victim or if she was a traitor. Well, she was a traitor to her race, that was for sure. But he shouldn't be too harsh. Spies are master corruptors, and Michael — or whatever his name really was — would surely know how to work a young, beautiful woman. Still, if she was spying for the Russians there was nothing he could do for her. Nothing.

He stepped out of his car and scrambled to the sidewalk to intercept her.

"Maryanne?" he said. She looked startled, then annoyed.

"What are you doing here?" she said, trying to walk around him.

"Stop," he said, reaching into his shirt pocket, which was now drenched with sweat. "I need to reintroduce myself." He showed her his FBI badge and her face paled, drained of all warmth.

"Are you serious?" she said, shaking her head. "Is this a joke?"

"No."

He let it sink in, waiting for an uncomfortably long pause.

"Am — am I in trouble?" she finally said in the tone of someone who knew they were in trouble. O'Connell called it the "guilty treble."

"You need to come with me," he said, opening the passenger side door of his car. "Let's go somewhere we can talk."

✳ ✳ ✳

The trees of the National Cathedral grounds offered cool sanctuary against the blazing sun. She sat as if she could sink all the way into her seat, like his daughter had after she'd cut off her sleeping sister's braids. He felt a flood of conflicting emotions, from concern to condemnation. And attraction. She was, even in her stormy state, beautiful. He gripped the steering wheel and stared straight ahead, willing his brain to focus. He needed to be clear-headed.

After a silent car ride, they found a bench and took a seat, nodding to a pair of Episcopal nuns as they sauntered past. Otherwise, there was no one else around.

"So," said Donovan in a low voice, "still wrapped up with Michael, eh?"

Maryanne rubbed her hands together so hard he thought she'd remove the brown from her skin. "Yes, we're, um still together."

"Together," said Donovan, sounding unimpressed, though he could feel the anger swirling in his ribcage. "How well do you know him?"

"Pretty — I mean very well. As you said before, he's one of the good ones."

"Heh."

"Still mad that I'm dating a White man?" she said, her voice rising slightly. "It's none of your business."

"Oh, yes it is," said Donovan. Keep your temper, he scolded himself. "He's not who you think he is."

She blinked and swallowed.

"What do you mean?" she said, her upper lip suddenly sprouting beads of sweat.

It had been a while since Donovan had interrogated someone, and for some reason, she intimidated him. Her soft eyes, long lashes, and gentle smirk made his mind wander to places they hadn't since he'd been married. Plus, her skin glowed and her body looked softer. He had to stay focused.

"I know that you know he's NOT one of the good ones. That he's bad. Very bad. And that if you're caught up with him, when he goes down, so do you."

Maryanne's cheeks hollowed in and out, like she was suffocating. He took her hands — her very soft, small hands — into his and looked her in the eye. "Calm down," he said. "I can protect you. But you have to tell me everything."

"There's nothing to tell."

"Maryanne," he said, his training coming back into focus. "You have to think about more than yourself. What about your family? If you go to prison . . ."

"Prison?!" she exclaimed.

"Keep your voice down," he cautioned. "Never know who's listening. Yes — prison. Federal prison. Treason is a serious charge."

Her face melted in understanding. Yes, she knew what he was talking about. And she was clearly scared. The disappointment hit him like a ton of bricks. He wanted to think she was just an innocent patsy, a Pollyanna. Clearly, she was more involved. But she was still a victim. He suddenly had the urge to find Michael and beat his head in.

"So much has happened," she said, the tears flowing. "It just got so out of control."

"Take your time," he said, his anticipation as electrified as sitting at the top of a roller coaster.

As Mary tearfully recounted the past few months Donovan felt venom pricking his tongue. *That son-of-a-bitch*, he thought. *Pregnancy? Defection? How could she be so stupid?*

"What were you thinking?" he said. "And did you agree to obtain any information for him? Anything at all?"

"No, nothing. All I shared was where I worked."

Donovan rubbed his chin. They never offered something for nothing. "Has he ever been in your house?" he asked, his mind running like a hamster on a wheel.

"No."

"Have you heard any static or whooshing sounds on your phone?"

She shook her head 'no.'

He looked up at the trees, which rustled as a crow landed on a lower branch. It had something shiny in its beak. "Crows like to give little gifts," his daughter told him last week.

He looked at Maryanne's tear-stained face and wished he could kiss the tears on her cheeks. "Has he ever given you any-thing?" he asked gently. "Like, a gift."

"Yes," she said, clearly trying to regain composure. "A car. And the leather valise that's in your vehicle."

Donovan sprung from his bench and ran back to the car. He could hear Maryanne's confused shouts behind him, but he turned and put his finger to his lips. "Quiet," he mouthed as she approached.

He pulled the valise from the car and emptied its contents into the seat. Then he started feeling around the interior, under the lining, in the brass feet, and finally the piping and handle. Then, he felt it.

Son-of-a-bitch, he thought, retrieving a pen knife from his glove compartment. "Be quiet," he mouthed again. Then he took the knife and ran it under the piping, retrieving a slender device that looked like an electric bean with wires. Maryanne's mouth dropped open. Donovan shook his head and slammed a fist on the hood of his car. Then he took Maryanne's hand and led her several yards away.

"What was that?" she asked, chewing her thumbnail.

"He's been listening to you," he said. "All this time. Probably has a tracking device on your car too. Still think he's a good guy?"

"I — I don't know."

"Maryanne, listen. I know you're in a difficult situation right now. But I . . ." Donovan looked at his feet. "I can protect you. But you — you have to turn yourself in."

"No — no way," she said. "I didn't do anything wrong."

"Not exactly," he said. "You did harbor a foreign agent. But they'll go easy on you if you report him."

"He's the father of my child," said Maryanne. "I can't — I won't do that."

Donovan felt suddenly heavy, as if his legs were cast in lead. He couldn't make her turn on Michael, but he couldn't bring himself to arrest her either. At least not yet.

"Look," he said. "I'll give you 48 hours. But you have to make a decision. Otherwise, I'll be forced to bring you in myself."

Chapter 50

MARYANNE

Maryanne sat on the top step of the Lincoln Memorial, overlooking the National Mall which was still a muddy mess despite Resurrection City being cleared weeks ago. It was here that she'd let herself fall completely under Michael's spell. Where she'd thrown caution to the wind and let herself completely go. It felt like she might cry, but she had no tears left.

She'd completely betrayed Michael. Yes, he was a liar, and yes, he'd been spying on her. But she already knew that, didn't she? *Shouldn't be surprised that he was bugging me*, she thought. *Stupid of me not to think that anyway.*

She had to confront him. She needed to see the look on his face when he admitted to lying yet again — even though he promised there were no more secrets. How could she still love him? Maybe he was lying about that too. And then, the baby. He'd been so happy when she told his she was pregnant, and visibly crushed when he thought they'd lost it. He said he still wanted a family with her, and she believed that he wanted her to come with him to Russia. Would he still be happy?

She loved Michael, yes. But there had been so many withdrawals from her love bank she wasn't sure what was left.

If only she could just walk away. She stroked her midsection, gently, like it was already a baby in her arms. Oh, the decisions she'd made. Bad decisions. She looked at the empty landscape in front of her, which had teemed with hopeful Americans who, despite the odds, continued to hope for a better life.

She still wanted a better life. She deserved one. And despite her current situation, she had to believe she still had a choice.

If she told Michael about Donovan, and the FBI, maybe they could escape together. She could work for the Soviets and do the work she loved. But she'd never be able to come home. Never see her family again. And could she really trust the Russians?

Atkins had finally come through, but now that she was a target of the KGB and the FBI, not to mention pregnant, there was no way the offer would still stand. But Atkins was a straight-shooter and had given her no reason not to trust him.

And Agent Donovan. He was hanging a sword over her head, all while trying to flirt. He could have just arrested her, but it seemed he was more interested in getting his man. And he was probably going to get Michael, whether she turned on him, or not.

She just wanted to run away. Jump on the nearest rocket ship and fly to Saturn. Or at minimum, just lay under the stars.

Under the stars . . .

She looked at her watch. It was already 10am, which meant she was very late for work. But at least she was to report to NASA headquarters that day. Roger wouldn't be there, and it would be quiet. *You have a choice*, she said to yourself. She'd made her decision.

Chapter 51

MIKHAIL/MICHAEL

August 28, 1968
Southwest Washington, D.C.

Mikhail excitedly opened the door, expecting Mary-anne. But it was Roman. He looked like he had indigestion. He quickly closed the door behind him and walked over to the window to peek around the curtain.

"What's wrong?" said Mikhail.

"They got your man, Marlboro."

"What!?" Mikhail's stomach dropped and he couldn't stop the flood of panic that filled his brain.

"The FBI arrested him at his home just an hour ago," Roman said evenly, though the corners of his eyes stretched wider. "Raided his house, confiscated everything. "

"Did they find anything?"

"Don't know yet. Listen, you know him. Will he talk?"

"No — not immediately. He's too full of himself." Mikhail paced the floor, his temples throbbing. "But he has nothing to lose at this point. He might try and get a deal." *That stupid, arrogant svoloch!* thought Mikhail. *I should've killed him before Chicago.*

"There's no time to waste then. The Center wants you out. They want you out now."

Mikail felt like he'd just been hit over the head by a 2 x 4. Leave now? Of course, the heat was on, he had to go. But Mary-anne?

"What about — "

"Don't you worry about her. I'll take care of everything."

"But there's time. I know there's time to get her. . . . Just give me 30 minutes." *She's ready — she's got to be ready. I can't —.* "I can't leave without her." A ton of bricks sat on Mikhail's chest. "She's coming over."

Roman stroked his chin and looked at Mikhail. There was sorrow in his eyes.

"I'm sorry. I really am. But there's no time. The FBI could be on their way here right now for all you know. You need to go before she gets here. If you want to protect her, walk away now. I promise, I will try to get her to you."

Mikhail reached deep, deep into the recesses of his mental toolkit, and dipped his emotions into a frozen lake. He had no time for worry. He had no time to question. He had no choice but to trust Roman — to trust them.

He betrayed his Soviet atheist ethos and prayed. *Oh, please God. Please, keep her safe. Please bring her to me.*

✳ ✳ ✳

Twelve hours later Mikhail was on an Air France flight to Paris, though for this trip he was Pierre Martin, wine distributor, returning home. He even left samples for the desk agents. Using the airport was risky, but it was fastest, and he always had a backup plan if things went sideways. The Center made the travel arrangements, and his driver would have everything he needed.

After the conversation with Roman he'd gone straight to the warehouse and donned the disguise of the chestnut-haired French businessman. He checked the entire building for signs of human life, rats be damned, before dousing his arsenal with gasoline and setting it alight. So many identities, he had begun to lose track, though his favorites were Thurston the Texas Roughneck and Jeremiah, Bible salesman from Kansas. And of course, Michael, when he could just look like himself, and even be himself to a certain extent. Michael was his ticket to another life, one he never imagined. Without Michael he never would have met Maryanne. She placed all her trust in him, and now he was leaving without her. Roman promised that they would get her out "when the time was right," whatever that meant. He was not yet Americanized enough to question. It wasn't right, just leaving her behind. He told himself there was nothing he could do, but he felt the now familiar pull at his heart and fought back tears.

His ride to the airport was courtesy of one of Geoffrey's local assets, Stuart, a professional chauffeur. He picked up Mikhail in front of the Willard Hotel, several blocks away from the now two-alarm blaze that burned in Southwest. He'd ditched his car at Hains Point, wiping it down and leaving the keys in the hand of a passed out drunk just a few feet away. Washington was such a compact city that it was easy to travel on foot from here to there. No one at the Willard paid him any mind- he was just a wine-soaked Frenchman who had too much of a good time the night before.

"Would you do me a favor?" said Mikhail to the driver.

"Sure, man."

"At some point, in the next day or so, could you please deliver this," he handed him a sealed letter and scrap of paper, "to this address?"

Stuart nodded.

And with that, Mikhail bid goodbye to America.

He convinced himself that he wasn't abandoning Maryanne. No, it was just that for his safety, to secure their future together, he *had* to leave before her. His chest tightened, painfully, and it felt as if his ribs were collapsing inward. He was leaving, she would never forgive him. When he left for Chicago, he promised to return to her, as always. Promised. He cursed himself for not destroying the listening device in her bag, but it had apparently gone dead. She'd never find it anyway. But the thought of not being able to listen in — not knowing — of being indefinitely separated — left him feeling helpless.

There was no point drowning in regret. He had to think about the future. Once she was in Moscow, they could try for another baby. Make a family.

Maryanne was in their hands now. For his own sanity, he had to believe that they would deliver her safely to Moscow, and they would finally, truly, be together.

Chapter 52

DONOVAN

Donavan had just sat down at the dinner table when the phone rang. O'Connell rarely called him to come to the office after hours, so he knew it was important.

"What's so important that you dragged me away from my wife's gumbo?" said Donovan as he walked into the office.

"Come with me," said O'Connell, who looked like he was on his twelfth cup of coffee. Did the man ever leave the office?

O'Connell led him down the hall and up to another floor, where he knew the Counterintelligence guys were. It always irked him that they were separate from the COINTELPRO program, as if they were too good. *Information sharing* was treated like a dirty word.

O'Connell opened the door to their "war room" and turned on the lights. The walls were lined with photographs, documents, and maps. A cork board was covered with a detailed network diagram, complete with pictures and names, and the table was stacked with files.

"All of this," said O'Connell, "is for one Mr. Roger Elridge, Air Force Engineer and CIA conscript, assigned to the National Reconnaissance Office. They've been interrogating him for almost 12 hours now. Stubborn fucker. Keeps holding out for a better deal."

"Does that mean?"

"Yes, they finally linked him to your Russian, Michael. Eldridge knew him as 'Mr. Pender.' Still don't know his real name, though."

"So, the information I provided was good?"

"Better than good. Plus, it seems Eldridge had turned the tables and had spied on the Russian. Even figured out where he lived."

Donovan gritted his teeth. "Why didn't they bring me in?" he said angrily. "So, I just give them all of the information, do all of the footwork, and they don't give me any credit?"

He'd traced Michael's plate number to a crooked used car salesman in Laurel, Maryland. Caught the weasel freebasing in the dealership office with his secretary's head buried in his lap. Took less than ten minutes and his best scary Black man act to get the guy to reveal he was the KGB's favorite car dealer in the Mid-Atlantic. Turned the traitor over to the counterintelligence group, after which they went radio silent.

And now he knew Michael tried using a young, impressionable Black girl to spy too. But she hadn't caved. Well, not really.

"Turns out your cokehead's sketch corroborated that your Russian is KGB, whose real name we still don't know, plus some other suspects." He slapped Donovan on the back. "You found a cell, my friend."

Donovan blinked hard and walked up to the corkboard. So many connections, targets. He stopped at Mikhail's picture. There was a line to an empty square, labeled *Female, NASA employee.*

"Who's this?"

"Oh, that's some girl who he's banging or something. Eldridge keeps teasing us with her, saying he has information that will "blow our minds", but won't give anything more unless he gets immunity. Can you believe that?"

Donovan shook his head. *Think fast.* "Ah, that girl. I already looked into her. She's no one of interest — turns out she gets chatted up by a lot of men. Very pretty." What was he saying?

"A hussy?" said O'Connell.

"No, nothing like that. She's just a looker, that's all. I'll tell the guys not to waste their time on her. Seems like they've got enough info." He hoped.

Just then a group of agents entered the conference room, all steel-jawed and serious with shellacked hair. How they all achieved the same shellacked hairstyle amazed him.

"Hey Donovan, what's up brother?" said the one he remembered from the Academy as being chronically offensive to anyone not White, Anglo-Saxon, and Protestant. He was especially venomous toward Catholics, for some reason.

I am not your brother, he thought. "Hi Dexter," said Donovan.

"Guess what? We're going to get your Russkie. Right now. You comin' with?"

Donovan looked at O'Connell, who nodded.

"Hell yeah."

Chapter 53

MARYANNE

August 29, 1968
Northwest and Southwest,
Washington, D.C.

Maryanne walked into NASA and hadn't made it more than fifty feet before realizing something was off. Outside it smelled like damp smoke, like a forest fire put out by a rainstorm. Inside the entire building was buzzing with restless intrigue, and people spoke to one another in hushed voices as if they were at a funeral. The back of her neck prickled, like she was about to walk down a dark woodland path. Had she been found out? She kept her eyes down until she found Atkins alone in the old conference room. His head was in his hands.

"What's going on?" she said, heart in her throat.

"It's Roger. He's been arrested, and now our whole program is under a microscope."

Maryanne's hand flew to her mouth. Roger?

"For what?" she croaked, slightly relieved but a new uneasiness crept into her psyche.

"Can't say exactly. But Hoover's boys are combing through our program with a toothpick. Seems old Roger was playing fast and loose with classified information. So, they wanna know if anyone else in the building has been in the business of information sharing with the Russ — oops!"

Maryanne felt the ground dropping beneath her. Michael had been not only spying on her, but using Roger, her nemesis, as well. Had he seen them together? A headache hit her square between the eyes, and she felt her cheeks flooding with warmth. If Roger linked them together, *oh my God*, it would be all over for her. Donovan would have zero sympathy. She sat down, her mind paging through option after option. Russia . . . California . . . there was really only one option to choose from, and it had to work.

A curated, carefully calibrated version of the truth.

"I went out a few times with a man who I decided wasn't trustworthy," she said as resolutely as possible. "He didn't sound foreign, but after a couple of lies I decided to walk away." The words suddenly tasted salty as the reality of the situation set in, her choice becoming reality as she spoke. She knew had to leave Michael. There was no way she could go to Russia — no way she could turn her back on her family. If she left, she would never be able to come home again. She'd be a fugitive, and so would her baby. And she could never, ever trust him.

"So do you think he was some kind of spy?" Atkins said, his eyes wide. Love was one thing, but trust was another. She just couldn't rely on love alone.

"I don't know who he really is," she replied. And that was the truth. "All I know is that I want nothing more than to get out of D.C. and take the job in the desert. All I want to do is listen to the universe."

Atkins narrowed his gaze and rubbed the bridge of his nose. It was a risk sharing so much, but she had nothing — absolutely nothing to lose.

"I'm so sorry you almost got caught up in this," he finally said. "And we all make mistakes. But you've been an invaluable asset and I know that you are of the highest integrity."

"I know, I was just so — so stupid," she said, the tears starting to flow again. It was the most honest thing she'd said in weeks. "There's one more thing," she said.

"Oh that?" he said politely gesturing toward her belly. "Oh yeah, I figured something was going on."

Maryanne wanted to check her ears. Had she heard right? "But, how . . ."

"I have five children," he said. "And another on the way." He beamed. "I know what pregnant looks like."

Maryanne just stared at him.

"Look," said Atkins. "I don't know how this is all going to end up. We'll have to wait and see what happens. But I want this for you — for your future. Go home and I'll see you tomorrow."

Maryanne felt as if she'd passed through a black hole when she emerged into the bright sunshine. There was just one more thing to do before calling Agent Donovan. She walked slowly down 4th street toward Michael's apartment. She had to tell him that she was staying in the U.S. That she loved him but could no longer stand the lies. But deep down she knew he really did love her. She could feel it in every breath, every heartbeat. Being close to him, his warmth, his vibration, it would be nearly impossible to resist. She had to see him one last time. And she had to tell him to leave.

Suddenly a fast-moving caravan of dark cars whooshed by, screeching to a stop in front of his building. She froze. Men poured out of the cars with guns drawn, looking up and down the street, including right through her. They disappeared into the building. All except one.

It was Donovan. He was staring at her. He was also holding a gun.

Her heart leapt into her throat.

Donovan's mouth was moving, first fast, then slow, but she couldn't hear what he was saying. Then she realized he wasn't speaking. He was mouthing something.

Run.

She turned and ran back down the street, stopping to catch her breath at the corner. *I can't take any more of this,* she thought. *I just can't.* Maryanne couldn't run from the truth anymore.

She turned around and walked back toward Michael's apartment. Donovan looked at her like she was a defiant child.

"What are you doing here?" he snapped, looking around. "I told you to —"

"Did you get him?" she asked, unmoved by his meltdown. "Is he here?"

Donovan shook his head. "No — he's gone."

"So, what do you want to know?" she said, her face stone, but a smile spreading through her entire body. With Michael already gone, it was a good chance he was already safely away from danger. But she wanted so badly to say goodbye. Why hadn't he come to find her before leaving? She would have understood. *Maybe he hasn't left the U.S. yet*, she told herself. Maybe he'd call or materialize at her side like he'd done so many times before. She could still tell him about the baby.

She shook her head. *No, he'd never take the risk. Not even for me.* It broke her heart to acknowledge this truth.

Had it really been that long since she'd seen him? It felt like he was with her all the time, so consumed she was with the idea of him, and their future together. It felt so tangible, so real. Now it was but a paper tiger. She had to soldier on alone.

Chapter 54

MARYANNE

Maryanne was helping her mother make dinner when the doorbell rang.

"I'll get it!" said Gladys from the living room.

"I wonder who that is?" said her mother, in nervous anticipation.

"I know what you're worried about, but Daddy's fine," said Maryanne. He had been in and out of the house, staying away for long stretches. Rumor was he was halfway shacking up with the widow Rosalie one block over, who was as much of an alcoholic as he was. The house was quiet and serene when he was away. It's not like Mother missed him — she just kept expecting to hear he was dead.

"It's a serious looking man with a serious afro," said Gladys with a hint of amusement.

Maryanne wiped her hands on her apron. "I know who it is," she said, and walked toward the front door where Donavan was standing.

"Sorry to show up unannounced," he said.

"Who is this?" said her mother, looking stunned. "Is it? I thought he was gone?"

"No, Mother," said Maryanne, surprising herself by laughing. She'd never told her mother that Michael was White. "This isn't Michael."

Donovan crossed his arms and scowled. "I'm definitely not Michael, Mrs. Freeman," he said. "My name is Donovan, I'm with the FBI, and this is official business."

Gladys rushed to Maryanne's side and gripped her protectively. "What's going on?" she near shouted. "Mary didn't do anything!"

"Please," said Donovan. "Calm down. She isn't in trouble." He turned his attention back to Maryanne. "But we do need to talk — in private."

Maryanne led him to the living room, watching her feet move across the rug. It was all so surreal, Donovan here, in her house. She still cried over Michael every quiet moment, her feelings drifting between sadness and anger, his name both bitter and sweet on her tongue. How could she continue to love someone so treacherous? It was the life growing inside her — a constant reminder of what was and could have been.

"This will be hard to hear, but I think you should know everything," said Donovan as they sat down. "You were almost implicated as a co-conspirator in a Russian spy ring in the U.S."

"What?!" she cried.

"Everything ok?" said her mother, whose head popped from around the corner.

"Calm down," said Donovan. "I haven't finished. Yes, everything is fine."

"Who?" said Maryanne, shaking. "Who accused me?"

"Roger Eldridge."

"That slimy, no good piece of — of"

"Yes, I agree," said Donovan. "No one likes the guy. Not even his wife, who turned him in."

"So, what, now I'm going to be arrested?" Her voice started to rise again.

"No, no. Listen." He took her hands in his, gently, like a lover. She looked at him with surprise and pulled them away.

"I'm sorry," he said, flustered. "It's all going to be fine. I'm part of the investigating team and I told them that you were no traitor — that you found me as soon as you had suspicions about the spy and became an informant."

Maryanne narrowed her gaze and studied Donovan's face. He would have no reason to lie.

But there was something else there that unsettled her, she just couldn't put her finger on it yet.

"Why did you do that?" she said.

"Because you — and this child — deserve a chance." His hand flinched, like he was going to reach out again. "And because I care."

She understood the bags that swam under his eyes, and his hopeful gaze. *Oh no.*

"And — you expect something in return for your help? Well, if that's the case, no thank you."

She crossed her arms and let out a 'humph', probably loud enough for the kitchen eavesdroppers — her mother and Gladys — to want to listen closer. Her heart raced like a cornered mouse, afraid of what he would do. But this time she'd be ready.

His brow gathered in thought, and he turned his head. She thought he heard him sniffle, and when he turned back to look at her his eyes looked slightly reddened.

"I'd hoped you would maybe consider — but that's ridiculous. No, I don't expect anything in return. Look, we got someone who'd done real damage to our national security, and he exposed enough information to know there was a significant KGB operation going on. But he's such a disgusting character that I easily discredited everything he said about you." He shook his head. "It was time we focus on the real bad guys."

Maryanne had no idea what the last thing he said meant but decided not to ask. All she knew was that she'd be free.

"Thank you," she said. "You don't know how much this means to me."

He looked at her with mournful eyes. "There's just one more thing," he said. "The Russians — well — you know enough about them and their operation that you're dangerous. They're probably laying low now, but they don't like to leave loose ends."

Maryanne wrapped her arms around her midsection and felt her stomach drop. "What do you mean? Do you mean they'll try to kill me?"

Donovan squeezed his eyes open and shut. "I just want to you to stay vigilant. I can protect you if you stay in Washington."

Maryanne stood up and walked to the fireplace. On the mantle was a picture of her in a cap and gown on the day she graduated from Howard University. Another picture was of her in pigtails holding up a ribbon, standing next to a paper-mâché model she made of a comet. Her degree was framed on the wall, and her mother kept a book of her crayon drawings from childhood on the coffee table. Then she looked at her father's empty armchair, into which he had sunk further and further, weighted by disappointment and dreams deferred. This was it. She would choose to chart her own path. She turned to face him.

"I don't need protection," she said. "I just need space. Then I'll be fine."

Chapter 55

MARYANNE

May 1, 1969
High Sierras, California

Maryanne stepped out of her bungalow into the cool night desert air and deeply inhaled. The onyx black sky sparkled with infinite luminous beings — stars, nebula, comets. This was the blissful solace she'd longed for when she was trapped under the iron dome of Washington. This is how she had always wanted to live, under the stars rather than under the yoke of men. A grateful Atkins had come through with the perfect job and stellar recommendations. After tearful goodbyes, at nearly seven months pregnant, she set off for Goldston, California. She'd found the tiny house with brushy garden and bottle tree and immediately fell in love. It would be perfect for her and the baby, and a thirty minutes' drive across the desert to the trailer where she worked, digesting real time data. Baby Anna was almost born in the backseat of Maryanne's erstwhile and matronly landlady's sedan halfway to the hospital in Barstow. Luckly, they made it in time.

Abelene the landlady was also an empty-nester and was more than happy to keep herself busy helping Maryanne with Anna. Abelene also volunteered her daughter to watch the baby once Maryanne returned to work. It wasn't her mother or

Gladys, but these two desert-hardened women with soft hearts and not a racist bone in their bodies were a Godsend.

Maryanne sat on her porch swing and started to sing to little Anna under the night sky. The baby's eyes dart between her mother's face and the stars, and Maryanne flooded with love. It was a love she'd never felt before — not even with her mother, or Gladys. Or Michael.

After Anna's eyes fluttered closed, Maryanne put her in her crib then sleepily walked across the hallway to her own room. In the distance a coyote howled, and it tugged at her heart, though she didn't know why. Oh yes, Gladys loved coyotes for some reason. Something to do with their family -focused nature. It pained her to not be able to run home to tell Gladys her latest news or seek her advice when faced with a ridiculous decision. She also missed her mother, who had suffered a minor stroke and was bedridden for a month, and she couldn't be there to help her. And Michael. She felt like a piece of her life was missing, like there was still too much left unsaid. She had been convinced that he was nothing but a liar, that he'd ripped out and trampled her heart on purpose just to further his wicked purpose. But then, the day after Donovan came over, a young man delivered a letter.

Sitting on the bed, Maryanne opened her nightstand drawer and pulled out the piece of paper which she kept hidden under her New Testament. She carefully unfolded it, hands shaking even though she'd read it dozens of times already.

My Beloved Mary,

I am writing this letter with a broken heart because we cannot leave together as planned. I must leave immediately. It seems that I have been exposed and must get as far away from here — and you — as possible.

But do not worry. Nothing has changed — not how I feel about you and not about us being together. You will do great things in my country, and we will be rewarded. I cannot wait to

She read the letter several more times, tracing the script with the tip of her finger. Swoop, up, pen point. The paper was slightly crinkled in places where her tears had landed in the past, but she had no tears left to cry over him. He was perhaps waiting in vain for her, but she'd left D.C. in a hurry before the Russians could come looking for her. Only Atkins and Donovan knew exactly where she worked, though she'd given neither her living address. One day she'd take Anna home and she would finally meet her grandmother and auntie — even her grandfather if he was around. But for now, it was safer to lie low, albeit in a job she truly enjoyed showing up to every day.

At unexpected times she'd feel unnerved and look over her shoulder, or out across the long expanse of the desert. And she'd remember the feeling of being with Michael — in his arms, under his adoring gaze. But his love had nearly destroyed her life. Now she, and her little girl, were under the watchful eye of the heavens. She was exactly where she was supposed to be, and there was a universe ready to be explored.

Acknowledgements

I am eternally grateful to the following people:

Maddie and Spencer, the lights of my life, my intrepid peace warriors, my children. Thanks for tolerating Mommy's late nights in front of the computer, countless Uber Eats meals, and being my sounding board for story ideas. I love you both to infinity and beyond the outer limits of the universe.

Editors Nicole Meier and Jacqueline Cangro, who helped me polish and perfect my manuscript and elevate my voice.

Author Jennifer Close, whose novel generator course gave me the skills and critical eye to develop my story.

My incredible advisor and partner on all things marketing and publicity, Donna DeStefano. I'd be lost without you!

Friends Catherine and Colleen who have been cheering me on since day one of this project.

All of my colleagues at CSIS.

My incredible family, including my Mommy and Daddy, sisters Lauren and Mallory, my brother Dave in heaven, my brother-in-law Kwame, nieces Kylie, Shani, Kendi, and Nia, and nephew Dakari.

9 798218 510923